pretty lies

BETHANY-KRIS

Published by Bethany-Kris
www.bethanykris.com

ISBN 13: 978-1-989658-15-4

Editor: Elizabeth Peters

Cover Design © Mignon Mykel from Oh, So Novel

For anyone who wasn't ready when it happened.

CONTENTS

ONE

THE REALM OF boredom was a dangerous place.

At least it was for Cory.

"Joe."

"Mmm."

"Hey," Cory said, once more attempting to get Joe to as much as *look* at him.

It didn't work.

Fuckhead.

"Joe, I'm serious."

"Yep."

He was going to punch his brother.

Hard.

"*Joe.*"

He didn't even glance up over the newspaper in his hands. Joe did, however, smile and voice his thanks when his wife came around to the head of the table to set a mug with rolling steam coming off the rim down in front of him. Liliana headed back across the kitchen but now rhythmically patted the back of her two-month-old son sleeping against her chest. A task that was made easier after she delivered her husband's coffee.

He smiled at the sight of his nephew.

Babies weren't so hard to understand even if they were foreign creatures in a lot of ways. Who wouldn't want to be constantly warm, fed, comfortable, and happy if one was new to a big world and nothing seemed to make sense?

Shit, yeah.

Babies knew what was up.

Damian Joe "DJ" Rossi.

The first of his generation.

Cory loved that kid to death already, and he didn't even do anything at this point but cry, sleep, and eat. It was only the love he had for his nephew that stopped him from reaching across the table to punch Joe in the shoulder when he deliberately ignored his younger brother.

A few years ago, that wouldn't have surprised anybody. *Hell*, a few months ago Cory still could have been provoked into doing something crazy to Joe just to make his brother pay attention to him at any given moment that he felt the need. His ma, Lily, liked to say he had a bad case of middle child syndrome. The one-year age gap between Cory and his older brother made them closer than most siblings; they did everything together growing up *and* when they moved into adulthood. The nine- and ten-year gap between Joe and Cory and their younger sister, Monica, fostered an older brother complex that the world would just have to get used to.

But the brothers ...

Joe always looked out for Cory.

Not that he *had* to.

Or fuck, maybe he did.

Except—

Cory glanced his sleeping nephew's way once more—the baby was starting to blink awake as his mother wiped down a counter. He would hate to make the little guy cry when Joe cursed Cory out for being a shit. So, he kept his fists and *annoyance* to himself.

Later, though ... He could always get his brother back later.

"Have you listened to anything I've said to you in the last five minutes?" Cory asked, his hand faster than Joe's when he snatched the newspaper out of his brother's grasp before he held it out of reach entirely. "Because I know you're not *that* fucking checked out, bro."

Joe glared.

He didn't get the chance to speak, though.

"Language," came a quiet, feminine call from across the kitchen. Just as quickly, Liliana cooed to the baby, "How was that nap, *bambino?*"

Goddammit. He considered rolling his eyes. Except he liked his brother's wife.

Cory grinned at Joe instead while saying to Liliana, "Sorry, Lil."

"Mmhmm."

"Give me the newspaper," Joe muttered while holding out a hand, waiting.

He answered that with a shake of the newspaper, taunting his brother. "Talk to me first. I've got plans."

"You always have some kind of fuc—"

Joe's gaze cut to the side where Liliana watched them from behind the kitchen island like she was *daring* one of them to start up with their usual nonsense. Cory was being good; Scout's fucking honor and all that shit. It was just Joe who seemed to forget where he was. Liliana's new thing about correcting bad language in her house—although she'd never liked them swearing in the kitchen to begin with—made her seem *more* like Joe and Cory's mother than she already did.

And that said something. Considering their mother's name *was* Lily and all.

Cory had learned it was better to *not* point those things out to his brother. Despite what people liked to think and say about him, he wasn't dumb. Foolish at times because often, that's when he had the most fun.

Not stupid, though. He didn't like to wake up with aching bones, so he kept his mouth shut to his brother about how he'd basically married a woman who was *a lot* like their mother.

See?

Smart.

"You always have a plan, Cory. The problem is you rarely follow said plans because apparently *why bother* and then you cause a bunch of shi— *problems.*" Joe let out a hard sigh with his gaze blazing when Cory laughed at his *almost* slip-up again. "Knock it off—Damian barely slept last night. He's teething. I'm tired."

"That's a little early, yeah?"

Joe's brow crinkled. "What?"

"Isn't he young for teeth?"

"Apparently not," Liliana answered for her husband.

Cory hadn't taken his gaze off his brother. He decided to scale back his usual personality just a touch or two. At least for the moment. Sometimes, Joe was owed a break from his younger brother's constant torment, regardless of how much personal enjoyment Cory gained from it.

Screw it, he thought.

Forget the new property he wanted to buy with his brother to add to their portfolio. They could get back to the legal side of their business on another day. Besides, they weren't even supposed to be opening anything new for a while. He'd promised their mother to give Joe a break on any new real estate or other business ventures until they settled in with the new baby. It made sense, but this particular business that was up for sale had been too good to pass up. Except he would. He wanted to do something else for his brother instead. Joe could use some fun.

Right?

"You need a break," he said to Joe, switching tactics *and* topics in his next breath. Now he had a better idea, and the follow-through to get it done would probably be a lot easier. "Let's go to High Life tonight."

"We opened that club months ago, and it's still packed full every night."

"Good business, right?" Cory pointed at his temple. "Told you that one would be a banger."

And he was right, like with most of their business ventures.

"So, come and enjoy the place with me tonight," Cory said. "You didn't even open it with me."

"My son was three days old." Joe scoffed. "Are you serious? I've got a *newborn* here, man. I'm not going to party all night while my wife chills with a teething baby."

"That would be a dick move."

Something their father, also named Damian, would have his sons' balls for. He liked to tell the brothers that good men were made at home serving their wives and not in the streets with people who often forgot their morals for the sake of business. For a simple reason, too. Another man might not trust someone based on the things they knew from the streets, but the way a man treated his wife—publicly *and* privately—would always say a lot about his character.

It was a poignant statement. Considering his father was one of the three highest seated men in the Chicago mob—the *Outfit*—it really said something coming from him.

Cory kept it in mind. Not that he had a wife to remember it for. He also wasn't currently looking for one. Besides, one married Rossi brother was enough.

"Except you could use a break," Liliana spoke up, "and all he really wants is me at night, anyway, Joe. Why not go out and get away from … *everything*?"

He pointed in his brother's wife's direction, saying, "See. What was it you told me last week? The Outfit is running you dead, man."

Joe said nothing, but he didn't have to when the two faced one another at the table. Nothing he told his brother was a lie. The Outfit had both men by the throats when it came to work. That happened when one looked to move up in the mob, and they came from a family like theirs.

They never said as much, sure. It wasn't like they ever spoke about their intentions with the mob. Everything was always *unsaid*, but just understood. He blamed that on the fact this was all they ever knew.

Their uncles? In the mob. One, a boss. The other, sitting next to their father so that the two could act as the right and left hand of the man running the whole criminal organization.

Where else were they going but *in*? They didn't need to say it.

His brother was already in. Joe just wanted … a seat at the table, now. Cory, on the other hand, kept busy with his Uncle Theo and the man's arms and substance dealing he had going on in the city and elsewhere. All he ever did was work now, too.

Damn, he hadn't even gotten a new tattoo to add to his collection of full sleeves, a throat and chest piece, and an almost finished back piece, too. That was unheard of for him—every six to eight weeks of healing, and Cory was back in for another round in an artist's chair. His lack of new ink spoke to how busy he'd constantly been.

Joe was no better. Hadn't they earned a break?

Cory gave Joe a grin. "So, are we going out tonight like old time's sake, or …?"

"You know I'd feel better if I just got to have a damn nap, right?" Joe asked back.

That time, Liliana didn't correct his language. She did laugh, though.

"I mean, *yeah*," Cory returned, shrugging under his leather jacket, "but what's the fun of being twenty-five—"

"You're twenty-five."

"Twenty-six," Cory corrected, cursing himself internally because no doubt, Joe was onto his scheme.

"Really, you just want to go out tonight, but you want me to come with you, right?" Joe asked. "That's what this whole thing was about, wasn't it?"

Well ...

Cory looked Liliana's way for help.

She always did.

It's why he liked her the most. Next to his brother marrying her and all.

"He does need a break, doesn't he?" Cory asked. "You said it first, Lil."

"He does."

He went back to his brother. "The wife spoke. I'm really just trying to follow her wishes." His brother still said nothing. "Come on, Joe, all I do is *work* ... that's all you ever do anymore, too. Take a night."

Joe shook his head. "You're something, man. I hope you know that."

He did.

All too well.

●●●

"*Rossi!*"

The holler from the other side of the club's VIP section had Cory raising a hand in reply. He didn't know who had called his last name, or if they were even calling for him. The place was mob-owned considering it was the brothers' name on the paperwork, so really, it could have gone either way.

Lowering his hand from the air to bring the cup to his lips, Cory downed what remained of his tequila in one swallow. It burned all the way down, but he found satisfaction in that all the same. He was certainly fucking feeling the alcohol, too.

Then again, he was six drinks in.

And he'd mixed some.

Joe's dark laughter had Cory's attention moving away from the oncoming server. The chick would do her job—in this club, when a Rossi's cup was empty, it needed to be filled before they had the chance to pick it up again and ask someone to do it.

"You were right," Joe said at Cory's left.

"On what?"

He usually was.

No one liked it when he pointed it out.

"The DJ—he was the right pick for the place."

Cory nodded, his booted foot tapping out a beat to the shined cement floor—High Life sported a whole industrial look that he really preferred, though only a few of their mutual businesses went down that design route. In the VIP booth, the two had a view of the entire club laid out before them. Like this, they stayed clear of the dancing and drinking crowd filling the floor in front of the DJ with his booth and lights and the bar that never stopped moving.

"I seriously thought you just wanted him because he smoked a blunt with you when you were supposed to be doing his interview," Joe said in a chuckle.

"I mean, that was *part* of the reason."

Why lie?

That never got Cory anywhere.

Tipping his head to the side while the sounds around Cory blurred like his vision, his last drink had started to take hold. He eyed his older brother. In years, there wasn't that much of a gap between them. It was the changes in their lives that separated him from Joe more than he wanted to admit sometimes. Things like marriage, babies, and *adulthood.* Just in general.

He didn't blame or fault his brother for the differences between them now, but he still liked to close the space and remind himself they were still *those fucking Rossi brothers.* As everyone in their life liked to call them when they were younger and crazier.

"Hey," Cory said, the taste of tequila still heavy on his tongue.

"Yeah?"

Joe glanced his way.

Cory flashed his teeth in a grin. "You out?"

That's all he needed to ask.

His brother would understand.

"Would you hate me if I said yes?" Joe returned with a lazy smirk.

"Nah, I figured once I got a few drinks into you, then you'd be ready to head home."

"Oh?"

A shrug lifted his shoulders. "Is what it is, bro."

That was it, and that was all.

Joe didn't have the same priorities as Cory at the end of every day now, and he got that. He didn't need his brother to tell him to know that Joe's mind hadn't been very far from his wife and newborn son from the moment they walked into their club for a good time.

Besides ...

"I got you out to blow the fucking stink off you," Cory said, straightening up in the booth and eyeing the dancing crowd for something—or *someone*—interesting. He'd know what it was when he found it. "I'll count that as a win."

On another night, when Joe was less drunk and tired, he probably would have had a smart ass, cutting comment for Cory in reply. Instead, he just shook his head and smiled like he knew the truth.

"You know, if all you really want is to spend some time with me, you just gotta say, Cory."

Yeah, well ...

"I told Liliana," Cory said simply. "She came up with a better plan."

Because usually, he'd just cause some shit to get his brother's attention. It always worked before. He was trying a new thing—one that *didn't* end up with someone in trouble, mostly him and Joe, or worse.

He figured that was good.

Mature.

Whatever.

"Let Max know at the door," Cory said, "because I already had someone ready to drive you home when you were ready to go. He's probably got the car close by the entrance."

Joe sighed. "And what are you doing for the rest of your night?"

Cory's gaze finally stopped in its search of the dancing swell of people when he found a brunette with a shimmering, black club dress tossing back a round of shots right off the tray of a server. In towering heels that showed off all kinds of smooth, tan legs in that short dress, the woman spun around to join another female waiting. The fast movement made the blonde and red highlights in her long, wavy brown hair catch the lights overhead. The women started dancing again. Now that he had found her in the crowd, he couldn't seem to look away.

Not that he minded.

She was quite a sight.

Every inch of her—from the curves of her hips to the glowing sheen on the valley of her breasts where that dress dipped dangerously low, and even the red on her lips—screamed *fuckable*. He tried not to objectify women upon first sight. It wasn't a particularly admirable trait in a man, after all.

The brunette made it easy, though.

Damn.

She'd tossed back five shots one after the other. Not a flinch in sight. That meant one of two things to Cory.

The brunette was looking to forget something, or she wanted one hell of a night. Either way, he could provide both of those things. That was, if she was interested. He simply needed to make his way over to her and find out.

But first, Joe.

"Well?" Joe asked. "Do you need me to make sure *you* get home, too? Or are you not done here?"

Cory was already standing from the booth. "Not even close to done, bro."

The only thing he could guarantee was that he'd make it home to take his dog, Mace, out for a piss, because the animal depended on him. The pup was the only thing that ever gave him a real sense of responsibility. He would be drunk when he got home, likely, but he always had a mob enforcer waiting in the wings to do the driving when needed.

And that was it. Everything else was up in the air. He liked it that way.

"Talk to Max—it was my deal with Liliana," Cory told his brother as he passed by him in the booth to exit. "You're not driving home."

"Yeah, I got it. I don't know what caught your attention out there on the floor, but you know the fucking rules, yeah?"

Joe called that at his retreating back.

Cory just laughed.

He was *way* too drunk to be picking up a brunette in his club to fuck, if he were being honest. The way the room looked as he walked away—a little too fuzzy, maybe—told him that.

What did it matter?

Fun was still *fun*.

"The rule, Cory!"

"Yeah, yeah." He waved a hand high over his shoulder, and his fingers made the peace sign that quickly turned into just his middle finger standing up. "I know the rule—don't be stupid."

Sometimes, that was when he had the most fun.

He just knew better than to say it.

•••

The brunette had a name.

Cory just couldn't remember it.

He blamed his lack of memory on the fact that the second he got close enough to actually catch her attention, the girl was like a fucking spider web. *Beautiful* face. Intoxicating laugh. Sex appeal in every move she made. He got a dance from her. Made her laugh and smile and it all pulled him in closer to her. More shots were involved.

Then, she kissed him.

The second he realized those stained-red lips of hers tasted like sugar and Henny … Cory was done for. At some point between her round, pert ass grinding into his cock through his slacks on the dance floor and a kiss that had his lungs aching for more in the darkened hallway leading to the employee's private bathrooms, she'd told him her name.

Now, after he'd gotten her somewhere relatively private, had her sitting on a counter with her tight dress bunched around her hips while he buried his face between her thighs, he was trying to remember what it was.

Her name, that was.

Mel?

Lana?

Fucking hell.

Cory hadn't needed those extra shots.

Not that it mattered at the moment—his drunkenness made no difference to the fact that the brunette's legs shook as they tightened to his head while her demands came out high and broken and *perfect.*

"Don't fucking stop … *don't stop*," she breathed.

She rocked against him, *needy.* He loved them like that. So messy.

It was the only time he let himself love a woman, really. He often fell in and out of lust more than he cared to admit, but sex wasn't quite the same. Nothing got him off more than making a chick lose her control while he ate her out like it was the last thing he was ever going to taste.

On his tongue, she was hotter and *tart* as all her sounds echoed in the empty bathroom. Her manicured nails pulled tighter in his hair when he stuffed two fingers into her pussy. Those strappy stiletto heels of hers scratched against the fabric of his silk button down.

And then she was shaking.

Begging.

"*There, there …* there, *fuck, yes.*"

Her pussy, a slick paradise.

Cory had most certainly found heaven.

At least for the night.

All at once, as he looked up and a wild gaze—the color of his favorite dark chocolate—met his sky-blue stare. He couldn't really smudge the stain on her lips like he'd wanted, but he'd kissed her hard enough in the hallway outside the bathroom that she *looked* like he'd fucked her before he even got the chance to actually do so. Every breath she dragged in had her tits rising and falling heavily.

He grinned.

She licked her lips.

"I forgot your name," he admitted.

She shrugged her shoulders, the straps of her dress tangled down her arms, but she didn't seem to care at all. "I didn't even bother to ask for yours."

Fair enough.

A buzz echoed to their left.

She didn't look away from him, but his gaze darted to the side where her purse laid in a heap on the corner of the counter. Her phone had done that a lot since they left the club's dance floor. She ignored every call or text— acted like it didn't even exist.

"Someone looking for you?" he asked.

The lines of her face changed to something more sensual when she laughed. Beautiful wasn't a good enough word to describe how *feminine* her features were. From soft, plush lips to cheekbones that would undoubtedly look best in the glossy spread of a magazine, she really was something. The fact he had the taste of her pussy on his mouth currently made his opinion of her a lot greater, too.

"He can keep looking," she said.

Oh.

Well, shit. Who was he to step in this woman's way of getting back at— or maybe moving on from—some other man in her life? Hell, he might as well help however he could.

Wasn't that the gentlemanly thing to do?

"That's what this is?" Cory asked, tipping his chin up when he let out a dark chuckle that had her shivering under his hands that flexed at her inner thighs. "You're out looking for a rebound, pretty girl?"

"Just a fuck, actually," she countered. "Make it worth about a year of my wasted time, would you?"

That time, it was Cory's turn to laugh when he straightened to his full height to tower over where she sat trembling on the counter. The bathroom smelled like liquor and sex. Like a damn good night. One well spent.

Her legs widened when he grabbed her waist.

"Well?" she asked.

He liked that there was still a hint of a woman who could probably grab him by the balls and make it hurt if she really wanted to when she stared at him. At the same time, she was all sweetness and sex and sin under his grip.

Her breath hitched when he yanked her down to her feet. Those heels on her feet clicked against the floor. His lip curved upward to flash his teeth when he smirked, a wink only adding to the arrogance of his next words.

"Oh yeah, I can definitely do that."

He still couldn't remember her name, but it proved insignificant when he bent her over the counter and fucked her. He was sure she would have a line of bruises on her thighs from the edge of the counter and how hard he grabbed and pulled at her body.

Yet, she took all nine inches of him, and then asked for more. *Purred* when he pulled her hair and came harder when he wrapped his fingers around her throat.

So, shit.

He hadn't remembered her name.

No big deal.

Besides, he'd learned not to sweat the small things.

How important was a name, really?

TWO

THE CLICK OF Della's red, six-inch Giuseppe heels took her up the marble stairs to the entrance of a building in downtown Chicago. The towering skyrise housed hundreds of offices by companies that rented space for their own purposes. When the sun came around to the front of the building later in the day, the glass had a shimmer of gold.

It certainly made for an interesting sight.

She might have cared slightly more about the building and the companies using the place had she been there for any reason *other* than work. Despite the way she looked in designer shoes, black, high-waisted, skinny-legged pants she'd paired with a cream-colored silk blouse tucked into the waist, and a Hermès bag hooked around her inner elbow, she wasn't there to sit in any boardrooms or even behind a desk of her own.

Della still liked to look the part.

It helped in her career to … blend in.

Just beyond the entrance of tower's front doors waited security. Tightening her arm around the ten-thousand-dollar bag to keep it close, Della chose the guard on the end with a familiar face. It wasn't the first time she'd come to this building to do her business, and she seriously doubted it would be her last.

Something else that was good in her field?

Knowing people.

Or making sure people knew *her.*

Either worked.

That was why when the security guard turned to greet the next person going through his line, his smile deepened a bit at the sight of Della stepping up to bat. *So to speak.*

"Miss Costello," he greeted.

"Jethro." Della glanced down at her shoes, knowing the custom was to take them off if the guard asked. Safety, and all that. Crime in Chicago was higher than ever, and one couldn't be too careful. Problem was … well, *she* was also part of that crime. "You're not going to make me take these off, are you?"

"Probably not. Business today?"

"Unfortunately."

It was always going to be an unfortunate workday for someone else when she was called in to have a chat with them.

"Shame," he murmured. "Bag in the container. ID on the counter for me. Then, you may step through the scanner, please."

"Right, thanks."

She gave him another beaming smile and did as he asked. Stepping through the large scanner, Della kept her eye on the man while Jethro moved behind his desk to watch her bag go through the conveyor. Of course, the scanner blinked red. A couple of years ago, however, the building switched their systems so it no longer alerted the rest of the room to the fact someone was carrying metal into the building.

Like the gun and knife in Della's bag.

Or the blade at her thigh.

Jethro eyed her over the edge of the screen, and then wagged a single finger to invite her to pick up the designer handbag from the container when it was spit out the other side. As was custom for the arrangement she made with this man the first time she'd needed access to bring a weapon into this building, when she pulled out her bag, she made sure to leave a small roll of cash in the container that would disappear before he replaced it with the others.

"Lot of money in that bag today, huh?" he noted.

Della smiled. "Is it? I've not really counted."

Lie.

In the business of loansharking—her father's main source of income as a Capo to the Chicago mob—and collections when a client defaulted on their payment, Della had to know every single penny she had on hand, where it came from, and that was that.

Whose money it was, on the other hand, couldn't be questioned once she had been called in to retrieve it—the Costellos made sure of that.

"I hadn't realized you were only twenty-three until today," he noted, glancing down at her ID.

"And?"

Across the conveyor, the guard swallowed at her hard stare. Deciding to keep his mouth shut on any further comments, he simply said, "Enjoy your day, Miss Costello. I hope business treats you well."

"You, too, Jethro."

Her bag was back on her arm. The guard handed over her ID, and the world was right again. She could see the questions burning in his eyes. Especially the way his stare dropped to the identification card she now held. He was the same as every other acquaintance she'd made in her line of work—they always wanted to know the same damn things.

How did you find yourself here at only twenty-three?

It wasn't a simple answer. It never was when it came to the mob; how exactly should she explain that the illegal business of loansharking was a *family* venture, anyway? Frankly, Della didn't owe anybody shit.

"Anything else?" she asked, figuring she might as well put the man out of his misery.

Besides, a line was starting to form behind her of others wanting to get through the guard's scanners. And now she was running late, too.

That wasn't Della's style.

"Not a thing," Jethro murmured, picking up the container in such a way that he kept the cash inside hidden from any camera's view. He glanced at the line of people, shouting, "Next!"

Della headed for the bank of elevators on the other side of the entrance. *Time to get to work.*

When the elevator climbed the sixty flights to the floor that a CEO—Jared Tramen—had rented for the sole purpose of running his investment company from, Della switched back and forth from texting on her phone to talking into the small microphone that hung down from her one earbud. The two entirely separate conversations needed to end, and soon.

"Work done for the day?" her father asked in her ear.

"Almost. Just the Tramen debt."

"You're waiting for J, right?"

Her older brother—by only a *year*—he meant. If only her father knew how many collections she did on her own without her brother as a backup. Today didn't seem like the right moment to tell him the truth, really.

"*Adella Ivy,*" her father said in her ear.

Della had a good mind to roll her eyes and tell him to chill out, but her raising kept her from doing so. It didn't matter how old she was or that Frankie couldn't actually see her be rude. Her father wouldn't stand for any of it. Frankie came from a different generation where respect had been the word of the day *every fucking day*. He demanded the same from his children—it didn't matter if they were collecting his loansharking debts or going to an Ivy League college.

"Of course, I'm waiting for him," she lied smoothly.

A little white lie wouldn't hurt. Within the hour, she'd have the money, everything would be fine—as it always was when she did her job—and her father wouldn't know one way or another whether she waited for her older brother to get it done.

Who cared if it was *done?*

Right?

Besides, even J knew she could do this alone which was why he never said a thing when she did it. If her dad could figure that out, too, everything would be easy.

"Right, well, I'll let you get back to it, then. Be smart, hmm? Love you."

Della smiled. "Always am. Love you, too."

The elevator doors opened to expose a modernly decorated small reception with the name *Tramen* spelled out in golden script behind the woman sitting at a desk. With a Bluetooth in her ear, and her fingers flying across the keys, she didn't seem to notice Della stepping off the elevator. Since there was no one else in the reception area, she took a moment to end the *other* conversation she had going on in her text messages.

The last message from her friend popped up on the screen. The one she hadn't been able to reply to because her father called.

Jennika had simply written *are you still sad about your fuckhead ex?*

Fuckhead ex was a good way to describe Luis.

Small time gang leader with a superiority complex. Bad boy with *worse* intentions. Emotionally unavailable, incapable of being loyal to one woman which she learned way too late for her own good, and a problem in every other aspect of Della's life because despite how much she wanted him to be the *right* guy, he wasn't.

Hell, even her father hadn't known about him.

Not that he would have approved.

It took about a year for her to figure out Luis wasn't worth shit—but most men weren't, to be honest. Problem was, Della seemed to have a type with guys, and it wasn't the type of man she could bring home or count on to actually *come* home.

Usually tattooed. Ripped denim was a plus, leather a must. Combat boots were the cherry on top of a bad attitude with a give-no-fucks demeanor. Add on a pretty face to that mess, and she would eat right out of a man's hand. Apparently, her brain had not yet gotten through to her heart and vagina that things which looked like trouble almost always *brought* her trouble.

Perfect, right?

Yeah.

Luis was her latest mistake.

She wouldn't be making another any time soon because as far as she was concerned, it wasn't worth the effort. She was *not* chasing after another problem like that one. If only her ex would also get the goddamn memo, that would be great. So far, no luck.

Right now, Della had other things to focus on.

Instead of replying to her friend about the ex, she typed out, *I'm down the hallway. Incoming in less than five.*

That would give her friend—and partner in this business—just enough time to ready herself for Della's arrival, and if needed, make herself decent. Because where Della was the one who would go in and collect the debt when needed, Jennika was often the person they used to get her through the front door in many cases.

Sometimes, her friend ran her own side hustle with Frankie's debtors when she knew she could get away with it. A little blackmail or bribery never hurt anyone, after all, and as long as it didn't fuck with her business, she didn't care what Jennika did.

Simple as that.

It was the click-click of Della's heels on the tiled floor that had the woman behind the desk looking up from her work. She opened her painted-red lips to speak, likely to ask if she could help, but Della was quick to stop her before she could do or say anything at all.

"The escort Mr. Tramen has in his office is one of mine—I'm sure he told you to cancel his afternoon for him to spend it with her. He'll be expecting me."

Well, he wasn't.

But he should have.

As if Della's statement wasn't at all unusual, and it probably wasn't considering the CEO was in trouble with the mob's major loan shark, the woman gave a nod and went back to her work. Like not a single thing was out of place in her day.

Huh.

It said a lot.

Pulling the switch blade and Glock from her bag, Della readjusted the purse on her arm to keep it out of the way as she headed down a familiar hall. As was custom whenever her father took on a new client for loans, she and her brother always made a special trip in to see the individual in order to make the terms of their new arrangement with Frankie Costello clear. She'd walked this hall before.

Knew it well.

At the far end, a wall of frosted glass greeted her. Beyond the closed glass doors, Della could see shadowy shapes moving near something large and dark. She couldn't be sure if there were more people in the office than she was expecting. Given her conversation with Jennika and the plan they had in place, however, it should only be her friend and the CEO.

Della opened the door.

Her dark-haired friend in a dress better suited for a club, with makeup smoked out to the heavens to give her the sex appeal she loved so much, grinned over her shoulder from where she'd perched herself on the CEO's desk. Behind them, a wall of windows faced the skyline. In the chair, a man in a ruffled suit popped his head up from between Jennika's thighs.

A scowl on his face, Jared Tramen still had what was apparently his lunch smeared over his mouth as Della racked the gun while still holding onto the switch blade. The CEO didn't get the chance to say shit when her friend's heel met his forehead, and shoved him back into an office chair that was twice as wide in the high back as his own shoulders.

"Really?" Della asked Jennika when her friend shimmied down her skirt.

"I got bored."

Of course.

Or working an angle.

That was Jennika.

"What the fuck are you doing in here?"

Ah.

The man of the hour.

"Mr. Tramen," Della said, taking a single step into the office and kicking the door closed behind her, "we're here to talk about your debt to my father and how much you're willing to pay of it today. Careful, because before you speak, if the number doesn't please me. I'll take an inch. *Where* that inch comes will depend on your tone when you do speak to me."

In the chair, with a stiletto heel to his forehead, the man gaped.

As they usually did.

There were two types of men in the world, Della had learned … those who could *be* the boss, and those who only thought they were. More often than not, all it took was a woman to figure out which one a man was at the end of the day.

She enjoyed being the woman who did it.

THREE

"YOU'RE IN ONE piece," J said, greeting Della into his favorite booth inside the mid-town club he liked to frequent on nearly every damn night of the week. He gave her a one-armed hug, and used the same hold to pull her down to sit whether she wanted to or not. Chuckles passed down the table from her brother's friends. Or rather, those that he cared to have around when she was also nearby. All it took was a flip of his middle finger and the guys scattered. J—whose real name was Joel Peter, but fuck anyone who dared to call him that but for their mother—still didn't let his sister go from his grip. "Must mean the Tramen job went well today, huh?"

Della elbowed her brother hard in his kidney, earning a grunt from him but also her release from his grip. It didn't matter that they were twenty-three and twenty-four years old—not when the two of them were together and in a mood. They went back to being kids again who just loved to have fun with one another.

"If you're gonna be a brute, keep your hands to yourself, shithead."

"Bitch," he muttered as he picked up a glass from the table.

Whiskey, she thought.

He only drank whiskey.

"You fucked up my hair," she countered, flipping a loose strand of hair over her shoulder at the same time. It was a lie—her hair was fine. It did let her scan the floor of the club for her friend that should have already been there. "And the job did go well. Daddy called right before I went in, though."

Beside her, J stilled. "Oh?"

"He *asked* if you were going to be there. Well, if I was waiting for you. So, I kind of had to—"

"Don't lie to Dad, Della. I'm not going to out what you've been doing most of the time with work, and all, but … that's only because you should tell him you're not always following his rules."

Right.

Yeah.

She would get right on that.

"Where's Jennika?"

Tonight had been *her* idea, after all.

Just like the weekend before …

Although, that hadn't ended badly.

For her, anyway.

J picked up his phone, but his squint as he checked the screen told her that he wasn't very happy about it. "On her way, she says. The fuck you have to give her my phone number for, anyway? It's not like she works with *me*."

No, but her friend had a secret crush—that wasn't really so secret anymore—on Della's older brother that was nearly as old as they were, considering they'd been friends for about as long, too. Well, since their private high school days, anyway. With men in their life that just happened to be connected to the darker side of the world, the two were bound to come together at one point or another. Anyway, she was *trying* to help her friend out with J.

It wasn't working.

She did what she could.

"Indulge her," Della said, "even *once*."

"Adella—"

"Only Ma and Dad can call me that, *Joel*."

Her brother scowled.

Della winked right back.

"I'm not fucking Jennika," her brother said simply. "Because that girl is loyal to *no man*. And that's fine, if that's what a guy wants or whatever. I don't share, you know?"

Well …

"Your call," she returned.

She hadn't been seated more than a minute before a server came over with the house's drink for her and another glass of whiskey for J. The smile and wink that was shared between her brother and the server made Della think there might be another reason why J wasn't interested in her friend. She chose not to point it out or ask.

She loved her friend.

Wished she could help her.

J was still her blood. Her brother. No matter what. Way back when he had been doing work for their dad that she couldn't even consider trying herself, J was the one who dared to break the rules first which paved the way for her. He had her back no matter what.

So, she would always have his, too.

Pulling out the phone from her purse and dialing her friend's number, she muttered to her brother, "I'm just saying, maybe if you gave her a taste of whatever she wanted, she'd get over it. *And*, if she's distracted by her obsession with you for a little while, she might stop asking me about my ex for five damn seconds."

Della wanted to move on.

She was *ready* to do exactly that.

It was hard when someone kept talking about it, though. She knew Jennika meant well. That was the only reason why she didn't just outright tell her to knock it the fuck off. Her patience was still wearing thin.

At the mere mention of Luis, J's scowl from earlier came back with a vengeance. "I told you to tell that prick to—"

"And I did," she snapped.

Her friend's phone went to voicemail.

Where was she?

Ending the call, Della threw it back in her purse and turned on her brother in the booth. "I did tell him to get the hell out of my life—*you* were there when I did it, remember? Except he won't get the hint and *stay* gone because he keeps showing up whenever I think he's finally gone away, and I don't want him to start a problem for Dad."

Which was easier to do—both keep Luis away from her father and her father away from Luis—when her ex ran a small gang in the Heights, and her father ran his main operation *outside* of the city entirely. Especially when J and Della did most of the footwork for their dad inside the city, and he wasn't as hands on as he used to be with it all.

Keeping shit under his radar was simple.

J's gaze cut to her, the matching dark brown irises flashing with his worry and rage all at the same time. "He's small-time in the city—Dad's got a seat at the Outfit table as a Capo. It wouldn't even *be* a fair fight, Della. You don't have to handle the asshole alone. You're choosing to, yeah?"

So be it.

She could handle it.

Everyone else just liked to think she *couldn't*.

That was the problem.

"I'm not choosing anything because you think I *want* to get back with Luis," Della told her brother. "Just so that's clear. We're done—me and him, it's over. I'm over it. Last weekend took care of that, believe me."

Then, J grinned crookedly. He looked more like their mother, and so did she with high, sharp cheekbones, dark eyes, and angular jaws; his was simply the more masculine version. Although he couldn't take much from their dad. After all, biologically, J wasn't even Frankie's even if that's what all the papers said. He couldn't be when he'd met and married their mother when she was pregnant with Joel.

"What?" she asked when he kept grinning.

"*Right,* yeah, tattooed guy in the club's employee bathroom."

"Oh, my *God.*"

Her groan had her brother laughing.

"I drunk call you *every* time I go out," she said, "and then I have to remember it *later* because you don't even have the decency to tell me I do it the next day."

J shrugged like he didn't care at all. "I figure if you call me when you're drunk and spill all your secrets, then at least you're not doing it with someone you can't trust."

Well …

That was sweet.

Her embarrassment over drunk-calling her brother to spill all the details about her club hook-up the weekend before didn't last long. Hell, she only remembered brief flashes of it the day after. It took a couple days for all of it to come back. It wasn't like her to get so drunk that she would act foolish with a man, but it did what she wanted.

It got Luis straight out of her head.

Now when she was alone, her mind filled with thoughts of tattoos—wings on his throat; how those muscles there flexed when he swallowed—and the way he tasted when he kissed her after he'd ate her until she came. Before and *after* he'd fucked her.

Again.

Just for good measure.

It wasn't so much what she did—but *who*—that kept Della from wanting to talk about the hook-up. That was a secret better kept to herself, considering the man who'd picked her up hadn't seemed to know who she was, and frankly, from the rumors she knew about Cory Rossi … well, he was probably exactly her type.

Bad.

Rude.

Trouble all over.

Also, she was pretty sure he was a friend of her brother's—but that was business J did with the people of the Outfit that Della wasn't even allowed near. She knew just enough about Cory Rossi and the Outfit to know the men around him held the highest seats in the mob. Her father and brother kept all of that and those men far away from her. Or as much as possible. That way, no one who didn't really matter couldn't cause a problem about her involvement in the business.

She didn't know when that might change.

As for Cory …

She was going to keep pretending that didn't happen. Even if her mind and body wouldn't let her forget.

"Let's not ever mention that again," Della finally said, picking up the glass of liquor on the table that she had yet to touch. That moment seemed like the right one to down the whole damn drink in a single go. Next to her, J chuckled under his breath, but otherwise, said nothing more about her drunk calls.

Good.

Then, her brother's good mood vanished; in place of his previous happiness now rested a face made of angry stone. Della didn't even have to look over her shoulder to know what caused that look on her brother. Only one person made him *that* pissed.

Luis Ruiz.

"You having her watched now?" J asked as he rose from the table before Della could even get her glass set down. When she did, though, she was quick to stand and put a hand on her brother's chest to keep him from stepping around her to get out of the booth. "You must be, asshole, because how else would you know she was here tonight? She's only been here ten minutes—at *most.* You're looking to have a real fucking problem."

The dark chuckle behind Della had her giving J a look, one she hoped voiced for him to calm the hell down, before she looked over her shoulder.

The thing about Luis?

The man was devastating.

A little broken, too.

And he liked for everything else to be broken along with him.

Wrap that up in a package of gorgeousness and sex, and any woman who had a thing for a bad boy would run right after him. Della had not been an exception to the rule, but she wouldn't be stupid enough to fall for the trap twice.

So, his beautiful face made up of severe lines, with brows that dipped low in suggestion when he talked, and those lips that told the prettiest lies did nothing for her. That's how Della knew she was done. She looked at him and felt nothing.

"What do you want?" she asked.

Maybe if she just finally made it clear that she wasn't interested, because apparently ignoring his calls and getting rid of his shit a month ago hadn't been enough to do it, he would go away. Move on.

"Haven't found someone new to break, Luis?" she asked.

He smirked.

It was sexy, yes. Mix his swagger and charm with the power and control he exuded, and the man became a hurricane of everything attractive and forbidden. Except he also taught her a valuable lesson—she didn't like to be hurt.

"Just missing you, pretty thing," he returned gruffly.

Then, Luis's gaze cut to J behind her. Della's brother stiffened.

"Say it," he urged her ex.

"*J.*"

Her warning went right over J's head.

It had taken her all of ten seconds to realize that Luis had come at the worst time. After she got there, her brother sent the rest of the guys away.

Any protection he had inside the club was probably just out of reach, if he even had any. Was the place mob connected?

She didn't know.

But her ex?

Luis had six guys behind him.

All muscle.

She didn't recognize one of them.

Their tatts told her a lot, though.

Definitely gang.

"*What*," Della said strongly, meeting Luis's gaze, "do you want?"

Men always needed to be put back on task.

"A conversation, Dell."

She cringed at his nickname.

It'd never really been her thing.

Della—that's what she liked.

It's who she was.

"The lack of phone calls and shit didn't tell you I might not want to talk?" she asked.

He shrugged one distressed leather-clad shoulder. "Better to let you calm down, *loca*."

Nice.

The *crazy* comment—like it was meant to be affectionate—had her annoyed all over again in a blink. Not that it mattered. She wouldn't even give him anger anymore.

"*Just* a conversation?" she asked.

Because if she could get him out of the club, then she had a feeling that would be better for everyone in the place. She highly doubted J was slumming it in a business that *wouldn't* offer him some kind of protection being who he was.

No doubt, someone was watching.

Waiting.

Della wanted to diffuse anything before it even started. "If it's just a conversation, then you can walk me out."

"Were you leaving?" Luis asked, chewing through each word as the man always had to have a piece of mint gum, his grin firmly in place. "Because I thought you just got here."

She refused to indulge him.

In *any* way.

Luis wasn't affected, giving her a wink when he added, "Playing hard to get again. You know I love that, girl. We can chat while you call for a cab and that's it, that's all."

"Della—"

Fast, Della turned to grab her bag while also whispering to her brother, "Make sure there's a car for me. We'll get him the hell out of here."

J gave her a look, clearly displeased, but said nothing. He let her make her choices even if he *hated* them.

Della stepped out of the booth and before she even passed Luis by, he'd turned to walk with her *and* placed a hand on her lower back. A little too close to her ass. His hand flexed—fingers squeezing—on her body in the same possessive way he always touched her, but it did nothing for her now. The men who stood behind her ex spun on their heels to follow them out.

She didn't look back.

J would do what she said.

Wouldn't he?

"A conversation," Luis said, the crowd of dancing people parting for the *line* of tattooed men who now walked in front of them. "Let's have it."

"That does require occasional listening which was something you struggled with."

"Low blow, babe."

"Don't call me that. I'm not your *babe*, or your love or your fucking *loca*, Luis. All that really needs to be said here is that we're over. Which I already told you. It was cute the first week or so that you wouldn't give it up. Now it's just annoying because you're starting to be a problem, you know?"

She smiled up at him.

He stared back, cold.

Soon, the two of them were standing on the curb outside of the club. She turned slightly, just enough to watch the security come to stand at the door—at least ten of them. Some probably armed, if the place was in any way connected to mob business.

She felt safer at the sight of the men dressed in black. It meant her brother had probably done what he needed to do, and this bullshit she entertained with Luis could end.

Her attention went back to him when he said, "You know I miss you, yeah?"

"But I don't miss you. And that's the thing. We're *over*. It's okay to let it end like that. You can do your thing with somebody else, and you don't even have to *think* about me. Why aren't you doing that?"

He grinned. Once, that would have made her shiver. She still felt nothing.

"You lost your appeal," she told him. "It's not one of those things that comes back. It won't change. We're done."

"No, we're not."

His arm tried to wrap around her, but she took a wide step back, closer to the curb.

"I get it," Della said, "this isn't how it works for you, right? It's *you* who tosses somebody away when you're done with them. You're not used to being the one discarded. That doesn't change shit, Luis. You can't make me be with you, or want you, for that matter."

"You think?"

The question seemed innocent.

Even sounded like it.

Della didn't think it was.

"Don't cause a problem for pussy when we both know you've got a phone full of it that'll give you a lot less headaches than I will, Luis."

After all, his extra pussy was what ended this in the first place.

He didn't even deny it.

"Except you had to go and make me work for yours," he told her as a car pulled up to the curb with a guy in the driver's seat that she recognized. One of the guys who had been sitting in her brother's booth when she first arrived. The door was shoved open. Luis leaned in before she could step off the curb and get into the car. Just enough to catch a strand of her wavy brown hair between his fingertips when he said, "And since I earned it, I think that makes it mine, Della."

Up until then, she'd been *good*.

Didn't poke his monster.

Hadn't even *tried*.

"Fuck you, Luis."

The highest of disrespect, she knew.

He'd killed men for the same before.

She watched him do it.

Oh, well.

Della slipped out of his reach and into the safety of the car. Before he'd even stepped away, the guy hit the gas, making Luis jump back. The door shut with a *snap*.

"J says you're to go home—nothing else."

She glanced at her driver.

"He doesn't run my life."

"I do what the boss says."

Since when did someone call her brother *boss*?

Things were certainly changing, weren't they?

Della wondered if she might like it.

•••

"Home safe?"

"Yeah," Della said into the phone. "He just dropped me off at the townhouse."

"Lock the doors. He's not going anywhere but right outside your door for the night."

"What, like an enforcer, or—"

"Just don't ... ask?"

"When did things with Dad's business start to change for you?" she dared to ask her brother.

J sighed. "Last year."

"Huh."

A laugh echoed through the speaker.

"Just ask," he said.

"Well, are you trying to be like ... *in?* With all of it—the Outfit?"

"What else was I gonna do?"

Della climbed the front stairs to her townhouse, replying, "I guess we just never talked about it."

"Because nobody talks about it. That's the point."

Yeah.

Maybe.

Then, she had another thought as she dug through her bag for the set of keys that *always* managed to find their way to the very bottom. It never failed.

"I bet Jennika went to the club, and we weren't there—"

"She'll be fine. Girl goes there more than you know. Everybody knows her face."

"Oh."

"Mmhmm."

"Everybody's got secrets, huh?"

J laughed. "Whatever. Get some fucking sleep, ye—"

Her brother didn't finish his sentence. Or if he did, she didn't hear it. As she reached to put the key into the lock of her front door, she realized it wasn't locked at all. It wasn't even closed completely. She hadn't left the porch light on, so it was too dark to tell until it was too late.

And it was too late ...

She didn't even see that bat coming.

FOUR

"WHAT'S THE PLAN?"

In the passenger seat of the black '69 Shelby Mustang—that his uncle demanded to be the only thing Cory ever drove him around in—Theo smirked at Cory's question. "When do I ever have something like a *plan*, Cory?"

"But isn't that basically our everyday plan?"

Theo glanced over at him. "I mean—"

"You should just say *the usual*. Would have saved us this entire conversation."

"You're such a *shit*." Theo's laughter colored up the car. "Don't make me laugh before I have to do business, Cory. Makes it harder to keep a straight face."

"Sometimes smiling when you get work done is worse. Trust me—a man that can beat the hell out of you with a smile will fuck with your head worse than one who won't."

His uncle considered that.

Only for a second.

"Good point."

To another high-ranking man in the Outfit, a chat like that would have probably earned Cory a smack, *or worse*. Definitely a whole conversation with his father about disrespect and *boundaries*. All fun things.

Not.

Except this wasn't any other man. This was Cory's uncle. His mother's brother that he'd taken his middle name from. His *godfather,* too. People liked to say his carefree attitude and behavior came more from his uncle than his own father, Damian.

They probably weren't wrong.

It didn't matter that Theo had decades of experience and years on his nephew, either. They were always more friends than anything else. Even when his chance to dabble in the family business—*mob* business—came up shortly before his sixteenth birthday to mentor under his uncle, Cory didn't hesitate to say yes.

Next to a portfolio of businesses that he kept with his brother for the purpose of hiding, laundering, or washing cash, his main business with the Outfit revolved around working with his uncle. The Outfit's *front* boss, and the only man keeping the streets mean.

It appeared like Theo called all the shots to anyone who might be watching. Outside organizations. Officials. Even people on the *streets.* It was a rather significant seat in the Outfit's tiers of power because when all the attention was on his uncle and the business he did while on the streets, it kept their eyes far away from what was really happening *inside* the mob.

Like Tommas—a man he knew as his uncle but was really Cory's second cousin by blood—the *real* boss.

And all the illegal deals he had going.

It worked.

Well.

"You're going to kill this shit when it's you," Theo said absently as he turned to watch the familiar buildings on the east end pass them by. Their destination was coming up in three blocks, so whatever had his uncle in his retrospective feelings was going to have to be packed away in a few moments. "They worry all the time—think you won't be *ready.* Some shit, that. You'll be fine."

"What?" Cory asked, his grip on the wheel tightening.

Theo didn't even turn to face him when he scoffed under his breath and said, "Come on, Cory. Don't pretend like you're unaware of the shit you do. Trouble doesn't just *find* you. It's not like you're stumbling on it. You actively look for it."

Yeah, yeah. His self-preservation was shit, and he had little to no moral compass. Safe was *boring.* Same shit, different day. That also wasn't what he'd meant.

"Why'd you say when it was me doing this?"

That had his uncle turning in the seat.

Face to face, it was much more obvious to Cory how he had taken more of the DeLuca side of his family genes than the Rossi in appearance. The hard, sharp planes of his uncle's face was an older mirror of his own right down to the masculine grin and jawline that could cut steel. The only difference was the eyes.

Theo, with his brown.

Cory, with his blue.

"Your father is the underboss—your second cousin is the *boss.* You've mentored under *me.* Where did you think you were going when you joined the family? Did you think we'd place you boys where you couldn't *control?*"

Theo resumed his previous position in the passenger seat but now pulled out his black leather driving gloves because, in one short block, they had work to do. "I wasn't more than a couple of years older than you or so when I came into this position—unusual to be that young, but the circumstances of the Outfit then were a lot different than it is now. We did what we had to do for it to be *ours.* You've got a while more to go, though. I happen to like what I do. Either way, it *will* be you. And you will be fine."

Cory focused on the road.

His uncle reached between the front seats to offer an open-gloved hand to the Rottie sitting in the back. *Cory's* dog, Mace. He was being an extra good boy because it wasn't very often he got to drive around the city with his master all day while he worked.

Mostly because if he *did* attack, one couldn't get him off. A lot of the time, Mace didn't like to wait for the order. He was still learning.

The pup sniffed, then licked, Theo's open palm.

"You gonna be loud today?" his uncle asked his dog.

The dog chuffed.

"Big and scary boy, Mace, yeah, I know."

The almost *babyish* tone his uncle took on had Cory suppressing a grin. Dogs and kids, man. Those were the only thing that could turn his uncle into a teddy bear, but not very many people knew the secret trick.

"Shit, I wasn't even gonna let him out of the car for this one," Cory grumbled. "I didn't bring his leash and you know he'll act—"

"He's only a year old. He's still a *baby*," Theo cooed to the pup, scratching Mace's ear with his gloved finger. "Aren't you? Yeah, you're just a baby."

"He's eighty-five pounds of *muscle*. He eats two bowls of food a day. I don't think we can call that a baby."

"Well, he is. As for making him mind, it's all in the *tone*, Cory."

He *did* mind. Quite well. Just sometimes he liked to do what he wanted to do. A lot like Cory.

"Right, well … check it out. You were right; we didn't even have to go looking for the stupid fucks."

Theo faced forward in his seat as Cory slowed the Mustang coming up along a popular block corner where a few small-time dealers liked to chill on the street in between drops. Problem was, two of those dealers had an issue while dealing a little too close to a warehouse where the Outfit's stash of guns that they sold on the illegal market had been stored. There'd been cops up and down the row of industrial buildings for *days*, making any Outfit business impossible.

As for his uncle?

And why Cory was there?

Just to make a point.

Anybody else doing business in the city—whether with the Outfit or not—needed to make sure they didn't bring any problems to the mob. It was a good lesson to learn.

Cory put the car into park on the side of the street as the guys lingering on the corner nodded at the black Mustang, and its illegally tinted windows. How many fines was he up to for that now? *Four?* Theo stepped out of the car before Cory had even tossed off his seatbelt. He got out of his side at the time his uncle pulled a bat from the backseat *and* let Mace out.

Rounding the back of the car with a whistle falling on his lips while he shoved his hands into the pockets of his leather jacket, Cory had Mace hanging back closer to him. He leaned against the trunk of the Mustang, letting his uncle do what he had to do—if he needed to step in, then he would.

Twenty feet away, one of the dealers took a step toward Theo who was making his way to a red beamer—the guy's car that had caused the problem.

"Hey!" the dealer shouted. "What the fuck are you doing?"

Another guy stepped toward Cory.

He ticked his chin up at the man and grinned, arching a brow. Mace—all eight-five-fucking-pounds of him stood just two feet ahead of Cory with teeth bared.

"Try it, yeah?" Cory called.

The first smash of glass had the car's alarm going off when Theo shoved the handle of the bat through the back window.

"What the fuck are you—"

The guy darted forward, already reaching for his back where he likely had a gun hidden.

Cory whistled a shorter, higher sound.

For him and Mace, it wasn't about the tone at all. It was all in the whistle.

Mace went bark-shit crazy. Spittle flying and all.

With the Rottie and the gun Cory pulled out from his own back to hold at his front, Theo got his business done and the message across. He was sure the six-foot-four guy dressed in leather and combat boots with the scary dog and a gun helped with that. Another satisfying workday.

He doubted it was anywhere near over.

•••

"Get out," Theo said once Cory had parked the Mustang in the circular driveway of the Trentini mansion. "Have a smoke with me."

"All right."

It was the only time he did smoke anymore.

Otherwise, his mother never got off his ass.

Theo answered his ringing phone while he exited the car. Cory, on the other hand, let Mace out of the back for the dog to wander the lush, well-manicured front yard. The man down near the gate—an enforcer for the Outfit's boss who rarely left the property; the man even had his own rooms in the mansion—whistled low for the pup. It sent Mace running for the guy.

Since this was the last stop every day for Cory when he was acting as his uncle's driver, the people who worked on the grounds knew his dog well. And for the most part, they liked Mace. Those that didn't ... well, Cory figured maybe that said more about them than his pup.

But who was he to say?

Cory settled in beside his uncle where Theo leaned against the hood of the Mustang. He'd taken those leather riding gloves off, and looked as though it could be him who owned the mansion in front of them what with his black, three-piece Armani suit and the thin gold chain he kept around his throat that matched the rings on his fingers.

Theo passed him a smoke.

Cory lit it with a silver Zippo he kept on hand whenever he needed to light the occasional blunt. Pulling a drag from the smoke, he eyed the mansion and then the phone that Theo was quick to tuck away.

"What was that call about?" he asked.

It'd been over before it even began.

Theo shrugged. "Tommas—wants to have a chat."

"Isn't that why you're here?"

It's why he dropped Theo off at the end of any workday. A meeting between the front boss and main boss of the operation kept things running smoothly. Not to mention, he knew his father, Theo, and Tommas were all friends beyond *la famiglia*.

A sigh echoed from his uncle. "No, he wants to talk to *you*."

Oh.

"He'll be down in a minute. Wants to catch you before you leave, apparently."

That had Cory straightening up a bit. And maybe a little too warm under the collar of his leather jacket. Although Tommas Rossi was also his second cousin, but for the most part he'd called him *Uncle*, and his son, Tommaso, was one of Cory's best friends ... well, the older he became it seemed like all he called the man now was—

"Theo, don't throw that butt in my yard. You know good and well my wife will have a fit when she sees it. And she *will* see it."

"Learned my lesson the last time," Theo said, glancing up with a grin as Tommas closed the main doors at the front of the mansion behind him. Stepping down the marble stairs and then out beyond the pillars, the Outfit boss barely glanced around at his surroundings. He'd never behave like that anywhere else. At home, he felt the safest, Cory knew. "You're seriously going to put him with someone else? What the fuck am I going to do, huh?"

He didn't have a clue what his uncle was talking about. Tommas was also now looking his way expectantly, reminding him of his place against the other man without saying a word.

"Boss," Cory said with a nod.

Tommas smiled thinly, coming to a stop a few feet ahead of the car. "Evening, Cory." Then, his gaze cut to Theo. "And don't worry; I'm sure he'll occasionally find his way over to your side of things for … whatever. It's also not forever. Just for a time."

"*Right*," Theo said, lifting his cigarette for another drag.

"I missed something."

Cory's statement had the boss's attention back on him. It wasn't that it bothered him really, but he'd be a liar if he said it didn't put him on edge. There was no malice in Tommas's stare—simply a perusal of the young man in front of him. Cory always found himself wondering if the men of his family thought he … wasn't up to par. Because he didn't follow the same rules they did all the time. Because he didn't dress in suits when he preferred leather and combat boots paired with ripped jeans.

Because he wasn't like his brother—*Joe.*

Who wasn't wild; who never stepped out of line; who followed the path set out for him because that's what he wanted. Cory, on the other hand, zigzagged and *jumped* through his fucking life while everyone else waited for the inevitable fall.

So yeah.

He wondered.

Not that they ever said anything one way or another.

"You'll have some new business for a while," Tommas said, breaking the silence. "You'll be answering to a Capo that mostly stays outside of the city limits. It's the crew that works for him in the city where he makes all his money."

It took Cory a second.

"Costello?"

The loan shark?

Damn.

"Frankie," Tommas confirmed, nodding. "He's a good man—you know his son."

"J, yeah." Cory shrugged. "That's about all I know, though."

"Never really intersected with him for business," Theo said out of the corner of his mouth where the cigarette still bounced on his lips. It was just about gone now. "Which isn't a bad thing."

Right, because if the front boss was all up in your business to see what was going on and not just to collect money you might owe to the boss, then something was *very* wrong. Cory had enough to handle between his work with his brother, his businesses in the city, and his uncle that he didn't have time to be sticking his nose in the business of every made man of the Outfit in and outside of the city.

Simple as that.

"Anyway," Tommas said, bringing them back to the main point of Cory's new job—*apparently*. "He makes a steady, stable profit. Doesn't have much trouble. Well … usually. A problem came up recently. His daughter was attacked at her townhome in the city. Apparently, she's been running with his crew."

Theo coughed hard.

Tommas gave him a look. "What?"

"Been doing that for a while."

"Pardon me?"

Theo sighed and leaned further into the car. Pulling what remained of the cigarette from his mouth, he lifted his leg to snuff it out against his shoe before he pocketed the butt. "Your wife bitches about my butts in your driveway. Mine bitches about the ones she finds in my pockets. I can't get a fucking break, man."

"Don't deflect."

"Not deflecting. Sharing some truth." Straightening up, Theo folded his arms over his chest. Cory chose to stay quiet and watch the exchange. Sometimes, he learned more that way. "Listen, Adella's been working for her father for a while. Affiliations, and all. It's not a new development—she's good at what she does."

Adella.

Why did that sound familiar?

"J has a sister?" Cory asked.

Maybe he sounded too curious about the news. It wasn't that the guy had a sister that made him feel as much, but rather her name just seemed to ring a bell in the back of his head that he couldn't place. And whatever that bell was, it made his chest tight as fuck.

In a *good* way.

Strange.

Two pairs of eyes turned on him.

His uncle looked amused.

Tommas just seemed …

"She's your job, actually," the boss said. "And I expect you to behave as such, Cory. This is important—you're being put in front of another Capo. Somebody with a seat at the table. You understand, don't you?"

Yeah.

Of course.

But …

"You want me to *babysit* the loan shark's daughter?"

"Keep an eye on her. Work with her father on the issue, if he needs you to. If she does have a heavy hand in his business—Theo," Tommas added, pointing a finger at Cory's uncle, "I want more information about that—then I suspect she will still have work to do, no?"

32

"Is it because she's a chick?"

"Pardon?"

"A female," Cory clarified. "What, even if she's good at what she does, she still shouldn't be doing it because she gets wet between her thighs?"

Was he a little crass?

Maybe.

Facts were still facts.

"Is this going to be a nightmare?" Tommas asked Theo.

Theo chuckled. "Nah, Cory's *gold*. Just a little … crazy sometimes."

Tommas's gaze landed on Cory again. "It's not *just* because she's a woman, but men do tend to cause a lot more problems when their women are involved than when they're not in this life. As for this … Adella, and you watching her. Well, they're not sure what happened, and we doubt you're a familiar face to people she may be working with, so you'll make a good guard for her. You won't raise any brows or clue them into what Frankie might be doing behind the scenes. Clear enough?"

He looked to Theo. "I seriously gotta be a babysitter?"

Theo shrugged, helpless. "Have fun?"

Yeah.

Right.

The way Tommas was staring at him, there would be no fun being had. This was supposed to be all business.

Just perfect.

FIVE

"RISE AND FUCKIN' shine, little sister!"

"*Ugh.*"

Of course.

Of course, J would use the spare key for Della's townhouse to enter her place way too early in the morning. It was only meant to be used for emergencies.

When had her brother *ever* cared about details?

Never.

That's when.

His voice bounced along the downstairs corridor and up the stairwell. It traveled all the way to her master bedroom at the far end. There was a sort of glee to his tone that said J had probably been awake for a couple of hours and already had a good start on his morning.

Great for him.

It kind of annoyed her how some people—people like her brother— could be *that* chipper first in the morning, to be honest. She needed time to wake up, put on her face, and be able to pretend like she gave a shit. Which was hard to do when everybody else wanted to be morning people. Like that should even be a thing.

Damn them all.

She didn't even have time to prepare for her brother because just as she rolled over to her stomach in bed to pull the blanket higher, she heard his heavy footsteps pounding up the stairs. Their mother—Chloe—liked to say anyone knew when J was in a house because he walked like a herd of elephants. Frankly, their ma wasn't wrong.

"Don't come in my room," she mumbled.

Probably too low for her brother to hear. Not that it mattered. It'd never mattered to J.

He came storming into her room the same way he used to do when they were teenagers, and he needed to yank her out of bed for school because she refused to get up for her mother's calls.

"Seriously, it's *nine,*" her brother said, although his voice was slightly muffled from the fact she was still hiding under the blanket. Not that the reprieve lasted for long. He grabbed the edge at the bottom left corner and yanked hard enough to pull the blanket from the bed entirely. That left Della splayed on her stomach in the middle of the bed wearing an oversized

34

T-shirt, cotton shorts, and *cold* from the air that wrapped around her. "Get up, we've got shit to do."

"I hate you, J."

"Nah, you *love* me. It's the law of siblings or some fucking nonsense."

Right.

"Is it also the law that I can kill you for being annoying? If not, it should be."

She muttered that against her sheets.

Her brother only laughed.

The *asshole*.

"Damn, you really are tired, huh? That was your lamest comeback ever. Really, though. Get up. Dad wants to see you."

His tone softened a bit for that.

Della sighed. "I'd rather not."

It felt like all she had done since the attack—which left her with a bad bruise, a concussion, and a trip to the hospital where her entire family gathered like it was going to be her last night on earth—was talk to her dad. About *everything*.

From the business she'd done alone without her brother's supervision to the ex who showed up the night someone decided to hit her in the side of the head with a bat on her own fucking doorstep. And she was right about how Frankie would feel regarding her ex. Her father had absolutely not approved.

He wasn't *mad*.

No.

Just disappointed. As though that made anything better.

"Can't I have one day where I don't have to listen to Dad *worry* about me?" she asked.

It was a rhetorical question.

Her father would never stop worrying. That was most of the problem in a nutshell. It was also why, despite the fact she didn't want to get out of bed, she still would. And she would head across town to sit down for breakfast with her mother and father, too, even though it would only lead to yet another conversation about business, her involvement, and the details she'd been selectively leaving out for her father's benefit.

Or as he told her earlier in the week, *her* benefit.

Nonetheless, it all boiled down to the fact he was worried. So was her mother. J, too.

In the grand scheme of things, Della was fine. A baseball bat to the head—though they couldn't be sure if the attack was a product of her involvement in collecting her father's loansharking debts or her ex-boyfriend who just happened to show up on the same night it happened—

wasn't that bad. Not considering everything else she had seen or got too close to over the years.

Somehow, Della needed to show her father—and maybe her brother, too—that she was just fine, and this little problem of the attack hadn't put her off balance. She was ready to get back to work, what remained of the yellow bruise could be hidden by concealer, and when she figured out who exactly had done this to her, they were going to regret it in the worst possible way.

"*Go away.*"

"It's not that bad, come on," J said.

Turning her head to the side, Della eyed J where he had come to stand at the side of her bed. "The *second* something bad happened, what did you do?"

That had J giving her a look.

She stared right back.

"Dell—"

"You spilled *everything* to Dad," she said before he could come up with some kind of an excuse that really wouldn't help the situation. "You told him about everything. And what did that leave me doing? *Dealing with it,* J."

"He needed to know."

"No, he didn't."

"Yes, he did. Because what if the attack wasn't meant to be a singular incident? What if it had a bigger purpose? Even if it doesn't seem like that, we have to treat it like it does because that's the world we live in. You need to be safe and so, Dad needed to know all the details. He was going to learn that you've been working without me and running with guys who aren't shit, anyway. It was just a matter of time."

Maybe.

J had a point.

Still …

"It didn't have to be you that told him," she said, gaze narrowed. "Because I'm pretty sure there's some shit in the sibling code about not ratting each other out, but especially not when we're *adults*."

"I mean … keeping you safe trumps that."

God.

She hated when he did that.

"Get out of my room," Della demanded.

"Get up and ready to leave. We've got an hour and a half—we're doing brunch."

"Great."

"And chill the attitude."

Della heaved herself up from the mattress, but really just wished she had stayed right where she had been before her brother waltzed in to drag her from dreamland. It was only because she loved her brother, and they *did* have a close bond, that she didn't reach for the blade on her nightstand to *make* the asshole leave her alone, so she could go back to sleep.

"Besides," J said, heading for the door, "I think you're going to be … mostly happy today. Dad got some stuff figured out for you. You can do what you want; he gets what he wants. I can still do what I was doing elsewhere for work. You're just going to have to deal with it."

Still sleepy, she called out at his retreating back, "What does that even mean?"

"Get up and find out."

He slammed the bedroom door shut.

Just perfect.

J knew the right way to make Della move. All she needed was a hint of something going on that dealt with her of which she wasn't aware, and she started moving her ass to get ready for the day. Before long, she'd dressed in her staple skinny jeans, pointed-toe stiletto heels, had thrown her hair into a messy bun, and threw on a blazer that matched her shoes overtop a silk blouse. She took the most time on her makeup because that was a non-starter for Della.

It didn't matter if she was only leaving the house to have brunch with her parents and brother. *If* she left the house, her face was painted to the Gods.

Always.

Unsurprisingly, J was already waiting at the door with her purse held out when she came down the stairs. She snatched it from his grasp as she checked her phone for any message she might have missed last night or over the morning.

Mostly, from Jennika.

It wasn't like her best friend not to message her a half of a dozen times by the time Della finally rolled her ass out of bed. Yet another person in her life that she loved to death who also just happened to be one of those awful morning people.

Except there was no message.

Not even an emoji.

Della brushed it off but sent a message to her best friend all the same. *Back to work ASAP—brunch with Dad in an hour if you wanna come?*

Her parents wouldn't mind. More often than not, Jennika trailed along anyway.

"Your chariot awaits," J said, swinging open the front door to expose his muddy Jeep parked right behind her white Benz.

Della scowled. "Can we take my car?"

Not that she didn't like the Jeep. It was the *mud*, which she didn't know how her brother managed to find in a city, that bothered her more than anything. No matter how hard she tried to avoid it, she still got dirty whenever she traveled in her brother's vehicle.

Because of course ...

Wasn't that just her luck?

J only laughed. "Fuck no—I got business after brunch. I won't be showing up to that in your pretty little white *coupe*, sis."

She wished she was shocked.

But nope.

"Let's go, then."

•••

"Have fun, hmm?"

Della's mother smiled and winked at her husband as the two stood from their chairs. Always the gentleman, Frankie made sure to pull his wife's coat from the back of the chair and help her put it on before he leaned in for a kiss.

"And mind yourself," her father added with a chuckle.

"I'll try. It is Abriella, though ... you know how it is."

"Stay a bit, Ma," Della spoke up, drawing in her father's sharp eye. "I've barely been here fifteen minutes."

Chloe gave her daughter a smile from the side that said she knew exactly what Della was attempting to do. The longer her mother stayed for brunch, the less she would have to talk to her father about business ... and everything else that would surely follow. They didn't talk shop with her ma around, and right now, she'd prefer that.

Even if she was still curious about what her brother had said earlier.

"Maybe, had you gotten up earlier," Chloe returned, "we could have had a long breakfast."

Damn her mom. And Chloe's *all-knowing* motherly senses, as she liked to call it. She kind of loved her mom for it, too.

"Later," Chloe said to Frankie.

"Have a good time, sweetheart."

Under his breath beside her, J muttered, "I could go for a wine tasting this afternoon with the Outfit boss's wife instead of sitting here, too, but you know."

"Shut up. I could literally stab you under the table—my blade is right there in my bag."

Within reach, too.

Childish?

Yes.

At this point, who cared?

By the time her father had walked Chloe out of the restaurant and returned to the table, he wasn't alone. Jennika accompanied him, her smile growing at the sight of the food spread out across the large table in the private dining section of one of three restaurants her father owned in the city.

"Yes, I'm *starved*," her friend said, dropping into the seat Della's mother had vacated earlier. She reached for a croissant and an already-poured glass of orange juice that Chloe hadn't touched before adding, "Your text woke me up, thanks."

Della grinned, not at all sorry. "Since when are you not up before me anyway?"

"Sometimes. It was a good night."

Laughter passed around the table.

It wouldn't last long.

With that *slept-in* makeup look that women spent hours desperately trying to copy and a high, messy pony, Jennika didn't look at all tired or bothered to be there. She wore a long trench coat overtop a dress that looked more appropriate for a club than this place. Not that her friend, or anyone else at the table, really cared. Della just took note of it because well, when her friend went out the night before, usually she'd give her a call.

But she hadn't last night.

Who knew?

Maybe her friend had a new guy—despite chasing after Della's brother, she still enjoyed male company in between. Good for her.

"New plan," Frankie said, reclaiming his seat and the coffee he'd set aside to see his wife out. "On the work side of things, of course. I'm not taking any risks over the next little bit while we feel this out and look for information. If it was business, it might have been a one-time thing. If it was gang-related—"

"It wasn't Luis," Della said in a sigh.

Across the table, her father's dark gaze landed on her. Another day, and the sight of that might have been enough to keep her quiet. Maybe it was the lack of sleep making her foolish, but she kept talking.

"Is he trash? Yeah. He's not exactly the kind of trash who would come after me for telling him to fuck off somewhere."

Or, that's what she liked to think. Yeah, his pride was hurt. He would get over it. She was just a woman, and God knew he had dozens of those. Luis wouldn't put that much effort into sending a woman who rejected him a message like the one delivered to Della through a baseball bat to the head.

"I'm not so sure," her father returned, his tone measured. A good sign that he wasn't pleased but was still doing his best to keep it contained. "Nonetheless, because of his connections to *other* gangs in the city that have been problematic to the Outfit, I would rather not test the theory which means we're going to keep your involvement with him on the low."

"*Previous* involvement," she put in strongly.

"And isn't that a good thing?"

"Daddy—"

Frankie raised his brow, quieting her instantly. "I've been fine to keep my nose out of your business where men are concerned, for the most part, but this one might be a problem, and I won't apologize for doing what I need to do and pulling rank, Adella."

Full first name.

He only used that when he was serious.

"You're right," her father added after a moment, "we *don't* know that this … *Luis* … was the cause of the attack. It could have been related to business. We don't know otherwise, either. Which brings me to an impasse of one way or another, we need to handle business differently until we do get it figured out. Because like I said, I'm not taking risks. Money still has to move, it's the nature of the business, but it's *how* it'll be moving with you involved that might have to change for a bit."

Della sat straighter, her anger simmering just below the surface. She didn't like what her father implied.

"What does that mean?" she asked.

Sipping from his coffee as though he couldn't see very well that Della was starting to get a little edgy at the turn this conversation had quickly taken, her father pointed at Jennika while the girl smeared her croissant with butter. "You're to always work with your partner—we'll circle back around to the business you were doing without your brother another time, don't worry—and there's nothing wrong with letting Jennika handle things on her own otherwise. She knows what she's doing when it comes to collecting—"

"*I* know what I'm doing," Della said, snapping the words. "I get that you're worried and all, but I've been running with J since back when he was peddling shit from his backpack in high school. And what, the moment something bad happens as soon as he's not around, now you say I can't do what I've always done?"

"Except there's a target on your back now—that's why it was *you* that had a visitor in your house with a baseball bat and not someone else. They wanted the message to go through *you*. You're not seeing that, are you?"

A black Mustang caught Della's eye as it parked in front of the windows of the private dining section on the street outside. Never mind that the windows were tinted so darkly that she couldn't even see the driver; whoever it was parked in a No Parking zone. She had a good mind to admire the shiny vehicle and appreciate its beauty, but the conversation at hand was more important, so she went back to her father.

If he noticed her distraction, he didn't say.

"Della, I know you're good at what you do—it's too late to tell you to step back from it," Frankie said, his tone quieter but not at all softer, "but that changes *nothing*. Until we understand *why* it was you, and we take care of it, the business will be done to my spec. Do you hear me?"

"Okay, so Jennika is with me. J can—"

"Your brother has his own business to handle with other people and for me elsewhere. I can't pull him from that often enough to make me think it would be beneficial to both of you."

Just what all was her brother doing in the Outfit?

She knew now wasn't the time to ask.

"You, on the other hand, will also have someone to watch your back. When you're doing business, if you're going out to dinner ... even if you just want to go to the gym. His job is to keep an eye on you for the time being. Call him a bodyguard, if you want. He's certainly trained like one— unintentionally acts that way for a few other people in the Outfit, not that it matters."

He?

Like a guy?

"Why—because I need a *man* to look after me?" she asked, not at all hiding the contempt in her tone at the idea. "Because someone breaking into my house to ambush me is a good indicator of how well I can protect myself as a woman, right? Like the same thing couldn't have happened to you or J, huh?"

Even Jennika slowed her chewing at that statement. Beside her, J shifted in his seat and did his best to stare at anything but his sister and father. Frankie, however, kept his expression passive and nodded at something— or rather, *someone*—over her shoulder.

"So what if it is a man," her father asked, "as long as he does his job and keeps you safe while we figure out the details here? And if you have anything further to say about your new friend, you can say it to him— Cory?"

Oh, God.

No.

Please, God, don't let it be him.

A throat cleared behind her.

She knew that sound.

Heard his voice before he even spoke.

"Guess I'm a little late, huh? Sorry. Thought you said noon, boss."

There was no possible way for her father to know the true reason why the color drained from Della's cheeks when she dared to glance over her shoulder at the new presence. *Cory Rossi*, that was. The man she hooked up with in the club two weeks earlier. His gaze darted to hers, a raging blue so bright with recognition that she could tell two things: one, today he was sober; two, he remembered who she was.

She wouldn't lie. He looked good standing there. *Real* good. Black on black with hair slicked back; denim and leather added to his already edgy, alluring vibe. He *screamed* trouble in more ways than one.

"I did say noon, but my wife changed her mind about joining a friend, and she still wanted to see the kids. I didn't think it mattered when you showed up—the end result would be the same, Cory. Give my daughter the chance to calm down and see things rationally, and I'm sure you two will have plenty of time to get to know one another considering how much you'll be working together for the next little while as we handle this problem."

Jesus.

Her heart thundered.

Cory arched a brow.

That made her heart *stutter.*

Della did the only thing she could. "I need a minute."

Her tone suggested she was still pissed. It was *way* more than that.

As she stood, J's hand flicked up with two things for her to take. A cigarette, and a lighter. Her brother knew her damn well, and like everyone else at the table and in the room—including Cory when she passed him by—said nothing as she left.

Sometimes, people just needed a second to get it together. Della wasn't an exception to the rule.

SIX

"DELLA."

She stiffened, the cigarette between her fingertips—she only smoked when *everything* in her life felt like it was going to shit, or right after a good fuck—bounced from the shiver that raced through her body. She knew his voice entirely too well because she heard it in her dreams far more than she would admit. It was a little different in her dreams, yes. Rougher and breathier because the last time she'd heard it, he'd been fucking her. It was just her luck that neither her body nor mind wanted to forget it.

Whether or not he noticed her reaction to him saying her name when he stepped out into the back alley of the restaurant, Della couldn't say. She did her best to hide it, all the while avoiding his gaze as he crossed the damp pavement to lean against the wall beside her.

She didn't need to look at him when she'd already done that *more* than enough between the club, and *earlier* ... not to mention, her anger was still quite present. Oh, she understood good and well he was just there to do a job, but sometimes misplaced anger was a woman's second-best friend. Or it was certainly hers.

Della would bite at *anyone* when she was mad. A fault of hers she hated more than anything, but one she'd never been able to fix.

Yet, even staring down at the ground gave her a view of his black jeans tight to muscular thighs, and the scuffed combat boots tied around the ankles. His entire aesthetic was a drug to her senses, and he probably didn't even know it.

Fuck him for that, too.

"It's Della," he said, breaking her daze.

Not enough to make her look at him, though.

"Your name, I meant," he added. "I couldn't remember it. Not that night, and not until I stepped into that dining room and saw you. Not surprised, though."

"Why's that?"

"Pretty things are lies, girl. Pretty always lies. Nothing that looks pretty is *ever* what it seems on the surface. Of course, you weren't just some beautiful woman in a club—you had to be *more*. Can't trust pretty things. No offense, or whatever."

She tried to laugh it off.

He had been drunk. It didn't hurt her feelings. He also was kind of right.

It just wasn't a memory she wanted to revisit for too long because then he would see the heat start to climb in her cheeks, and she just couldn't afford that right now.

"Well, to be fair, I already knew yours," she replied, "or enough, anyway. I just didn't think it mattered. We were only having fun."

"Yeah, you're not wrong. Still, what were the chances, huh?"

Didn't she know it?

"But hey," Cory said suddenly.

He snatched her cigarette from her fingers before she could stop him as she was still staring at the ground like it was her new best friend. Not that it mattered because all she could see was the cloud of smoke he exhaled and his carved-from-stone profile while he peered down the other end of the alley. He'd slicked back his dark, tapered fade; the strands wet-looking but she knew that just kept his hair in place.

Despite the fact he'd taken *her* cigarette, he already had one stuck behind his ear. The ball piercings in the cartilage of his ear glinted in the small bit of light that was afforded into the alleyway. The silver hoop that hugged his lower earlobe matched the one in his nose. *God.* All the little details of his face that she'd forgotten came rushing back, and she could only see *part* of it. He truly was a godly man.

"With that out of the way," he added, not missing a beat or knowing that she was staring at him like a love-struck *girl*, "let me fill you in on what you seemed to miss back there with your father."

"Don't bother."

"I'm sorry, you thought I asked if you wanted to hear it? Because I didn't." He didn't even let her correct his attitude. Just continued right on, anyway. "You know, if your father thought you needed a man to just … *take care of you*, as you said back in there," Cory drawled, his words slow, and sensual instead of the condescending arrogance she expected, "then you wouldn't have ever touched his business in the first place."

"Excuse me?"

"Be real, babe. Women who get taken care of in this life don't even have to worry about chipping a nail on even the *suggestion* of something illegal most of the time. They're happy, *pleased* women, and I'm not saying there's anything wrong with that, but they don't touch mob shit, enjoy their privilege, and not much else. They're *fine* like that. It's how they want it. You get what I'm saying?"

Della chewed on that, considering … "I do, but—"

"Nah, see all you needed there was the *I do*, the rest is just you trying to save your pride because you threw a temper tantrum and kind of showed your ass. I bet it's hard being a chick in this business—they do say it's a man's world, right? But your father had already taken the familial aspect out of what happened to deal with you *and* the business side of things. It was you who hadn't, and it's okay to admit that."

Fire blazed through her.

Who did this guy think he was?

"How dare you—"

He kept looking down the alleyway, away from her so their gazes couldn't meet. She *wished* he would look at her then so that he could see the hatred glaring back at him that she felt in those moments. Instead, she was stuck scowling at the way the leather of his jacket molded to his broad shoulders and how his back flexed when he shrugged. Those tattoos peeking out above the collar of his jacket, and the plain black tee he wore underneath had a heady memory thrusting through her mind of how sinful that same ink had tasted under her tongue.

Like sex and salt.

Fuck her whole life.

And fuck her for being attracted to Cory Rossi, too.

"The fact you're *here*, that he offers you protection because you need it while you work, says he respects you the same he would any other employee of his that is valuable to him. And don't for a second think he wouldn't give someone else the benefit of protection, too, if he thought it might be a danger to his *business* or well-being."

"I'd like to think I'm more than just his employee. It's not like this is a traditional business or something. Maybe I do my own thing, or *could,* and some decisions could be left to me. Like whether or not I want a guy trailing me day and night."

"One of the *most* traditional, actually. And I didn't say it like it was meant to diminish what you do—just *simplify*. Because apparently you're the one here who can't do that."

Ouch.

That hit a nerve.

Della was determined not to show it.

And failed, it seemed.

Cory laughed under his breath, those stormy eyes of his darting over to her in the shadowed alley. *Finally*, their gazes met. Funny how earlier, she'd not wanted to look at him at all for fear of losing what sense of self-control she had left ... now, she didn't dare to look away. That same, hot and heavy feeling she felt hearing his voice raged through her much the same a dangerous storm would ravage the coastline. Swift, unforgiving, and *wild.*

"What, pretty girl, you thought stomping the streets and making a few calls made you the boss of yourself?" Cory smirked wickedly, and it did *wonderful* things to her insides despite the fact she wanted to wipe it from his smug fucking face. "It's understandable that you don't want to be called an *employee*, doing what you do and all, but at the end of the day, that's what you are. Nobody's the *boss* on these streets unless they've earned the right to be called it, yeah? Let your father do what he's gotta do here, sit back and learn from it, and maybe you get a little closer to the respect you think you want around here, all right?"

Della *blinked*.

Words didn't form.

The anger bubbled.

And yet, he was also right.

No one had really said it to Della in so many words, or by being as blunt as Cory had just been with her, but she heard the way people around her hinted at it. She wasn't *in* with the family business like her father and brother were because she hadn't earned it. Not because she was a woman, or the men in her life were being overprotective, but simply because that respect wasn't yet hers.

She'd not paid attention to what they were trying to tell her until now. Maybe it hurt her ego a bit to have it be Cory who told her outright what it was, and how it would always be, unless she worked to change it.

Della decided that instead of making an even bigger ass of herself in front of the man who looked like walking sex on a stick beside her *and* made her insides twist with good and bad things … for once she swallowed her pride.

"So, you're my new shadow, huh?" she asked Cory.

He grinned.

Goddamn.

It had been his grin that made her walk off the dance floor at the club with him, ready to let him do every sinful, dirty thing he wanted to her.

Good to see it hadn't changed.

Like she needed another problem.

"Seems I am," Cory returned.

"I might make your life a living hell."

That earned her a chuckle.

Every part of her felt it.

Did he know the effect he had on women?

Or did he just not care?

"You don't know much about me," Cory said, pushing away from the wall in one confident, fluid motion before he stepped forward and opened up the exit door wide as if to hold it for her to enter, "but I like a good challenge, Della."

She held his stare and walked inside.

Noted.

SEVEN

WHISKEY ON ICE was a drink Cory didn't enjoy when he first tried it as a *much* younger man. Rather, all he understood about the drink was the fact it took a few slams of a whiskey bottle to get him tipsy. The taste and appreciation he had for the aged, amber liquor now, however, couldn't be matched.

It's why he liked to start every good evening with a glass of whiskey on ice. He nursed his current lowball, sitting shoulder to shoulder with his older brother in a strip club that offered an interesting view, neon and black lights for ambiance, and brick walls with ornately detailed tapestries that gave the place a rich vibe.

A vibe he didn't believe to be true, considering the owner of the place was in debt three-hundred grand to a fucking loan shark.

That wasn't on the docket of business for the evening.

"And that's it?" Joe asked.

Cory looked over at his brother and nodded. "Yeah, man. That's the job—watch Della Costello until they figure out who exactly attacked her—they got ideas, but they're not telling me much about them—and whatever else."

Joe hummed, absorbing everything Cory had filled him in on with what had happened in his life over the last week. According to his brother when Cory asked earlier about his week so they could catch up as they usually did on Friday nights, his week consisted of little sleep, too much work, and taking Liliana out for dinner because it'd been *months* since they went out together.

Adulting was hard.

Cory wasn't here for it at all.

"And this is the place you picked for us to meet up because?"

"Frankie doesn't want Della to be aware and all, but her daddy knows every, last detail of her business and what she's been doing because J didn't hold back when shit went down. He passed the info along to me that this would be on the docket soon. So, yeah. The club's a work thing—something on her upcoming schedule."

Joe nodded, tipping his drink back for a swig while his gaze scanned the crowd gathering near a particular stripper's pole. She could certainly shake her ass. Cory had to give her that. Then again, wasn't that kind of the point?

"So, you're scouting the place?" Joe asked.

Cory grinned his brother's way. "And catching up with you. Been a busy week."

"That it has. I guess they don't plan for you to stay under the radar while you're watching her, huh?"

"Not really."

It wasn't like Cory blended in, after all.

"I'm just there to be there and keep anyone from trying shit," Cory said. "Whether or not they see me while I do it isn't important."

"So, is Frankie testing her with you at all?"

"How so?"

"Kind of answers that, then, doesn't it?"

"Does it?"

Joe rolled his eyes. "I just thought maybe he didn't think she was capable of handling her job—wondered if he also had you checking up on that and maybe that's why you're here doing the scouting, you know?"

Ah.

Cory sucked air through his teeth in a hiss, considering how he wanted to respond. The men in this life, even his own brother really, were so accustomed to a woman never dipping her hands in business that when they did stumble upon one that was, their curiosity came out to play.

And sometimes their problematic sides, too.

"Actually, no," Cory settled on saying. "From what he knows, seems she's made herself known quite well amongst the clients and anyone else that might have a hand in the trade within the city. J's been less involved over the past little while, but for a bit it was them and her friend—Jennika ... that chick, well, I'm not familiar with her, anyway."

Joe's brow dipped. "So you're here ... just to *scout*, like for yourself?"

Cory laughed, a shrug falling from his shoulders. "She's my job—watch her back. I know she's going to be coming here, it's a new strip joint to me, I didn't know the layout and yeah. I'm doing my fucking job."

That actually had his brother turning to angle himself so that he could stare at Cory from the side. Cory just watched a server close in on a table nearby with a tray of drinks in her hand because her balance was fucking amazing. The tray had at least fifteen drinks.

"Are you being ... *responsible?*" Joe asked, changing direction in their conversation all at once.

Cory hesitated on his next drink of whiskey. "No, I'm just—"

"You *are.*"

"Fuck off, Joe."

A chuckle started to form because out of the corner of his eye, he could see his brother's teasing grin. The *asshole.* But damn, he loved Joe all the same. His best friend until the very end; they would always have each other's backs.

And his brother's teasing? Sometimes, Cory needed that. Even if they were grown-ass men now.

Cory shook his head as Joe laughed while he resituated himself in the booth, so they both faced the crowd again. "Fucking hate you."

"No, you don't. On the real, though," Joe added quieter, "you do worry Ma a lot less now. And fucking *everybody* appreciates that, Cory."

His cheek twitched with a smirk.

He held it back.

"Yeah, well, love Ma and all. Less headaches, that helps, too."

Because it meant less *yelling*.

And bitching.

And not just from his ma, no. From all of them. Joe, and his dad, and ever since his sister became a teenager, Monica didn't stop running her mouth either.

"Anyway, the job is good," Cory said. "Really, the chick is probably going to be a little annoying, but she's sure something to fucking look at. You know how much I like that. Certainly makes being at the beck and call of a Capo—you *know* I hate that—and her pretty mouth worth it."

Joe coughed out a laugh. "As long as you're only *looking*. Don't start any kind of shit by mixing business and pleasure. Hmm?"

"Like you did with Liliana?"

That quieted his brother.

"Consider it a warning about the trouble it can bring," Joe replied.

Cory didn't know what gave it away to his brother that something had already happened with Della. Maybe it was a certain look on his face. Or it could have been the fact Cory opted to stay quiet when he'd normally tell Joe to mind his business. Or hell, it was probably just the fact nobody knew a Rossi brother better than his own goddamn brother. The truth was always in their eyes, in their silence, or a quick lick of the lips. They didn't have a single tell, it was many but only someone just like them would know it.

"Wait, you've already fucked her, haven't you?"

Cory's jaw tightened.

He still said nothing.

Joe scoffed. "*Cory*. You did, didn't you? *How*? It's been a few days since you even met the girl!"

"*Very* much a woman, thanks. And shit, it happened before. Weeks ago, at a club. You were there that night. Remember, I got your wife on my side to trick you into going out?"

That had his brother groaning and resting into the booth's leather back. "Why are you like this?"

"It's not a problem. It isn't going to be one. Adults can *fuck*, and it doesn't have to cause an issue. It's everybody else that seems to think they can determine who someone should or shouldn't be fucking that seems problematic to me, Joe."

"Sweet Christ."

"Well—"

Joe gave his brother a look from the side that silenced him. "Just don't let it get in the way of the job, yeah? Tommas is watching you, Cory. The boss put you there. That's *important.*"

"I know."

And he did.

He did.

Cory settled into the booth, knowing soon his brother would want to get back home to his wife and newborn son. And damn, he, too, had an early morning.

With *Della.*

Yeah, he wasn't about to forget her name again.

"So," Cory muttered, eyeing his brother from the side, "this is growth, huh?"

Joe grinned in a way that reminded his younger brother of years ago when they had still been ignorant enough to tear up the streets without care. "Sometimes, it's still fun—just in a different way."

Right.

He'd remember it.

•••

Cory was thankful that he kept his liquor limited the night before when he strolled down a familiar street the next morning. He was never a morning person, not when he preferred to sleep in until the sun was higher in the sky, and the rest of the world had awakened, too. But he was also a fucker who, when he set an alarm, the damn thing would have him up and out of bed whether he wanted or not.

This morning would have been a lot more difficult to deal with—and his mood might have been a bit darker—had he needed to scope out a townhouse with a goddamn hangover. Instead, he had good stride and a decent mood while he kept his hands loose in the pockets of his leather jacket.

On the street, nothing was amiss. Not that he really expected it to be. He'd already found Della's cute, little white coupe. Parked inside her garage where he couldn't get inside and making it far more unlikely that someone would try to mess with it.

He'd also done a walk around the block. Checked at the rear of the place. Stayed away from her windows—he wasn't *that* kind of prick.

To be safe, though, he wanted to get a feel for where Della lived. Especially seeing as how for the unknown future, he would be coming here quite a bit whether to see her home or out in the mornings. The whole babysitter aspect didn't appeal to him that much, but he wouldn't deny the fact that a part of him looked forward to the rest.

Della, that was.

Very much Della.

The thing about Cory—something that made his mother convinced he would never settle down—was *yes*, he enjoyed having fun with women, but he rarely found one that interested him enough to have fun more than once or twice. He often fell in lust; never in love. It hadn't escaped his notice that his thoughts regarding this job and that woman consistently drifted to the fact he'd be spending more time with her.

And that he liked the idea.

Hmm.

Cory's gaze narrowed at the thoughts, but he shrugged them off as he came up to his parked Mustang. Still running, the smoke puffing from the tailpipe, and the purr of the engine settled him while the warmth under the hood heated through his black jeans when he rested against the car. Keeping one eye on the building in front of him, he acted as though he didn't notice the familiar guy approaching from the left.

In fact, he didn't say a thing at all until J came to lean against the Mustang's passenger door. He matched Cory's stance with his hands thrown loosely into his pockets, although the other man wore a blazer, and watched the townhouse in front of them.

"She'll be up and around by nine—probably see her come out by nine-thirty at the latest."

"Nice," Cory said. "Not a morning person?"

"Not at all," J said, laughing under his breath. "Shit, that's the whole reason she didn't want to go to college. Couldn't get the classes she wanted in the afternoon. They were all scheduled for the morning."

Huh.

Cory passed the other man a look. "Been what—couple months since we hung out?"

J shrugged, smirking. "Yeah, the Outfit's got me running like crazy. Tommaso tried to get me out when the boys were in town last month, but you know."

"Priorities, yeah?" When a man wanted to be made, his priorities changed first. Then, Cory said, "I get it. We'll have to figure something out. Better question is, what brings you around here this early?"

That had the man's gaze traveling back to the townhouse and the stone stairs hugged by iron railings on either side that led to the front door. "Been getting up an hour earlier just to be able to get over here and check out her place every morning since the attack. Felt like a shit that night—I wanted to stay in the club, deal with the shit in there because of the gang and figured the guy who took her home would be okay because I knew him. He was okay—wasn't his fault, he did what I told him. Still thought it might have gone down differently had I been here, though."

Cory considered that. "The person was inside the townhouse, right? Broke in?"

"Yeah, my guy had just started to pull away."

"You usually walk her to her door?"

"Well, no, but—"

"So, it would have been the same. Don't keep replaying it, J. That fucks you up."

Della's brother let out a hard breath. "Yeah, I know."

"And I'm here, now. Kind of my job to do this and all."

J grinned. "I hear you."

Cory held out a fist, and J bumped it with his own.

All was good.

It usually was in Cory's world.

Cory tipped his head J's way, asking, "So, are we thinking the attack was related to the gang?"

"We're looking at business angles, too."

"The gang *was* there at the club where she was, right? Why was that, anyway?"

J cleared his throat. "Just details—Dad isn't sharing, no offense."

All right.

He'd already been told his job wasn't to handle the issue unless ordered otherwise; his duty was to keep Della out of any trouble.

"Who are you working for lately?"

J laughed darkly. "Adriano Conti, man. And when they say he can break anybody in, they aren't fucking lying. I've been doing work for Georgie, too, though."

Yeah, Cory knew it.

Every Capo in the Outfit had their ways. A man had to go through all of them on his way to being made. The mafia and its semantics. Although really, it just meant when one man stood up for another to nominate for their *in* to the family, everybody stood up for him at the same time. Things had changed over the years from how it used to be. Cory's father had told him more than once the changes had been for the better.

"Better get going," Cory said. "I heard he doesn't like people to be late."

"Guess so. Update me on her, okay?"

Cory nodded. "Will do."

•••

By the time Della did finally stroll out of her townhouse—her brother was wrong, it ended up being closer to *ten*—Cory had a warm cup of to-go coffee heating his palm that he sipped. Another coffee, triple sugar and cream because most people liked it sweet, he thought, waited on the hood of the car for Della, if she wanted it.

He'd had the coffee delivered by a service. The guy that dropped it off to Cory on the side of the street got a chuckle out of the fact that in the notes for the delivery, it had been written *to give to the guy wearing a leather jacket on the street at …* The address had been listed below.

It was too early.

Cory needed coffee.

Seeing Della walk down the steps in a gray wool dress that hugged her curves with a trench coat tossed over her shoulders, and black, knee-high boots that matched the purse in her grip definitely had his day looking up, though. With her hair curled and loose, that pretty face of hers painted like perfect porcelain, he thought she didn't look at all like a woman about to go and collect a debt for her loan shark father.

Then again, maybe that was the point.

She looked good.

He had to admit it.

Della's gaze landed on him as she stepped through the gate that led to the sidewalk where he had remained parked for the duration of the morning. He was positive she'd seen him out there waiting. It wasn't like he tried to hide it.

Again, not what he was supposed to do.

Her smile faltered slightly at the sight of him. Cory, on the other hand, grinned and reached for the coffee he had waiting for her.

"I hope your preference in coffee is something sweet and creamy," he said, dangling it in front of himself like a treat she could take if she wanted.

Della didn't.

Not right away.

Cory knew the only way this was going to work with him and her was if she trusted him. No exceptions, she had to know he would have her back first—always. It would be made a lot easier, though, if she *liked* him. That would give her a reason to trust him.

He didn't want to make her life miserable.

Not that it wouldn't be fun.

He had a feeling a lot about this woman was fun.

"Well?" he asked.

Della sighed and took the coffee. "It'll do—chai latte next time?"

Cory nodded. "Absolutely."

This close, he could appreciate the maroon shades she'd used to smoke out her eye, the sharp, black-winged liner and the lashes that fanned across her lid and made her features look all the more sinful. Even that dark wine shade on her lips had him watching the way her heart-shaped lips pursed when she brought the cup up for a drink.

Head where it needs to be, Cory.

Was it so bad that he was attracted to her? Was it also bad that it was obvious she couldn't stop looking at him as though she liked what she saw? He couldn't find a reason to say it was.

So …

Nope.

"I know you don't like this whole situation," he said, "but what if I could make it better? At least, for your first day with me watching your back while you work?"

Della quirked up a brow. "How so?"

He tipped his chin down to the car. More than once, she'd look the vehicle's way, too. He understood why, no question. It was a hell of a car.

"You can drive," he said.

She smiled.

And wasn't that a beautiful fucking sight?

Cory thought so.

"Where are the keys?" she asked.

EIGHT

DELLA WASN'T particularly happy about the whole *babysitter* thing, but it was made slightly more tolerable for Cory's first morning by the fact he made an effort to seem like he was *only* going to do his job. The coffee didn't hurt, either. Oh, and the fact he let her drive this beautiful beast of a car when she *knew* how precious and rare these models were?

That *really* helped.

From the corner of her eye, Della watched Cory when the traffic ahead of her slowed on the bridge to nothing more than a crawl, and she could afford the distraction. Of course, the traffic would keep them from getting to their destination until around noon. Not that it mattered—this job of hers had always been an *all-day* kind of thing. Her father ran a team of loan sharks that handled the business of illegal loans to everyone—he had guys sitting in seedy bars making numbers move and then those like Della, handling a different sort of clientele. At the end of the day, their job was still the same. When one had to chase people for money, it took patience to get the work done.

Getting Cory in her view took thoughts of what waited for her later away in the span of a quick breath that escaped her. His tattooed hand lifted and swept under his jaw with a light touch. A jaw made up of hard, cut lines and an inked throat that bobbed in the best way when he swallowed.

"Something interesting?" he asked.

Fuck.

The man hadn't even looked away from the window to notice her staring. Was she just that obvious or could he *sense* it?

Was he that type, too?

Perfect.

"I just ..." Della scrambled for a lie, not willing to deny her staring because why bother? "Hadn't really noticed how many tattoos you have."

Actually, that wasn't entirely a lie. She hadn't given the ink peeking out of the collar of his shirt, or the color marring his hands much attention until that moment. Not because the intricate artwork didn't stand out—everything from bleeding hearts, to the face of the Madonna and even tiny skulls across each of his knuckles on his left hand—when in fact it *did*. To her, his tattoos also appeared less like an extension meant to distract others but rather ... to make them more interested in the artwork than the man, and more like it was a part of him.

"How much ink do you have?"

He hadn't taken his shirt off the night in the club. He'd barely shoved his leather jacket off when he was fucking her. She'd liked that just fine, too.

Cory shrugged. "Entire sleeves, just a bit on my fingers and palms left now to cover. Chest and full back piece. Still a work in progress."

Huh.

Her first thought?

She'd like to see.

Before she could open her mouth and say something stupid, however, a buzzing noise had Cory digging in the pocket of his leather jacket—the same one he'd worn every time they met—and pulling out a phone. His thumb cut across the screen in fast motions before a *click* sounded, and he was swiping more. The matte black pod in his left ear buzzed, and he grinned at whatever message or call he was listening to.

Della was fine to leave him to his … *whatever.* Well, right up until he talked back, holding his phone up closer to his mouth while he talked.

"Nah, Monica, just take him around to the pad, okay? He'll find whatever it is he wants, and then he'll be good. Kick ass unless you need me to come to do it—love you, yeah."

His thumb came off the screen. A *zing* sound came from the phone. Message successfully sent, probably.

The words came out of Della's mouth before she could stop them, and she didn't even attempt to cool her tone. "Monica, huh? She know?"

Cory let out a laugh. "Know what?"

It was his blasé attitude that bothered her more than the arched brow and his devilish smirk. Della was all for adult people doing whatever they wanted—as long as everybody was willing and happy, and it didn't hurt anyone, what did it matter?

She didn't like men who dogged, though.

At all.

If that's what Cory did, then she wasn't going to give him the satisfaction of him telling her that she was just another mark on his list of people he ran with behind some poor girl's back, either. So, she opted to be a bitch instead of telling him how much of a piece of shit she thought he was.

"Couldn't have picked something else to throw over that T-shirt except the leather jacket that looks like it's seen better days, huh?"

That had him looking offended.

Cory grabbed the sides of each zipper and opened the jacket up a bit while staring at her. She refused to look at him, then, paying more attention to the road since they were finally off the bridge and now, she had a sea of cabs in front of her.

Jesus.

"What's wrong with my jacket? It's vintage Saint Laurent. It's scuffed and worn and *broke in* because that's what you do to a jacket like this. It's what makes it a staple."

Yeah, she knew that.

All about it, in fact.

And if she were being an honest woman, she would say his jacket with the YSL patch on the chest, the row of safety pins along the pocket, the white *FUCK U* graffiti on the left wrist of the sleeve, and slightly frayed belt kind of pulled his entire vibe together. She liked it. Far more than she should.

"This jacket was the *shit* when I was young and stupid, damn," Cory muttered, settling slightly but not looking her way now. "Our whole group of friends fought over it for years—if you could take it off somebody and put it on yourself, it was yours. Finally got it when I was sixteen. It was a size too big back then, but I didn't care. A soul hasn't taken it off me yet."

And they wouldn't, she bet.

Della huffed. "I like the jacket."

His crooked grin from the side caught her eye.

She didn't acknowledge it.

"Yeah, I know," he said.

Then, he laughed a sound that was enough to make Della's air catch in her throat. His gaze slid toward her, his eyes an icy in the morning daylight yet still blazing with heat, when he said, "Just say what it is, yeah?"

"What, what is?"

Cory's tongue snaked out to lick along his bottom lip, a grin curving that too-sexy mouth of his in a grin when he told her, flat-out and unashamed, "You know, woman. That we just had a whole conversation about my jacket so that we wouldn't have to talk about the fact you got in your feelings that I was on the phone with *Monica*."

He flipped his phone around and held his hand high for her to see the picture of a dark-haired, teenage girl taking a selfie with a rottweiler. Never once did he move his gaze from the road ahead of them, entirely unbothered.

That annoyed her more. Especially because she had to look twice to make sure she was seeing what she was seeing on the text message thread, and she was sure he didn't miss her doubletake. Wasn't it supposed to be her making his life hell?

"Yeah, little Mon. Who is also my baby sister, by the way," Cory added, finally glancing at her with a pleased smirk. "She's keeping an eye on my dog, Mace, this week. Depending on how long this job for your father takes me, she might keep him a little longer."

Then, Cory tucked his phone away and readjusted himself in the seat, so he could lean one arm against the door while he watched her drive. That was not better for Della at all. "So yeah, that thing you did—back to that. Let's talk about that."

Shame raced through her.

It might have felt a little good, too.

Cory winked.

"Fuck you, Rossi."

"Yeah, babe, maybe." He flashed his teeth and nipped the air before he added, "Later, if you're *really* good."

Della went slack-jawed.

The nerve on him.

Cory's hot, heady laughter filled the car. Why did he have to look like that when he laughed? All sin and good looks with charm and charisma wrapped up in black denim and leather? Never had the world threw a challenge at her quite like this man.

"I'm fucking with you," he said after his chuckles died down, his stare flicking up and down her from the side while she tried to pay attention to the road. Traffic was getting thick. "But you don't look like you mind that much. Gotta pass the time somehow, right?"

At least he was honest.

"Honestly, I only got in my feelings, as you said, because I thought you were being a shit. It's just … women need to watch out for each other. And yeah, I didn't know if that's what you were doing. Whether you had somebody waiting on you while you chased ass across the city, that's all. Or if you were that kind of guy, I guess."

Cory chewed on the stick of mint gum, and she watched each flex of his jaw out of the corner of her eye. "All right, fair enough."

She noticed he didn't say whether he was that type of guy. Then again, they weren't anything to each other, and he didn't have to tell her fuck all.

Still …

Why did he have to look so good?

Sound so good?

Why did he have to be at all?

She knew he was only flirting with her, and yet, the man was so entirely overwhelming that even this felt like foreplay. On another day, that might not be so bad for Della. Right then when she had to be in the right headspace for business, and the situation she found herself in with Cory, to begin with?

She couldn't focus at all.

"You're …"

He chuckled. "A lot, huh?"

Oh, good.

He knew it, too.

"Want me to dial it back a touch?" he asked.

"A bit."

"Whatever you need, princess. Wouldn't want to be a distraction while you do your job."

At first, she thought he might have been poking fun. Instead, he righted himself in the seat, switched the song to another on the playlist, and asked, "How close are we to your first stop today?"

"Three blocks."

"Who is it?"

"A doctor with a gambling and sex habit, oh and a private clinic that he uses to treat wealthy patients."

Cory whistled low. "Yeah, damn. Where's your friend?"

"She'll meet me there. You just—"

He gave her a smile from the side. "Don't even think about me. Do your job. I'll do mine."

Right.

He was her walking wet dream come true. All she could think about was him.

Della liked it a whole lot that he was looking at her with the same glint in his eye that she was sure he found in hers. Somehow, this was going to be a problem. She was sure of it. Life hadn't proved her differently with men like Cory yet.

•••

"Oh, our new friend is joining us today?" Jennika asked.

Della stood next to her friend in the luxurious waiting room of a doctor's office. No clients—or patients, she supposed—waited in the leather seats, and the girl behind the desk had already noticed their arrival and had picked up her phone to make whatever call she needed. This wasn't their first rodeo here, after all.

"Ignore him," Della said to Jennika, referring to Cory who stayed a few paces back, closer to the bank of elevators that had brought them up to the office. Despite what her father wanted, she was not letting Jennika collect payments from debtors on her own. Not that she couldn't do it, but sometimes the girl got out of control. Simple as that. "Plan is still the same. We've got the strip club later in the week, too, but that's your choice to come along."

"Your dad wants—"

"The guy always pays. Never any trouble. It'll be fine if you don't want to come."

"Okay." Jennika sighed and gave Della a pout before she grinned with a gaze that darted to the man behind them. "So, I can't play with *him* later, then?"

A hot shot of *something* scored straight through Della's gut. She knew exactly what it was—that possessive streak of hers couldn't be contained. Not that she had any reason to be feeling something like that. Shit, she hadn't even felt that way in the car earlier.

"No," Della said, the word clipped.

If her friend noticed, Jennika didn't say.

Thankfully.

"It's cool," Jennika said, taking a step forward in her black, bodycon dress with matching black pumps that showed off red soles with every step she took toward the receptionist's desk, "because he's too busy looking at you, anyway."

What?

Della glanced over her shoulder. Sure enough, Cory's gaze met hers where he still stood at the elevators. He tipped his chin, as though he were silently asking *what's up* and flashed those white teeth of his in a smile.

He was *her* bodyguard. Right? Wasn't he supposed to watch her?

But ... like *that?*

"Dr. Kohoney is available to you ladies whenever you're ready," the receptionist chirped with a quietness that spoke of her fear. *Well,* Della understood why. The last time they were here, she left the woman's boss unconscious and bleeding on his desk. That's what happened when someone came up thirty-thousand short on their loan payment.

Jennika hadn't even made it to the woman's desk. She changed her direction to head for the hallway leading deeper into the office with a wink and grin back at Della. She followed her friend even though it should have been her leading the front. Behind her, Cory walked at a snail's pace but didn't say a thing. She had to keep checking just to make sure he *was* coming along.

Della wished she could say she was surprised to find the good doctor already had stacks of cash sitting on the desk in neat piles, ready for Jennika to pick up with a whistle that cut through her stark red lips.

Della stayed just beyond the private office's door. "Count it."

Jennika glanced her way. "Yeah?"

She only stared at the doctor who sat behind his desk, sweating a little too much for her liking. The soles of Cory's leather shoes—she noticed he'd not worn his usual combat boots today; maybe he thought they'd be walking a lot—squeaked on his last step directly behind her. She didn't turn around; didn't want to acknowledge him. He wasn't there to scare those who owed her father; that's what *she* was there to do.

She didn't want people getting it confused.

"Yeah, count it," she confirmed.

The doctor—a one, *Jeffery Kohoney*—desperately needed to keep his secret life hidden from his current wife that was dragging him through divorce courts after learning of his multiple affairs. *Shit*, the woman hadn't even scratched the surface yet of what her husband had done.

"It's all there," the doctor said, coughing.

Della tipped her head to the side. "You said that last month. You were four thousand short, then, too, which tipped you just beyond thirty-k short on your interest overall."

"I caught it all up. And the interest you wanted." His hands rose higher, palms up. "I swear."

"But can you keep it up?"

That was the real question.

The man swallowed hard.

Della only smiled.

Letting her purse hang from her wrist, she pulled out the switchblade she always kept close at hand to fiddle with while Jennika did the counting. The silence in the room seemed to grow and swell, reminding her of every single reason why she enjoyed doing what she did. While she had the chance to check, she found Cory admiring the framework on a piece of artwork next to the door in the hallway. He glanced her way, that eyebrow of his darting up before he quickly went back to his … whatever he was doing.

Hey, he'd not stepped in.

Didn't say a thing.

She appreciated that.

"It's all there," Jennika finally said fifteen minutes later.

Her friend lifted her large purse to the desk.

Della nodded at the money, and then to the doctor. "Pack it up. It was good seeing you today, Dr. Kohoney. My father appreciates the business."

The good doctor smiled.

It wasn't at all true.

"Of course, Miss Costello."

Pressing the switch on the hilt, she closed the blade on the knife and dropped it into her bag. Without waiting to watch if the money would be quickly packed up—she knew it would; Jennika's job was to handle the cash, mostly. Turning on her booted heels, she left the office without a look back.

Cory was quick to follow, but not without glancing back.

"She that type—you both good?" he asked.

"What do you mean?"

"Jennika. I mean, you kind of have to trust her if you're leaving her with money."

"It's always been her, J, and I. Usually just me and her, now. But yeah, we've been friends since we were in high school."

Cory nodded, but his gaze never left her. Even when she wasn't looking at him, Della could feel his stare. That was more unsettling than anything else.

"Why do you keep doing that?" she asked as they came back out to the reception area. In front of the bank of elevators, the two watched one another. "Stare at me like that. I get it. You probably know it, too. I'm attracted to you. You're attracted to me. There—it's been said."

Cory grinned. "I don't see the problem."

"Can we not make it into a *thing?*"

He said nothing. That same cocky smile played on his mouth. She needed the strength of saints to deal with this man.

"Could you make it less obvious, then?" she asked.

"Do we get what we want that way?"

Goddamn him.

"Cory—"

She turned his way as the elevator opened, ready to tell him to dial it back again. His next words stopped her from saying anything *and* told her he wouldn't stop staring any time soon.

"You're kind of all ... put together, you know?" A chuckle escaped that sinful mouth of his when he added, "You seem it, anyhow. But you can cut a man, too, I bet. Didn't miss how the good doc kept rubbing the scar on his hand and looking at your blade, right. Or how you get pink in your cheeks like when we were in the car. Except you're a little wild, too, huh? The club. It's like—shit, you don't stop changing faces, Della. Don't blame me for being interested in which one is about to come out and play."

Now, it was her swallowing hard.

Cory just shrugged. "So, what's up next?"

Right.

Work.

Back to work.

•••

Nothing ventured, nothing gained.

It was a motto Della had adopted recently. Though she was walking a line of fire with what she hoped to gain through the venture she would attempt today, if it worked out, then what did a little burn matter? At least, that's what she would tell herself if everything crashed and burned straight to hell. Because if nothing was ventured, then nothing would be gained.

So, when a chance presented itself to have a sit-down with a connection she had made—during the spell of her relationship with Luis—to another gang leader in the city and discuss what, if anything, the man knew about her attack and Luis's possible involvement, she decided to have it. *Without* her father or brother's knowledge.

Why?

Because that was her contact's request. He didn't want to fuck with the mob—didn't need the Outfit in his shit.

But her?

He'd talk to her. And if he had something good to tell, or Della thought she might be able to solve the issue, if there actually was one, with Luis through Thion Dirks, then she would do exactly that. If it meant her father no longer felt like she was in danger and all their current problems went away to remove Luis from the picture altogether, then Della was willing to do that.

First, she needed to talk to Thion.

Or Dirks, as he preferred.

Unfortunately, the only time Della had been able to find to meet with the gang leader of the west end was after her meeting with the strip club owner that couldn't seem to get himself out from under her father's thumb in his constant debt. Which was fine, in a way, because no one would think it was strange for Della to be here—she stopped in once a month to collect money from the owner, anyway.

She simply hadn't mentioned her other meeting.

What did it matter?

Jennika decided to go and have her nails done with the promise of picking up the rest of the cash to deliver to Della's father later—Frankie would be expecting it. Everything else that day went perfectly fine.

And Cory?

Well, in the duration of her meeting with the owner of the strip club, she'd lost track of him. In the flashing purple and red strobes, dancing girls on their platforms and poles, and the black lights overhead, it was hard for Della to discern what was what through the crowd.

Soon enough, she did find him.

Sitting in a corner booth, a woman danced in a fishnet bodysuit that hid nothing but for a scrap of fabric, one might call it a G-string. Even that was too nice. Cory wasn't even watching the woman, though. He was looking straight at Della. His gaze slid to the woman who dipped low with her ass high at the same time, and then right back to Della. His jaw flexed rhythmically; a sign he'd popped in another piece of gum from the pack she noticed he liked to keep on him.

She had to give him credit.

Even if part of her wanted to rip his eyeballs out—for being there at all; also because he put her on edge without doing a thing; and *maybe* a little because the stripper was too close to him—he'd done everything he said he would during their first week working together. Didn't step in on her business. Never made his presence more obvious than it had to be. Kept his distance.

So far, he kept his word.

Points in his favor.

It was the crowd of men dressed in black and leather that pulled Della's attention away from the man that seemed to be on her mind a little too much lately. They strolled into the main floor of the club with an aura that screamed *we own it all* and *back off.* Another time and that might have excited her.

Now, it only meant one thing.

The first words to come out of her mouth?

"I should have known."

Because that wasn't Dirks at all. Her meeting had been canceled, it seemed. There stood Luis. Someone was definitely going to get hurt.

NINE

"THAT'S NOT GOOD," Cory said aloud, his attention switching from one conversation to something else entirely all in a single second.

The stripper on the platform in front of his current position in a corner booth continued working the pole as though he'd shown her any attention in the last half hour that she'd been dancing for him. Not that he had been watching her.

She wasn't his job.

The thing about Cory, though?

He liked to multitask.

He might be working, but he also had a whole life outside of the Outfit's business. Not to mention an entire family that demanded more of his attention than he could sometimes give. Which was why when Della finished her meeting with the strip club owner and then didn't move from her table like she planned to enjoy the drink in front of her, Cory figured it was safe to call his mother for a chat so that she wouldn't leave a million messages in his inbox complaining that he wasn't around enough.

He wasn't sure he made the right choice.

The guy that just walked through the door?

Yeah, Cory knew that fuck.

Being privileged enough to walk the streets with one of the men running them meant Cory was given front row access to the way the underbelly of Chicago was really ran. Or for that matter, the people who made it all work.

It wasn't just the Outfit.

The city was full of smaller gangs that battled for different territory to deal drugs, control, and more. Generally, the Outfit supplied said gangs in one way or another. However, that was simply in the business of *trade*. As long as no trouble was made, everybody was cool.

That's how this shit was done.

So, when Luis Ruiz came into the club, Cory knew exactly who that asshole was. Not just because of his work on the streets, however. Small-time gang leader who made decent coin, and kept a small crew of guys to do a lot of his up close and personal dirty work. Probably the same crew of men that entered the club with Luis.

Which wouldn't be concerning and didn't immediately make Cory think they were going to have a problem. It was when Luis walked across the floor of the club with a gaze and grin that said he recognized Della as she stood from her chair at his approach which did.

Cory got fucking concerned, too, when Luis came close enough to reach for Della, and the man's hand cupped the side of her face and neck with a possessive touch that spoke of familiarity between the two. *Affectionate history.* Not that his hand stayed there long before Della grabbed Luis's wrist with a single word clear on her lips as fire burned in her gaze.

"*Don't,*" she'd told him.

She didn't let him go, though. Or rather. Luis had reversed the hold so that he had her wrist, now, and held it between them so she couldn't step back. Della didn't look the least bit afraid.

Strangely, Cory found himself annoyed that someone had touched her *and* pleased as fuck that she had no problem telling a man to keep his hands off. Problem was, he had more important things to deal with than what his fucking cock was trying to get up to.

Cory's brain raced to catch up to whatever he missed—he knew he'd missed something big—when he remembered to get his mother off the phone.

Yeah, definitely not going to be good.

"What's not good?" came the sweet, familiar voice in his ear.

"I gotta go, Ma—work."

Lily sighed in the Bluetooth. "I haven't seen you in *two* weeks. The very least you could do is make time to talk to me on the phone, Cory."

"That's why I called—"

"I'm going to talk to Damian about this."

Jesus H. Christ.

"Ma, I love you, but I gotta bounce. Sorry—don't tell Dad."

He hung up the phone before Lily could say a thing otherwise. He'd pay for that later, but right then, he had the better idea to snap a photo of the scene across the strip club. He swiped right on his screen, taking the picture to his messages before sending it off to someone who might be able to tell him exactly what the fuck was going on.

"No pictures!"

Shit.

That stripper had finally stopped shaking her ass in front of him.

So, hey.

Maybe he wasn't so good at multitasking after all. Apparently, the stripper hadn't realized that he was having a whole conversation on his *phone* because he'd been using the Bluetooth in his ear. Or she just didn't care until he brought up the phone with the camera ready.

His phone dinged with an incoming text. J wasn't kidding when he said he wanted Cory to keep him updated on Della. Her brother responded to Cory's *first* update of the week faster than he thought he would.

J's reply to the text image of Della and Luis? *Fuck. That's her ex.* That was all J said. It was all Cory needed to know, too.

The stripper snatched Cory's phone from his hand with a palm raised to swing at him at the same time everything clicked. He rolled away from the hit with his mind running a mile a minute while he climbed out from behind the table. The stripper was shouting for management and security.

Cory headed for the people now looking his way. Della's eyes stayed wide.

Luis, on the other hand, looked ready to *go*. Go a round or two with Cory. It seemed like he wasn't the only one with recognition of who was in the room. *Good.*

Gang involvement, they said about Della's attack. Possibly related to her work for her father, but that was iffy. The connections didn't matter. He didn't have the details.

Luis was the gang involvement. The *attack*—or that's what Della's people thought. Cory just hadn't been given the asshole's name, or *which* gang, or the whys. He was only supposed to be her backup, right?

The gang involvement was an ex.

Yeah.

Cory understood exactly why Frankie Costello hadn't made the situation clear. He didn't want people knowing his daughter had connections to a gang when she was also working under his umbrella in the Outfit.

Smart, really.

No one wanted someone to think a small gang might be infiltrating into Outfit business, even in that sort of way. Then, others might think they could join.

Or force their way in.

Still.

He wondered if he wasn't told because Frankie thought Cory was a little too close to the boss, and he didn't want Della's involvement with the gang—regardless of *what* their relationship was—getting back to Tommas. Or was it something else?

Cory would figure that shit out later.

And get his damn phone back, too.

Whether it was because *Della* was a recognizable face in the club to the owner, or Cory just looked like fucking murder strolling across the floor, the security didn't follow him. He didn't miss how Luis's men had all scattered, too, taking different positions in the room to make everything a bit sharper to Cory.

They moved to the doors.

To the hallway.

Right behind Luis.

Cory recognized what the men were doing—flanking their boss, covering the room, and making sure they had the upper hand in whatever was about to go down.

"*Rossi*," Luis greeted when Cory was but a step or two away.

He didn't drop the man's stare as he circled around to stand at Della's side. Nor when he slung a leather-covered arm around her side to pull her slightly closer to him. His gaze *did* drop then. Straight to the hand that Luis was still using to keep a hold on Della.

"Let me go," Della demanded, her tone quiet but firm.

The club had gone silent.

Even the music dropped off.

Cory wasn't paying that shit any mind. Not when it felt like violence was about to bubble over right in front of him and he couldn't afford to focus elsewhere because of it.

"You heard her," Cory said.

Luis dropped Della's hand, but he wasn't even looking at her anymore. He was too busy trying to burn Cory down to the ground with his glare.

It almost made him chuckle.

"Lu," Cory replied, the nickname coming out easy.

Like he'd used it before.

Because he had.

Only those closest to the man across from Cory would know and use that nickname.

Once, they had been that close.

"Been a while," Luis said.

Cory shrugged. "Some years, yeah. How's it been?"

"Getting better."

Della's dark eyes darted between the two men, clearly realizing she'd missed something. Cory wanted to laugh at that, too, because *damn* ... he'd been missing a lot, it seemed. Welcome to his current fucking life.

Luis cleared his throat, and his jaw flexed with a shudder that Cory recognized all too well when he said, "I heard she had a babysitter lately—you know how it works out there. Word always travels fast. Common goals mean when we don't have a problem with another gang, they'll probably help a guy out. Dirks says hey, Della, but you know ... *priorities*."

That had Della jerking forward a bit. Not noticeable enough, though, because Cory tightening his arm on her had brought her closer. There was no hiding the way her body molded into his side. He didn't miss how Luis's gaze stung, either.

Cory's mouth grazed the side of Della's ear when he told her, "*Chill,* we're not mad, babe. We're all walking out of here the same way we walked in, and Luis knows it."

The man didn't want to fuck with the mob. Cory was sure of that.

The two of them already had history—they both grew up on the streets, just in different ways. Luis didn't come from the privilege Cory had, but somehow, they ran with the same crew of truant, delinquent teenage boys for years. Luis, like a lot of guys, never gained an *in* to some of the things Cory had been because of who he was and his family's connection to the mob. Luis never forgot it. Well, that was part of it.

"*Babe?*" Luis asked, directing the question and a cocked brow at Cory.

It felt like a challenge. Cory might welcome that.

That stare; the man's tone. It told Cory *everything*. Luis was jealous as fuck. It might be a problem.

That was fine because all Cory cared about at that moment was getting Della the hell away from the guy and then he could deal with everything else, too.

Della opened her mouth to speak. Cory was quick to jump in before she could with, "Yeah, *babe*. See, you don't expect the chick you sent someone to beat with a bat is gonna stick around and wait for you to come back, did you? How's it feel to be an afterthought, Lu?"

"*Cory.*"

Della's hiss barely registered.

Luis's nostrils flared, and his fists tightened into balls at his sides. Cory didn't move, but he was quick to step back, slide his jacket off, and pass it to Della's shoulders. He pointed at the door—two of Luis's men stood at either side.

"We'll head that way, and you'll go yours," Cory told the man. "And shit is not gonna start while we do it, yeah?"

Luis's lips flattened in a grim line. "Things have changed, huh?"

"Things changed the day I took the jacket, and you didn't wanna follow the rules anymore."

The jacket Della had on.

The one that ruled his teen years.

All his friends.

"Remember?" Cory asked, a smirk coming out to play. "Now we got bigger problems between us, man—bigger boys, bigger issues."

All at once, Luis's gaze skipped to Della. That anger of his melted away, and in its place was a charming smile and a possessive glint. He didn't reach out to touch her—smart, considering Cory's arm was back around her waist. He might have ripped the man's hand off and beat him with it had he tried to touch her then.

Shit was bad between Della and Luis.

Cory remembered her mention of the ex the night they hooked up. Add in the attack. This whole fucking shitshow.

And *yeah*.

He didn't need to be told to know.

Shit with them was *bad*.

She didn't look happy he was there. She didn't seem like she wanted him within ten feet of her. Cory wanted it clear to Luis that he was going to be a huge fucking wall to get through if he wanted that to change.

Whether Cory was fucking Della or not ... well, that didn't matter. Luis could think it was fact, though.

"We're not done here," Luis said to Della. She tensed in Cory's arm. "Not even close," he added sharper.

•••

Cory drove.

Della hadn't even asked.

Which was fine because he would have hated to laugh and tell her *fuck, no.* His one goal after leaving the strip club was to put distance between themselves and the men he knew Luis would have following them. Whether or not he could lose them ... it was hard to say.

The Mustang shifted beautifully under Cory's hand when he finally hit the freeway and pressed the pedal down. Hell, he might drive an hour out of the way before turning back but if that's what he had to do, so be it.

Della remained quiet.

Until she exploded.

"*Why would you do that?*"

Cory had been waiting on it; bracing for it. The woman didn't hold back.

Damn. He chanced a glance her way, thinking stupidly, *beautiful when she's angry, too.*

The smart part of him kept that quiet. The not-so-smart bit said out loud, "Do what—get your lying ass away from your ex that *fucking everyone* decided to not tell me was the cause of all this shit and the entire reason I'm watching you? An ex, who by the fucking way, was a pretty good friend of mine for years? Is that what I did?"

Della blinked.

Cory let out a hard breath and focused on the road. It took her a while before she spoke. He rather liked the silence.

Mostly.

"You made a bigger problem back there acting like you did," she said. "He's an obsessive asshole, but he can be handled. Except you just had to go right on ahead and—"

"That's all you think he is?" Cory asked.

Della snapped straighter in the seat. "What?"

"Just an obsessive asshole? You're not that dense—you can't be. If he's willing to cause problems with the mafia because he's just in his feelings about whatever the two of you had, then he's got a hard nut for you. And that's not a great thing."

"That's why it doesn't make sense."

Cory dared a look her way but quickly went back to the road. He was driving too fucking fast as it was, so like this, both eyes needed to be looking forward. Nonetheless, his quick glance showed him every drop of her confusion that soaked her features.

"Nobody wanted to listen, though," Della said. "Not after it first happened. He's not going to convince me to go back—if he had someone there to send me a message after I told him to fuck off for what should have been the last time, then why bother with this at all?"

"What?"

"This stupid *game*," Della said. "Cat and mouse. Like he's having fun, and believes if he just shows up enough, everything will change. It's *crazy*, and it doesn't make sense."

It took Cory a second.

He waited another just for good measure.

"You don't think the attack is related to him at all," Cory said.

"Or maybe it is, I don't know. But even back there, when you mentioned the attack being *his* call, it just … something in his face doesn't sit right with me. He's a good liar—I know it better than anyone. But he is still a fucking *liar*. He didn't deny it, but he didn't say he did it, either."

Yeah.

Shit.

Cory had to think about that, too.

Even still …

"Maybe so," Cory agreed, "but even if he's not the fuck who did it, he's still going to be a problem for me or you."

Della glanced his way. "Things just changed, didn't they?"

Oh, yeah.

Big time.

Fuck.

"All my history is bad. Especially with that guy."

Della let out a sigh, her fingers playing with the edge of the jacket he'd still not taken back from her. He wondered if she managed to miss the comment he had made about the leather piece back in the club. She didn't.

"When you put the jacket on me—that was important, wasn't it?"

Akin to a dog pissing on his property. Cory didn't think she'd appreciate the sentiment.

Nonetheless, the action drew the fucking line. Let that fuck cross it— Cory *wished* Luis would. Not like he needed another reason to end the man at the moment, but shit …

"Meant a lot between me and him right then," Cory replied.

It was really all he had to say.

"That was a *lie*. You antagonized him."

"Nah, I let him know what really matters, Della."

"But you made it seem like we—"

"We'll deal with your people tomorrow," he said, knowing she wouldn't understand, and he had zero desire to argue in circles. "I'll work it out—we don't have to go through that bullshit tonight."

Della nodded. "Okay."

She didn't ask where they were going, then.

He didn't offer.

TEN

"AT LEAST IT'S not a dive."

At her comment, Cory glanced at Della sideways as she shrugged off his jacket, handing the item over to him. "Really? That's what you were worried about?"

She eyed the entry to his apartment, considering his question before answering. Maybe her nerves were a little too frayed because of Luis, or it could have been that once she realized Cory was bringing her to *his* place, she didn't know what to expect. Or rather, what *he* expected.

"I mean—"

He gave a shake of his head, not even bothering to let her say anything at all. "Doesn't matter, girl."

She had to stare at his back when he headed deeper into the apartment. The skyrise in downtown Chicago was decent. A doorman downstairs and a whole lobby with three women working a reception desk for those in the penthouses. She almost considered asking Cory why *he* wasn't in one of the penthouses on the higher floors, but maybe that shit wasn't his style. The guy had to have some kind of money, considering who his family was and all, but he didn't really show it that much.

Della found herself curious.

Not that she had any business being that at all.

Wonderful.

"I can go home," Della called at his retreating back. "I'm not staying here."

That had Cory turning around.

Smirk firmly in place.

"Yeah, you are," he returned.

Excuse me?

"I *have* my own place," Della said, knowing good and damn well that she couldn't just let this man railroad her every step of the way while he was made to watch her. "I don't see why I can't just go home tonight."

"Because that's the first place Luis's guys would go, Della. Don't worry, I'm sure he had someone follow us to make sure you were really going wherever I was. I don't doubt he knows you're here. It's a lot harder to hit an apartment skyrise and get out clean than it is a fucking townhouse with a shitty little gate in front of your place keeping them away from the door."

Well...

When he put it like that.

It wasn't like Cory didn't make good points. Della just … she really hated feeling like someone else was making the calls when it came to her. Especially if that person was a *man*. They all thought she couldn't handle herself. That she was stupid or silly. A *girl*. They could and would do it better—she didn't even get the option to show them how she might handle a bad situation.

Hell, Cory called her a *girl* moments ago.

Problem was, they had yet to let her prove differently.

Della was over it.

"Someone could be *outside* while I was home," she snapped.

Cory arched a brow. "Yeah, *me*?"

She shrugged. "Isn't that your job?"

He just laughed.

"I don't see what's funny, Cory."

"You wouldn't."

He turned to head further into the apartment. Her annoyance blew to higher proportions.

"You're just like the rest of them—you don't care to hear anything I want or think."

That had him swinging back around.

Fast.

He took two steps toward her, that gaze of his still keen and sharp on her like he was absorbing what she said and thinking about it before he replied. Coming to a stop midway down the hall, he let out a hard sigh.

Reserved?

Over it?

Della didn't know.

She was all of it and more, though.

Her mood couldn't be helped. It wasn't made any better by the fact that the man a few steps away from her in worn leather and ripped denim frustrated her to no end—had done so all damn day—and yet all she could think about right then was how *good* he looked.

She couldn't even just be pissed. No, she had to feel all the other shit he had bubbling inside of her, too.

"Listen," Cory said, never moving from his spot down the hall as he spoke, "you can be pissed all you want about whatever you have going on, but you're still not leaving my place tonight. For one, because when the sun's down, guys like Luis rage the worst. If he gets in some kind of mood tonight about what happened, we don't need to make it easier for him to find you. For two, you got feelings about shit I can't help—clearly—but at the end of the day, I'm making the final call on where you're going and what you're doing. Because my job is watching your back and keeping you *safe*. End of discussion."

Della's jaw tensed, holding back a *fuck you.*

He honestly didn't deserve it.

She knew that.

Still …

Turning, Cory waved a hand over his shoulder. Dismissive and cold, she thought. "I have some calls to make—you can take the bedroom at the end of the hall to use for the night. Tomorrow, we'll handle the rest."

Like her father.

Right.

She heard what he didn't say.

Chances were, things weren't going to get easier from here for her. With Luis making another move, even if it was just showing up while she was working, Della knew exactly what her father was going to do.

Safety came first. She was locked in with barricades everywhere. To a point, she understood the need. That didn't mean she liked it.

"And," Cory called, already gone from her view though his voice traveled from another room deeper in the dimly lit apartment, "when you feel like it, I would appreciate knowing if you have any other meetings with people or work that you plan to do behind Frankie's back so that I can at least be kept in the loop, you know? If you're going to play dangerous games, Della, I need to know about it."

Dammit.

•••

"Sorry, I should have just done that job with you," Jennika said on the call. "I tried to tell you that your dad was going to be pissed but you didn't want to listen."

"What difference would it have made?" she replied to her friend. "Someone else there for Cory to worry about, I guess."

"Yeah, but still."

"It's over with."

"No, it's not," Jennika said in a sigh. "Not even close. It's Luis, babe. Now he's got something on his mind—he's always been like that."

She wasn't wrong.

Della just didn't want to think about it.

"And speaking of *Cory …*"

"What about him?" Della asked, trying to keep her tone normal.

She didn't need Jennika getting on *that* bone because her friend wouldn't let it go. If she thought something was up between Della and Cory, she wouldn't hear the last of it.

"You're staying there for the night, huh?"

"Not by choice," she muttered.

"You know, you say that like it's a bad thing but ... have you *looked* at that man?"

Regularly.

Too often.

Even when he knew she was.

Della couldn't help it.

"I'm just saying it wouldn't hurt to have a little fun," Jennika said. "Get your mind off the ex that keeps chasing your ass all across the city."

Right.

Chasing my ass. That was a good way to describe whatever cat and mouse game Luis thought he was playing with Della. *Not.*

Thankfully, the beep on the call—which told her she had another call coming through—saved her from deflecting or outright lying to Jennika. She checked the screen just to see who was calling.

J.

"I have to go—J's calling."

"Mmhmm," her friend hummed, the teasing tone clear.

"*He is.*"

"Yeah, probably. Always worrying about you. They all do."

Della sighed. "I know. Call me tomorrow, okay?"

"Soon as I crack my eyes open."

"So, like noon?"

Jennika laughed, said her usual *bye, bitch* and then hung up the phone. Della had a laugh on her lips when she answered her brother's call.

"Someone's happy?" J asked before saying anything else.

Della calmed—a bit. She still smiled. "Just ... Jennika. She called."

"Right," J said, something in his tone that she couldn't quite decipher. Not that he gave her any time to think on it for long before he said, "I was having a drink with Dad when Cory called."

"He handled—"

"Yeah, I know," J interjected, "except Dad had questions, Della."

Della blew out a hard breath. "Like what?"

"How Luis knew you were there? Where was Jennika? Or why you stayed longer at a place to collect a debt when you know to get in and out? These are the kind of questions he should ask considering that's the shit keeping you safe when you work. You wanna keep doing it; he's trying to let you, but—"

"How pissed is he?"

J *eh*'d under his breath. "About what you'd expect."

"I only wanted to see what kind of info I might be able to pull about Luis. I had Cory there, right?"

"Yeah, but what if he *hadn't* been there, Della? *Shit.*"

"Well, we're never going to know, right?" she shot back. "I apparently can't handle anything myself or even *try.*"

"Hey—"

"Just … let's not and say we did," she muttered, turning back to stare at the items hanging on the bedroom wall.

Not the bedroom she should be using, but …

Della surveyed the photographs on the wall of the hallway in Cory's bedroom. The hallway outside led to the other bedroom and the bathroom. Which was currently closed with the sound of water running from behind the door. Cory headed straight for the shower after stepping out on the veranda for a blunt while he made the calls he needed to.

She almost joined him.

For the smoke.

Not the shower.

Although, she might like that, too.

God.

She needed to stop.

"I just want to know why you did that when you know we're handling it?" J asked, bringing her back to the topic at hand.

"Because something isn't right with this—*Luis.* I wanted to figure out what it was because everybody else is just worried about keeping an eye on me."

It took her brother a second. Then, another.

"What do you mean?"

"Luis. This. Something doesn't fit."

She couldn't put her finger on it and didn't know where to start looking.

"Della," her brother murmured.

"What?"

"You don't know what we're looking at. We haven't told you. You think we haven't noticed shit isn't right with everything happening?"

She swallowed hard. The fucking *mafia.* It never let a woman in.

"Listen, I gotta go," J said. "Keep your head down—we'll meet up with Dad tomorrow and whatever else."

She didn't know if Cory mentioned he brought her to his place. At the moment, she also didn't care to mention it herself.

"Sure," she replied.

What else could she say?

•••

"Are you snooping through my shit?"

Della laughed, but only because she could hear the amusement in Cory's tone. Turning from his nightstand with a tablet in her hands, she tried to punch in a four-digit code only to have it give her another error message.

"Well, I *was*," she said, "when you were showering. Now, I just wanted to get some music playing because I have no idea how to run your stereo out there. And if I have to stay here all night when you didn't even offer to smoke with me earlier, the least you could do is make it entertaining."

Looking up from the tablet to give Cory a sardonic smile just because she could and she enjoyed being a smartass occasionally, Della's breath caught hard in her chest. Leaning in the doorway of the bedroom, the man had nothing on but a gray towel wrapped around his waist. He rubbed his palms together, whatever lotion that was in his hands smearing over his freshly shaven jaw and down the strong column of his neck. She couldn't have stopped the traveling of her gaze even if she wanted to.

For the first time, she had a good look at his ink.

The full sleeves made up of eagles, wings, skulls and different flowers. The large chest piece was much like his sleeves in that there was no cohesive theme. Just art everywhere. She bet she could spend a night tracing all of his tattoos and there would still be more to enjoy.

In color. Black and white. The lotus. Piercing bars in both nipples. The ink went down to his navel, a patch of uninked skin peeking out at her above the band of the towel. That fabric hung loosely at his hips—barely holding on at all, really. The railroad path of abs and the cut V of his groin had Della hot in a flash.

God, why?

He truly was the very incarnation of sex for her. Every part of her knew it and that was half the problem. He looked like a drug she could take and have a damn good time indulging, but where was the limit? She didn't know how to draw lines. What happened if they crossed one?

"You wanna smoke?" Cory asked.

Della's gaze darted up, and other than the pleased grin curving that sexy mouth of his, he didn't say a thing about her ogling. "What?"

"Didn't know you smoked. Not sure if you were the type. You wanna?"

Della's throat jumped when his hands ran down his throat one last time. "I—"

"Or we can talk about what you found when you were snooping, too. Lady's choice, babe."

He winked. Those white teeth of his glinted at her when he flashed them in a sinful smile. She also realized then that the lotion he'd been putting on after his shower had a scent—a heady musk that reminded her of smoke and spice and *sex*.

His scent, she knew.

Just missing the jacket.

A weaker woman would have dropped to her knees.

Right fucking then.

Della held out.

Barely.

Instead, she decided to play his game because what choice did she have? If he was going to keep her there, she might as well make it worthwhile.

She set the tablet down to the nightstand—they could get music later—and pulled a perfectly rolled blunt where she'd hidden it in her bra. That was, after she found it in his nightstand.

"I already found your stash," she said, "but I didn't find much else. A closet of designer names. Box of rubbers in your bedside table. The sketchbook on your dresser was a surprise."

"I draw as a hobby—I'm not that great at it."

"You're not horrible, either. What else?"

Cory chuckled. "My kicks game?"

His shoes, he meant.

Because if she'd been in his closet, she would have had to see those shoes of his. Though she'd only seen him in combat boots or black shoes, the man had *piles* of them in his closet. All different brands and styles and color. Honestly, they needed their own space because he'd run out of room in his closet.

"It's *rude*," she said. "How do you even fit that many shoes in there?"

Cory grinned. "I'm trying to find a bigger place, actually. Ma's harping about a house—but that's only because she wants me to have babies. Dad's on her side because you know, that's his wife. Joe tries to stay out of it, but he thinks I should spend some money. Monica just wants a place to crash on the weekends when she's out too late and doesn't want to have to call somebody to get her in the city."

Then, he shrugged. "I just want some shelves for my shoes, so."

"Your family—they're close?"

"All of us. Me and my brother, though … it's a bigger thing." Cory nodded to the dresser. "In case you missed it, there's a lighter in the mug on there."

She had.

He'd smoked outside earlier, but didn't seem to have a problem with her lighting up right there in his bedroom. She kept one eye on him as he headed for the walk-in closet until his inked, muscular back disappeared and all she was left with was the imprint the image of his body had made in her mind.

Goddamn.

The smoke in her lungs burned, but the weed had that *good,* heavy smell when she blew out a thick cloud to the brushed-nickel light fixture overhead. His whole place was kind of like his bedroom, really. Earthy tones. Dark-colored fixtures. Leather furniture. A game system in the living room. No TV in his bedroom. Gray hardwood. His family everywhere.

Like he wanted to see them always.

It reminded her of her own, really.

As annoyed as she was with her current situation and the way her brother and father were dealing with it, at the end of the day, they were still family. Still *blood*. That's what counted the most for her.

Della pulled hard from the joint, holding the smoke in to let it do its thing as she asked, "So, are we going to talk about your connection to Luis?"

In two seconds, Cory came back into view. Or rather, he leaned backward enough for her to see his cocked eyebrow in the doorway. "Are we going to talk about yours?"

Well ...

"I kind of already told you at the club."

He considered that.

"Right—make it worth about a year, huh?" His gaze flicked up and down her as she released a thicker cloud of smoke than before. The weed was smooth though, so she wasn't coughing.

Della shrugged, the weight of her dress feeling heavy when all she wanted right then was to be *light*. The smoke was doing a good job getting her there. The way Cory stared at her certainly helped, too.

"He's exactly the type to make you think you're the one while he's fucking a different chick on every block. I bolted. *Fast*."

Cory laughed. "Not a bad idea."

"Yeah, well. Here we are. What about you?"

He sucked air through his teeth and dipped back out of her view while she went back to work on smoking the joint. Already the room was starting to get hazy with smoke and it would soon travel out of the opened doorway into the hall.

"We ran with the same crew of friends from around fourteen, fifteen, sixteen. We were seventeen and eighteen when shit changed. A lot of the guys went in different directions. Haven't seen Luis in a while, and I'm cool with that. Could have been a while longer, really."

"Sounds like old history."

"Playground shit," Cory returned from within the closet. "But it doesn't matter. Guys like us don't forget about what happened regardless of where it happened. I took the jacket—he wanted to change the rules. It was getting old anyway. Most of the guys were already up and gone doing their own thing. My uncle dragged me off to follow him, so I wouldn't keep getting my ass in trouble. That's the end of it."

"What *rules*?"

Cory came back to the doorway. Only now he had gray sweatpants hanging low from his hips. Low enough that she could see the definition in his groin, and the dark dusting of trimmed hair that peeked out around the waistband.

"That's the playground shit."

Cory tipped his head to the side, eyeing the smoke in her hand while Della openly stared at the beautiful man across the room. It might have been the weed, but she was a lot less annoyed with being at his place. It wasn't so bad.

Neither was he.

"Let me hit it," he said, striding forward.

Della already had the joint held out for him to take. Instead, he closed the space between them in a breath until his mouth hovered above hers and all she could see was the glint in his eyes and that wicked grin of his.

"Shotgun it," he murmured.

Della let out the lungful of smoke she'd been holding in, not even thinking it over before she did so. Cory inhaled it, and then Della put the joint to his lips for him to take a pull anyway straight from the blunt. His gaze locked onto hers and didn't let go.

She liked that too much.

"Are you going to let me?" he asked, voice raspy from letting out his smoke while he spoke.

Della licked her lips. "Let you what?"

"*Hit it.*"

Of course.

Her first thought?

Yes.

This man was dangerous.

Cory clicked his tongue when she hesitated to reply. "Why not, Della? We both know you want to. So do I."

She blinked.

This man.

This damned man.

"Are you supposed to be fucking me considering your job and all?"

All he did was shrug.

Della laughed.

"What does it matter?" Cory asked. "What's it hurt?"

"Still just having fun?"

"Why do anything different?"

Della took one last pull from the joint before handing it over to Cory for him to do whatever he wanted with it. He could stub it or throw it—she didn't care. He tossed it to the metal trash bin that sat beside the dresser without even looking to make sure that it hit the intended target.

He couldn't look when he was too busy kissing her.

His mouth found hers with hungry lips that kissed her hard and gave her no mercy. The way his tongue slashed along hers had Della pushing back for more. His hands found her shoulders, and her back met the closest wall.

Right next to the dresser.

There was something about his mouth, though.

His kiss.

How he took from her mouth without question, and she was helpless to do anything else but give him what he wanted. Those hands of his curved around her throat and then slid down to her shoulders. His mouth dragged across her cheek, his voice gruff in her ear as he pulled at the sleeves of her dress to rip them down.

"Need more of that skin," he told her. "It's so fucking soft—been thinking about that for *weeks*, babe. Like that pretty pussy, too, and those dimples in your back when I had you bent over the sink. All of that—I need it."

Shaky air rattled into her lungs at his declaration. She'd been blitzed that night, yeah, but not so drunk that she didn't know what and who she was doing. He'd acted as though he might have been, but it seemed he remembered a lot about her and that night than she thought.

Every word was a promise.

She drank them all in.

He licked her throat.

Tasted her collarbone.

Every swipe of his lips and tongue against her shivering, heated skin followed his hands pulling her dress down further. He didn't even fuck with the zipper in the back—the stretchy wool fabric pulling down under his handling with ease.

Then, the dress fell down to her heels.

Cory straightened up fast. His stare dipped down to her chest where black lace cupped her breasts and then lower to the same lace that hugged her hips. Her fingernails grazed under his jaw while he dragged in a sharp breath, and his stare came back to hers.

"You want it?" he asked.

She liked that he did.

That he made her *keep saying it.*

She wanted him.

She just wanted to fuck.

"Do you?" he asked, tone raspier. "Go ahead, it's all right there. You want something—*grab it.*"

She kissed him, then. The same way he'd done to her with all that hunger and need that burned so deep in her chest because that's just what he did to her. She thought he might like to know it, maybe. Her hands slipped down his chest and stomach to the waistline of his sweats. He backed her harder into the wall when her fingers wrapped around his semi-hard length and tightened with the first stroke. He hardened fast when her other hand palmed his balls, and her teeth found his bottom lip.

"*Fuck.*"

That breathy cuss fell down on her when she lowered to a crouch. His sweats came down by his own hands before they tangled into her hair, piling it high in his fist. She'd forgotten the size of him, how her hand couldn't reach all around his girth. That he was long enough for every stroke inside her cunt to feel like he had every inch of her impossibly full.

She stroked him again.

His thumb found her lip, popping her mouth open until the tip of his digit grazed her tongue. He pulled it out just as fast, and she took his cock into her mouth instead. All she needed was that little taste of his skin in her mouth and then *more.*

Salt and sex and *man.*

She loved the taste of that.

"*Goddamn.* Yeah, babe, shit look at that."

His cock filled her mouth.

She watched him lose control up above.

A beautiful sight, really.

He fucked her mouth until water sprung to her eyes. She was sure her mascara and liner was ruined. Certainly the lipstick she'd had on. Yet, the man above her stared down like he had found heaven underneath him.

She could have watched him like that for hours, but he pulled away from her just to yank her up to stand against the wall again. He stepped out of those sweats while their kiss started a whole new war. His hands slipped over her body, under the cups of her bra and then between her thighs. Knowing and skilled, he stroked her pussy over the lace just enough to get her whining against his hot laughter that echoed in her ear.

"Get on me," she heard him say. "I want you all over me, Della."

That was how she found herself riding Cory in the middle of his bed in her heels. His palms flexed on her ass with every rise of her hips. That way, he could yank her pussy right back down on his cock. Harder and faster until she was shaking and breathless because she was so fucking close.

He knew it.

Taunted the orgasm to the surface.

He only gave it to her when his thumb slipped against her ass to push and tease until she was backing into that, too.

She rode him faster through it.

He fucked her harder.

And after the tremors and her high cries had settled, he pulled her high until she was sitting on his face, and he ate the next orgasm right out of her.

Then they were right back to fucking in soft sheets until he painted her stomach with white ropes of cum with her name in his mouth and smoke still clinging to the air.

She only wanted more.

All over again.

This was supposed to be just them having fun. That's what he said.

God.

She wanted that to be true.

Except when they finished, sticky and hot and all out of breath, on theirs backs in his bed … his satisfied chuckles broke through the haze and she stared over at him. She ached in all the right ways. Her hands couldn't stop from reaching over to trace lines with her fingertips across the expanse of his inked chest.

It was *easy.*

He sucked her right in.

Like a hurricane.

No doubt, she looked a mess. Ruined makeup. Slick with *him.* Smiling, though. And he stared at her as though he liked it. All tangled in his sheets. Cory grinned back.

Yeah.

"We need more smoke," he said, laughter heavy. "See, *that's* why I had a blunt in my nightstand. For when you *really* need it in bed but don't want to get out of it. I have to get out of bed to get another—I blame you."

He had a point.

All she managed to say after a giggle was, "Fuck you."

So many of their conversations always seemed to end the same.

She barely knew him at all.

Cory stuck out his tongue between his grin to say, "Oh, yeah, yeah. Again, definitely. We're doing that again, babe, but with you on your knees when I'm slipping it in nice and slow. I need that ass *high.* Maybe fuck that, too."

She shivered all over.

Because wouldn't that be so easy?

He forgot all about that other room she was supposed to be sleeping in. She realized how easy it was for her to forget about it, too, while she looked at him.

He grabbed the tablet she had earlier. Hip hop filtered through the device, reminding her that he hadn't forgotten she'd been looking for music. The guy on the beat that talked up his hard work and material aspirations was a favorite of hers, but she didn't tell Cory that.

She wasn't surprised he liked the musician too, though. Too much of him seemed just like her, but the flipside of the same coin.

He said they were just having fun. Right—*just fun.*

The problem with that was she knew how men like him worked when it came to women. Fun could mean making a woman fall head over heels for him because the chase was the best part. And once that was over, well who cared about something like someone's heart? It had all been just *fun*, right?

Men like Cory Rossi only did one thing to women like her.

Break hearts.

ELEVEN

"HEY," came the quiet call from down the hall.

J lingered at the end of the hallway leading to the storage rooms of the restaurant. Half inside and half outside of the exit door at the end, the man pointed down their way. "Dad's having breakfast in the private section whenever you're ready."

Then, J tipped his head to the side, gaze on only Della. "You got a minute, though?"

Della looked to Cory.

He shrugged. "Go ahead—I can chat with your father alone."

He didn't mind.

Seemed the Capo and Cory had shit to go over now. *Respectfully*, of course.

He was still a little bitter that no one thought to tell him the issue was a fucking *ex* of Della's, who also just happened to be an old friend of his— they might not have known that, however—or anything really. A lot of information had been kept from Cory, and he didn't like that at all. Too much, truthfully.

He wanted to know *why*.

"You sure?" Della asked. "I can handle—"

"Anything put in your path, I know. Go chat with your brother."

The soft smile she shot him made Cory think that maybe he might be able to break through some of the walls this woman had erected around herself. He'd never really wanted to do that with anyone before … didn't care to learn what made someone what and who they were at the end of the day.

But she did.

Cory didn't know what to make of that.

"We'll be out back," J called down to him.

Cory nodded and then turned his attention to where it really needed to be. On the arched entryway that lead into the private dining section. The enforcer posted just beyond the doorway gave Cory a nod when he passed, not speaking a single word. That was fine with him—they were both there doing their jobs, and he didn't care to make pleasantries while he did his. Inside the room that sported large bay windows with heavy, richly colored tapestries that overlooked the front street, he quickly found the man he was searching for.

Frankie Costello sat at the very end of a long dining table that was filled with chairs on either side of it, with his platter of breakfast spread in front of him. Currently, he was adding sugar to a black coffee and staring in Cory's direction.

No smile.

Just waiting.

"Frankie," Cory greeted.

Della's father waved a hand with the steaming spoon he'd just used to stir his coffee. "Find a seat, if you like. Or stand. Your comfort isn't my concern, but you're welcome to it nonetheless."

Huh.

Just like that, Frankie reminded Cory of the Outfit boss, Tommas. Maybe it was the demeanor of men in power that all had the same ring, but he heard it all the same.

"I don't really need a seat. Spend most of my time on my feet, anyhow."

Frankie chuckled and did smile a bit at that. "Ah, yes, Theo's little *protégé*, hmm? The streets will always keep you running."

That had Cory raising a brow. "Is that what all you made men call me when I can't hear?"

The other man's stare flicked up from his food to meet Cory's. "It's not meant to be a bad thing."

Okay.

Cory still wasn't sure how he felt about it.

Seemed like his whole life lately.

"Where is my daughter?" Frankie asked as he went back to his food. Or rather, the piece of toast he started to slather with red jam.

"Chatting with J."

That earned another one of those small smiles.

"He worries about her. A lot."

"Like you," Cory returned.

Frankie dragged in a heavy breath. "Hard not to—this business has never been kind to women. I walk a fine line of wanting to challenge the status quo and needing to make sure Della is safe. I'm not sure I do it well."

"But you try. That counts."

"I hope so."

"And she stayed with me at my place last night," Cory added.

The scraping of the butter knife along the toast stilled. To his benefit, the man didn't look up or give anything away at Cory's statement. He didn't *need* to out the fact that Della remained with him for the night—people would draw conclusions, but especially the woman's father—and he was okay with that. He didn't intend to hide his business with Della because he didn't think it hindered his ability to do his job. He wouldn't, however, find himself in shit because his personal activities offended someone else's sensibilities.

Might as well get it out of the way. Right? He thought that was the adult thing to do.

"Is that going to be a problem?" Cory asked when Frankie stayed quiet.

The older man cleared his throat, dark eyes finding Cory's with consideration, amusement, and *annoyance*. "When they said it was you they were sending for this job—everybody hears about the Rossi brothers, Cory."

"And?"

"You do things a little differently than the rest of us, don't you?"

"I am who I am, Frankie."

The Capo nodded once. "Don't let it be a problem, how about that?"

He could work with that.

Cory came to stand a few seats down from Frankie and folded his arms over his chest, the leather of his jacket tightening against his tense back because time was up. The chitchat was nice and all, but he wanted to get down to business.

"Last night," Cory started.

Frankie grunted under his breath. "Mmm, my daughter stepped out on business to handle some of her own, I hear. Didn't go as she planned for it to, apparently. You weren't aware she was going to have a meeting *after* her business was over at the strip club?"

Cory shook his head. "Just as surprised as you. Luis wasn't the intended point of contact there, according to her, but the asshole has his ways. Any reason why you all didn't think I should know the full details of what you were dealing with here between Della and her ex? Like the entire fact that the issue *was* an ex?"

At the table, Frankie cut through boiled eggs while his jaw clenched at the mere mention of Luis's name. Cory didn't miss that—shit, he *felt* that. Seemed the chick's father didn't have much of a care for her ex, either.

Luis had that effect on people.

"Are you asking because you feel some kind of way about—"

Cory made a harsh noise, not even going down the road the man was suggesting. "Cut the shit—I'm not that petty, Frankie. It's not that deep. I just think I might have been able to do something to fix the situation or help you with it had I been given full disclosure."

"Cory—"

"Guy's got a hard nut for her, Frankie. Not in any way that's good, either. Just the idea that she was with me last night about sent Luis's head shooting off his fucking shoulders."

"Is *that* going to be an issue, you think?"

Cory considered that. "We've got history—me and him."

"And that means what for Della …?"

"Best option is for me to remain where I am, doing what I'm doing. See if we can get shit calmed down and go from there. Especially if Luis thinks we're together. The bigger issue I want to know is what the fuck does he want?"

Frankie's brow dipped low. "That's obvious, isn't it? He wants her. Why else would he go through all this fucking trouble?"

But was that it?

"Is that all?" Cory asked. "A little fuck like Luis is going to come after one of the Outfit's most successful Capos because he got a taste of your daughter's puss—"

"Watch it," Frankie said sharply. "And Luis's got more reach than you think."

Cory straightened his mouth out. It always got him into trouble. Or so his ma said.

"Apologies."

"Thank you," came the grumbled reply.

Frankie also had a point—Cory hadn't kept up with Luis's growth on the streets or rather, his gang's growth, more than knowing he still fucking existed and what he was usually doing to hustle. He was still waiting to chat with Joe and see if his brother could find more detailed information that might help him out here to connect some dots.

"It doesn't entirely make sense, think about it," Cory said.

Frankie didn't meet his gaze.

That told Cory a lot.

"And you didn't answer my question—why wasn't I given the full details?"

Still, all he got was silence.

Cory waited it out.

"You're a smart and quick young man, Cory," Frankie said, reaching for the cup of coffee with steam edging upward from the rim, "so why don't you tell me a reason I would have to keep valuable information like that to only those who needed to know? Your only real job here is to watch Della's back—keep her safe. *Not* solve my fucking problems. Go ahead and consider it, I have time to wait."

Yeah.

Just like his uncle, Tommas.

"You're protecting something," Cory said.

Della, of course.

Because she was who she was working in a business that would take every chance to eat her up and spit her out. No doubt, she could handle it. That didn't mean people like her father wouldn't still protect her at all costs from every angle they could.

Frankie shrugged. "For one."

"What else is there?"

"You answered that yourself, didn't you?"

Cory had to think about that.

All at once, he understood.

It was the entire thing.

The attack.

Luis.

Della.

The *motive*.

"Something just isn't right with this," Cory said out loud.

Frankie brought his cup up to his lips, muttering, "Hard to find what isn't right when everyone knows something is wrong and might want to take advantage. Loose lips. Sinking ships. That whole bit. Think about it."

Cory was.

Too much.

•••

Cory considered his conversation with Frankie after he stepped out of the private section and leaned against the wall of the hallway. He needed a moment to understand what it might mean for Della—not to mention, his job here. He didn't get much time to think about anything before the rear exit door opened slightly. The conversation from familiar voices traveled down to his spot.

He stilled at the words he heard.

"Just, shit … hey, I'm not trying to be an ass, you know?" J said.

Della let out a hard sigh. "Aren't you?"

"Or you could see it as me looking out for you. Don't see this as me trying to pry into your business—*you* offered. I'm only voicing an opinion. And it's not like anything I said was untrue, Della. You don't have the greatest history with guys. You tell me you jumped into bed with—"

"That's enough."

"Look, I'm sorry. Okay?"

Cory's gaze stayed trained on the wall across from him, but from the side he could see how Della's hand around the side of the exit door loosened. So much so that the door closed a bit. Not enough to shut out the conversation, unfortunately.

"I *know*, okay. I *do*," Della told her brother. "I just don't need everybody else to point it out to me, too. Jesus, I just got out of a relationship with a raging asshole and *shocker*, he just happens to be an old friend of Cory's. To top it all off. Men like that aren't worth shit. I don't need you to tell me. I already know. Don't worry, J, I'm not about to make the same mistakes again with Cory Rossi."

Ouch.

Cory didn't have long to acknowledge the ache that spread in his chest or just how much Della's words stung. Frankly, he wasn't even sure he had a right to feel anything about it at all when the two of them barely knew each other, right? She was his current job—he'd said it himself that this was just fun.

Except it wasn't that which hurt. It was her *assumptions*. Because she didn't know shit, not about him.

A couple of seconds later, Cory straightened up from the wall just as Della pulled open the exit door and stepped inside with J following close behind.

"Your father said you were welcome to join him for breakfast—both of you," Cory told the siblings.

If the two knew he had overheard their conversation, they didn't act like it. Neither did he. Everybody seemed fine like that.

Just perfect.

"What else?" Della asked, walking closer.

"Cory," J greeted, passing him by.

"J," he returned.

"Mind the things you handle, yeah?"

Cory met the man's gaze, murmuring, "Always do, J."

It was all about the unspoken words.

And what they meant.

"Well?" Della asked.

Cory's attention went back to her. He thought about what Frankie told him, knowing the man had a point. If there was something bigger going on and Luis or the attack on Della was just … smoke and mirrors, then there was a point to keeping information close at hand.

"I'll be hanging a little closer," Cory said. "You go, I go. That's the motto."

Della scowled.

Damn her for looking pretty like that, too.

"I don't want to appear scared," she said. "Luis doesn't frighten me, Cory. He's the type to like that too much."

"But he does *bother* you."

That much was obvious. And those were two very different things.

Della swallowed hard, tipping her head up to meet Cory's stare. Just a foot apart in the hallway, he found she was too close … yet not close enough. Except her earlier words made him bitter in more ways than he cared to explain.

"Luis has always been obsessive and—"

"It's more than that, clearly."

Della's expression hardened. "So, you see it, too."

Yeah.

He sure did.

"Go have breakfast. I'll be ready to leave when you are."

He could see she wanted to ask more. Cory had other things to think about.

Too much, really.

•••

Cory's watchful gaze swept the dark street as movement from his right followed the creak of the car door being opened. The figure slipped into the passenger seat without much fanfare at all and if someone hadn't been paying attention, they would have missed it altogether.

So was his brother's way. It's why they called Joe the Shadow.

"Thought you weren't coming—look at the fucking time," Cory said.

"Your bitching has started early. Good to see."

"*Hmm.*"

Just like that, Joe shot Cory a look from the passenger seat that spoke volumes without saying anything at all. His brother could tell just by his demeanor and tone that something was up and no doubt, he was going to pester Cory until he spilled his guts.

"What is it?" Joe asked.

"Nothing—hey, I need you to do something for me."

"Yeah, yeah. That's why I'm here. Your attitude, though, is why I'm gonna stay."

Of course, it was.

On another day, Cory wouldn't mind indulging his brother. Joe was a good sounding board—he always told Cory what shit was upfront with no-nonsense. He appreciated the bluntness because he offered Joe the same.

Problem was, his attitude came from one thing.

One person.

Della.

Because he still couldn't get her comments out of his goddamn head. Maybe ... just maybe, because Cory was who he was and he was proud of it, he didn't want to admit that a passing comment from a woman he wasn't even trying to chase had him feeling like a bit of a prick. Or like the last thing he wanted was for *her* to think he was exactly that.

Stupid.

That's what it was.

Cory didn't want to be doing this shit at all right now—not because Della wasn't interesting enough to be worth it—because it put him off his game. Instead of focusing on keeping an eye on her place a block down from where he'd parked after the sun went down, he kept getting lost in his thoughts about all the other shit that had nothing to do with his *job*.

That had to be the most important thing right now.

"Listen," Cory said out of the side of his mouth to his brother, "tonight's just not the night for anything else but business, bro. All right?"

Joe took a second.

"Yeah, all right," he finally replied, adding, "and shit, I would have got here earlier but since you're *busy* and some people—Ma and Monica, you know—need extra attention from me, so they'll relax for a damn minute."

That had Cory grinning.

"Ah, Dad got onto you to distract Ma, then?"

Joe shrugged. "Yeah, but Mon missed you last week, really. I had to listen to her tell me all the details about her group of friends, and whose messing with who, or which chick is trying to get lead on the squad and why she ain't shit ... Cory, I just—"

"It's a lot to keep up with."

But he did that with Mon—Joe, spent his time with their little sister in other valuable ways—because she trusted her brother. Enough to tell him *anything*. So much so that she counted him as her best friend. Fuck anyone if they thought to use or hurt Monica Rossi because the first people she would come to was Cory and Joe.

They would rage.

Blood would spill.

Joe grunted under his breath. "Man, that's why I didn't fuck with chicks more than once in high school. Too much nonsense."

"Fucking hell."

Cory's laughter followed Joe's; it colored the car, taking his mind away from the shit that hadn't left him alone all day. For that split second, he allowed himself to have that clean slate because soon enough, he'd be right back to business as usual.

"What do you need?" Joe asked, bringing them back to task.

He let out a steady stream of air, gaze cutting back to Della's place. Earlier, when he'd brought her home after a full day, she'd not asked him in. He didn't suggest that he wanted to, either.

"Luis Ruiz," Cory said. "He's who Frankie Costello is having the issue with. The attack on Della—why I'm watching her right now."

That had Joe's brow lifting.

Cory nodded in response. "Yeah."

"So ... *yeah*? Really."

"Yep."

"Shit. That's been ... how many years ago?"

Clearing his throat, Cory said, "A few. Wouldn't have hurt to be a few more. Certainly didn't expect to run into him like that. Might have handled it *slightly* better had I gone into it knowing everything from the start but what the fuck does that matter, you know?"

His brother made an inquisitive *huh*. Cory's attitude had come back fast and heavy but this time, it wasn't about the same thing as before.

"I missed something from the last time we talked. Fill me in," Joe said, resting deeper into the passenger seat. "Might as well get comfortable."

"That's why you're here."

"And to do something for you."

Cory shrugged. "That, too. We're getting to that—"

"You want me to find what I can on Luis, current and past?"

"Basically. I'm busy. Also not getting the full story from people. My job is supposed to be *Della*. I just like to know shit, Joe."

"I know. Still, fill me in."

Cory rolled his eyes, but did what his brother wanted. It passed the better part of a half-hour in time to go over everything with Joe that had happened in just the past couple of days, not to mention the overall picture he was currently seeing.

"It'll take me a bit to get it all without raising flags," Joe said after Cory finished, "but we'll know what Luis's been up to since the two of you parted ways back when … or mostly."

Cory didn't reply.

He'd barely even cared to listen.

Joe didn't miss it. "Seriously, what is up with you?"

Della had turned off the lights in her kitchen. Cory had a moment where he thought *should have just asked to go in, man, fuck the pride*, and he went quiet.

Joe gave him a look from the side.

Cory pretended like he didn't see.

"She thinks I'm like her ex," Cory said, the words bitter as they passed his lips. "Like Luis. Same type of dude, Joe. And I don't know, I'm not all that different if you look at what I've done and where I came from and all that shit. In some ways, we're exactly the fucking same."

Joe hummed under his breath. "At least you know it, though. The problem comes when people aren't self-aware, Cory."

"Except that's not the problem."

"What is?"

"That I don't want her to think I'm anything like him."

Joe's brow raised high, that look in his eye enough to make Cory point a single finger at his brother with a stare that *stung*.

"Don't say a thing," Cory uttered.

His brother's palms popped up in surrender. "Saying nothing, Cory. But *shit* ..."

Cory made a thick *ugh* sound under his breath before turning the key to make the car's engine roar and the lights flood the road. "Call me when you got something and get the fuck out of my car, man."

Joe's laughter chased him out of the car, but he leaned back in the door before slamming it shut just to say, "It'll be great, Cory."

"*What* will?"

All he saw was his brother's shrug before Joe turned and disappeared into the waiting shadows on the side of the street.

Prick.

TWELVE

CORY RESTED THE three brown paper bags of groceries onto Della's counter. Without as much as a *there you go* in her direction, he spun on his boot heels and headed out of the kitchen. Like he intended to leave— probably to go back outside and sit in his car. The same thing he'd been doing all week. Ever since the breakfast with her father the morning after her run-in with Luis.

Nonetheless, it seemed like Cory had been ... off since that day. *Definitely* avoiding her, she'd noticed. Considering he made every effort to keep a distance while at the same time making sure she stayed home as much as possible.

Today was an exception.

Only because Della was about to lose her shit. Entirely. One could only stay hidden away behind four walls for so long when they were used to being out and about before everything went bad. She'd tried to play by the rules as much as she could. Jennika was handling work—Della did her best not to say anything about that. She hadn't seen her brother or father all week, either.

Della hadn't realized when Cory said he'd be sticking closer, it also meant that she would be on lockdown in her place. Not to mention no one was telling her anything. Not her brother, father, and even Jennika refused to meet up for something like an innocent, quiet lunch because everyone didn't dare breathe the wrong way.

Or some nonsense. That's what it felt like.

Della knew everybody was just trying to ... handle the issue. Keep her safe. Or that's what she assumed because it was hard to tell when she wasn't doing anything and everyone was telling her exactly that, too— *nothing.*

Maybe she didn't do well with no control. Yeah, that was probably it.

So, that morning she decided to just head out. Not to work or cause trouble. No, she simply needed to get the hell out of her house, do something for herself, and *breathe.* Cory hadn't exactly been happy about it, but he clearly hadn't seen an issue when he let her go and followed behind like he was supposed to. It should have been a good day.

Back home after getting a new, red stiletto manicure, a blowout, and some groceries ... except Cory was currently making it hard to be happy. Or rather, maybe it was starting to get to her.

Cory's silence, that was. And his fucking mood. Whatever that was about.

"Thanks, I guess," she called at Cory's back as he moved to leave her kitchen.

His next step hesitated. He shot a dark look over his shoulder, that sharp jaw of his tensing when he asked her, "What, are you not done running around the city for the day, or …?"

Ouch.

She didn't miss the attitude there.

Della wanted to pretend like Cory's hot and cold demeanor didn't bother her, but that would be a terrible fucking lie on her part. She shouldn't be feeling *anything* for this man at all, but more often than not, that's exactly what she found herself doing.

Feeling too much.

When he wasn't looking, she did.

When he was silent, she wanted to ask why.

Except for all those strange urges she had regarding him were made more difficult to contain because all he'd done for the week was keep a distance and that damned attitude. Not that it should make a difference in the first place.

He clearly got what he wanted, right?

Seemed like it.

Della wasn't perfect—she knew it. Stubborn, *picky*, controlling and a pest when she wanted to be. But she actually tried *not* to be that bad when it came to Cory because she did understand he was only doing his job even when he pointed out fifteen times that she was supposed to be at home— *today alone.*

Now, she was just done.

Over it.

"You know what," Della told him with a wave of her new manicured nails, "never mind. See you later."

Cory didn't move. "Excuse me—you're dismissing me, really?"

"Not like—"

"Nah, I get it, Della. Don't bother explaining."

Okay.

"What the fuck is your problem?" she asked, unfazed at his burning stare still locked on her.

There, it was out.

She said it.

He could explain or not.

Cory said nothing.

Della wasn't having that. "Seriously, how did we go from laughing together in bed to you barely speaking to me all week unless you had to? Or is it that you got what you were looking for so now you're not even going to *pretend* to be a decent guy?"

With a dark laugh, Cory turned around all at once. He took the three steps to stand up against the kitchen island, directly across from her with those paper bags between them, just to place his palms along the edge while he leaned over closer to her.

"That's what it really boils down to for you, right?" he asked, his voice a dangerous murmur.

Della's brow dipped, her mouth opening to form words that she wasn't even sure she should speak, "What are you—"

"You should really mind your conversations more," Cory interjected fast. "What you said to J at the restaurant a week ago—about me?—yeah, I heard that."

A heavy weight found Della's chest.

It sat there.

Then it spread.

Her words didn't form.

Oh.

Why did he look hurt, though?

Had she misjudged …

"And why do you even care?" Cory asked her. "About whether or not we're fucking *talking*, you know? If the first thing you see when you look at me is a bad dude, don't worry about whether or not we're having conversations, Della. It's all good."

She went quiet.

He didn't seem to mind.

Della finally understood the meaning of tension so thick it could be cut with a knife. Cory looked like the very last thing he wanted to do was stand there for another second and talk to her, but he didn't move. Pride, maybe.

He had a lot of that, she noticed.

So did she.

This time, though, Della was sure *she* was the wrong one.

His face said that.

"If this was only supposed to be fun," she said, deciding to let her thoughts out to play, "then why are we doing this—fighting like this—right now?"

Cory's cheek twitched. "I don't know."

Huh.

"I'm sorry," Della said, though she knew without an explanation, it probably wouldn't mean very much to him. She took one step away from the island, breaking his gaze first. "But really, thanks for bringing my groceries in. I gotta … think."

As lame as that sounded.

She could feel Cory watching her as she stepped away from the island entirely. He didn't say a word, though.

"And I am done running errands for the day," she told him.

His sigh echoed behind her.

She didn't turn around.

•••

When *thinking* the rest of the previous day and then night away didn't work, she decided to meet up with J. Because if there was anyone in the world who could look her in her face and tell Della all her shit without being scared, it was her brother.

She figured she needed it.

Della knew it really wasn't safe for her to be wandering Chicago for the second day in a row when she wasn't even supposed to leave her house, if possible. Even J had to point it out when she texted him to ask where he was going to be that morning. Nonetheless, she let her brother know that *no* wasn't an option—she'd simply texted *I need your time*. That was their code for "*drop everything, I need someone to listen to me.*"

When she was a teenager chasing stupid boys and finding more trouble than they were worth at the time, her brother told her those exact words. She could still remember the way J had stood in the doorway of her bedroom's bathroom while she puked in a toilet, spilling the liquor she poured down her throat. He had cleaned and *sobered* her up, and then let her know exactly what to do if she ever needed her brother after that moment.

"If you have shit going on or you need someone to listen, Della, all you gotta say to me is *I need your time, J*," he'd told her, "and I'll be there. That's what brothers do."

She didn't forget it and had used it a time or two. It was good to know that silly little thing between her and J still worked after all this time. Because the moment she'd texted him that morning and didn't give him the option to say no, she had an address to meet up with him in the shipping district where a new row of warehouses had recently been built.

Stepping out of her car, Della ignored the roar of a familiar engine pulling up behind where she'd parked on the side street. About thirty feet from the warehouse where she needed to meet up with J. She did dare a peek over her shoulder, but only to find a *very* pissed off Cory stepping out of his car before he slammed the door and made a beeline toward her.

Well …

Of course, he'd be pissed.

She hadn't exactly explained much that morning, just left. He hadn't been driving the vintage Mustang for a couple of days the past week, she'd noticed, so she hadn't even thought to look for him when she figured he would just follow like he always did. Sometimes he changed cars.

Today, he *did* have the 'Stang.

And the staple leather jacket.

As well as a scowl.

Mostly, Della didn't want to explain to Cory she was going to see J when, *undoubtedly*, he would ask why. Since part of the entire reason why she wanted to see her brother was so that she could work out the nonsense she felt about Cory, she didn't think it would be helpful to tell *him* that fact.

So, she said nothing.

Just left.

Technically, he followed right behind her, so it wasn't like she broke the rules. That's what Della was going to keep telling herself. Maybe she'd explain to Cory later, if she felt like it. And maybe she wouldn't. What would it matter?

He didn't know now.

Nothing bad had happened yet.

"Della, *hey*," Cory shouted at her back.

Yep.

He was really pissed. The heat in his tone said it all. *Okay*. So, she would explain. Just *after* she talked to her brother. And gave Cory a chance to calm down.

Just around the corner was the warehouse with three bays that faced the road for trucks to back right up. Della blinked at the sight of a familiar woman leaning against the hood of her black Benz coupe. Even Jennika's brow raised at Della coming her way, but it quickly faded into a smile as she pulled a burning cigarette away from her painted-red lips and exhaled the smoke to the sky.

"Hey, what are you doing here?" Jennika asked. "Thought you were supposed to be hiding away at home this week until Frankie says otherwise?"

Della grinned, shrugging one shoulder. "Yeah, well ... same to you, what are you doing here? Especially dressed like *that*."

She didn't say it to be rude; Jennika winked like she wasn't offended.

The black, skin-tight cashmere dress hugged Jennika's curves and clung in just the right ways to the rest of her body. It dipped low at the breast, and the hem of the skirt stopped above her knees and her knee-high, heeled leather boots.

That was the kind of shit they wore when they worked.

They didn't work around *here*.

Jennika gave Della a sly smile—one she recognized. Whenever her friend found a man she liked, or reclaimed an already won conquest, she smiled exactly like that. "Oh, you know … fun stuff. And a bit of work, too. Later."

What?

That's not right, she thought.

Hadn't J said …

"Are you sleeping with—"

"When you got a second," Cory said, finally catching up with her and coming to stand behind Della, "then I'd really like to have a chat with you, yeah?"

He still sounded really pissed.

She probably deserved that.

Della didn't get the chance to deal with Jennika *or* Cory because a familiar face popped out of the black metal door between the right and middle bay of the warehouse. Her brother called out, stopping the conversation entirely to say, "Didn't know you were bringing a guest."

His gaze swept over the people down the side of the street, her included.

Why wouldn't she bring Cory?

He *was* her bodyguard at the moment.

Before she could come back with a smartass remark, J added with a wave to her specifically, "Get off the fucking street before you draw attention, Jesus."

Della headed for the warehouse.

They could follow or not.

She came here for a reason.

It didn't matter if she had more questions to ask … she came here for a conversation that she desperately needed to have. J was the *one* person she might be able to have it with and come out better for it. The rest? It could wait a minute. Not much longer, though.

•••

"What exactly is happening here? Or … *out there*," Della corrected, nodding toward the closed office door. She considered what had been inside the warehouse.

Cars—a lot of them. Cardboard boxes piled high between each vehicle. Which probably made it hard to see anything through the dirty windows on the three-bay doors at the front of the building. Steering wheels with the front caps that had been popped off, a pile of airbags sat forgotten in the corner, and other than J, the place looked like a ghost town when it came to other people. Except for all the personal items she noticed here and there as she walked to the rear of the large building with her brother—other people *were* here. She just didn't know where they were now or their purpose.

J glanced up from the papers on the desk as he sat down. "What do you think?"

"I don't want to guess."

"Drugs," her brother explained, words clear and tone dry. "Pills, to be specific. Packaged bags get put in the steering wheel after the airbag and sensors are all removed. It's transported across the border when it's time. But because it only takes one person knowing—the wrong person—a crew of four or five handles each shipment to keep any talk at a minimum. If you get my drift."

"Oh."

J shrugged. "I'm only telling you right now because you're here and you've seen it—if I gave you enough time, you'd put it together on your own."

That made sense.

And it was kind of ingenious.

All of it.

"Just because I'm making sure shit gets done with this job," J said, "doesn't mean I make the rules. When we're told to keep it quiet, that's what we do. It's for the good of everybody to do it—none of us want to go to jail for twenty-five plus years, you know?"

Della suddenly had an understanding about why her brother wasn't telling her a lot about his work whenever she tried to ask—he couldn't. That was just the reality of the matter. It didn't make a difference that she and J had worked together for ... well, the entire time Della had been involved in the business, really. That didn't factor into what was going on here at all.

All at once, she felt selfish.

A little stupid, too.

She hadn't even attempted to make sure her brother *could* sit down and chat—she didn't give him the option at all. No doubt, J was taking a serious risk by allowing her to come there. No one was around, sure, but she bet someone could show up.

That's how work went.

Even she knew it.

Damn.

"You needed to talk, right?" he asked. "Talk, before the crew gets in this morning or the Capo decides to make an appearance."

Della gave her brother an apologetic smile. "Sorry—I wasn't thinking, but definitely not about anything that wasn't *myself.*"

J chuckled, grinning. "I mean, you get like that sometimes."

"Thanks."

Her sarcasm wasn't missed.

J smiled wider when he replied, "I do what I can."

Even so …

Della gave the sparsely decorated office a second glance, and her brother dressed in his slacks with his pressed dress shirt rolled up to the elbows. She thought about the scene out on the floor of the warehouse, and the man who was probably still angry out there and waiting for her. *Yes,* she wanted five minutes to talk to her brother so that J could set her straight, like he always did, but Della had to realize not everything was about her.

The world didn't revolve around her.

Everybody's time wasn't her own.

"It can wait," she told her brother, "I just …"

She hesitated, considering how to pose part of her problem.

J seemed to already know when he cocked a brow and asked, "Is it Cory?"

She gave her brother a look.

He stared right back, unconcerned.

All these men were the same.

Arrogant.

Difficult.

Too quick for their own good.

"Well—"

J didn't give her time to talk before he said, "I noticed he didn't look happy. Also, when you texted, you did finish it off with *I just suck at men.*"

"Could you say it with less … *judgment?*"

"No judgment here, sis."

Right.

Just a brother who loved her.

Della sighed. "We *can* talk about it later."

"Summarize. Maybe you'll feel better."

Would she?

That was the real question.

Folding her arms over the tweed coat she'd thrown on, Della steeled her spine. Better to just get it out. "He heard what I said about him to you—you know, that he's not any better than Luis, basically. I think I hurt his feelings. We had a fight. I feel bad. Also confused. Seems like him and I have managed to make something out of nothing. So it's nothing, really. Just my usual nonsense. We can talk about it later."

J would tell her she was being ridiculous.

Or something.

But *later.*

"Okay, we'll get back to this later," J said. "But that's usually how great things start—from nothing."

Della's head popped up. The floor had been interesting to stare at for a moment, but now her gaze was drawn to her brother behind the desk. "What?"

"I know I told you to look after yourself where he's concerned, but I meant that for you. Because maybe you need some time after everything. Not because Cory isn't a decent guy, all right."

Huh.

Well, then ...

"So, it's just me?" she asked.

J gave her a look. "I didn't say that, either. Our past shapes everything. Until people prove otherwise, why should you give them a chance?"

Della dropped his stare. It was easier. "That's a fact if I ever heard one. Not that it matters. Cory probably thinks I'm fucking crazy with the way I've whipped back and forth the past few weeks. I *sound* crazy, J. Like, I *can* hear it myself. I'm not that out of touch."

That earned her a laugh from across the room.

Her brother grinned. "I hear that's Cory's type, actually. His brother told me once he liked chicks as crazy as him on his best days. Doesn't mean you gotta be crazy like him. Just your own special brand. Maybe you're making something out of nothing after all and that's entirely the point. Maybe something in you likes something that it found in him. Or vice versa. Like I said, lots of great things come from nothing, Della."

When had her brother become so wise?

It was like everything in her life was changing from one day to the next. This was why she came here, though. She needed her brother to tell her the truth. Look at her crazy, make sense of it, and lay it out on the table for her point-blank-period.

J flipped his palms up, still looking like the cat that ate the cream. "I'm just saying. Plus, what are the chances you might be in a state over all of this because of what's happening with the business side of things?"

That had Della thinking. "What do you mean?"

"Cory's here for *work*. At the end of it. Lately, work has been its own problem for you. If you're not able to do your own job, you feel like people are stepping in on it over you—*men*. Are you mixing the two things instead of dealing with them separately? Everything that's just business stays *just* as business. Private problems stay private. That kind of thing."

He had a point.

She'd not considered that.

When she didn't respond right away, J was quick to come with more of his wisdom although she didn't have the first clue where it all came from. "You realize those are not the same things, right? What you're handling with Cory and what's going on around you and him because of Luis and his bullshit ... they're not the same and we all have to handle them like they're different, including you. One is personal growth. The other is business. Different things and that's okay. Just sucks for you that it's happening at the same time, you know? Makes it messy."

"And confusing," she muttered.

J nodded. "Still … give it a chance to clear up or pass."

Della sighed. "Yeah, maybe you're right."

"I am. It's what I do."

"You're awful."

J grinned widely. "Yeah, well … what can you do? Call me—we'll meet up when I'm …" He glanced at the closed door behind her, probably seeing the scene waiting behind it but not wanting to go back down that road. "… not busy. Yeah?"

Actually, Della already felt better.

This was why she loved her brother.

And maybe now she could apologize to Cory because she understood exactly what she needed to apologize for to start with. Wasn't that always a good thing?

She thought so.

"Okay," she replied. "Later, for sure."

"Yeah, you probably need a night out, huh? Heard you been locked down all week."

She groaned on her way to the office door as she reached for the knob. "Don't remind me. That's ninety percent of my damn problem."

"Likely. You never were one to hide away. I'll talk to Dad. See what we can do."

"Don't make promises."

"I tend to keep them when I make one."

Right.

And he usually wasn't a liar.

Speaking of which … that reminded her.

With her hand tight around the knob, but hesitating before she opened the door, Della glanced over her shoulder, asking, "Also, why did you lie to me? I know she's not your type … but did you really have to make a whole show when you said you weren't fucking her?"

J's brow dipped. "What?"

Why was he playing dumb?

"You said you weren't fucking around with Jennika—not loyal to a man, remember?"

Something lit up her brother's face that she didn't recognize from him— embarrassment? No, that wasn't right.

Before J could reply, a knock echoed on the office door. Della let go of the knob and stepped back when her brother said, "Let them in."

Della was entirely unsurprised to find a *very* annoyed Cory waiting behind the door. He passed her a look, but then gave J a nod. Her brother returned it with a greeting in kind.

Then, Cory's attention was back on her. That cold stare of his said it all; it also bothered her the most. She really needed to step up and own her shit where Cory was concerned. Her brother had made good points. Frankly, this man also hadn't given her a reason to *not* give him the benefit of the doubt, either.

"Can I please have a fucking minute now?" Cory asked.

J cleared his throat even though Cory wasn't looking at him. "Uh, there a problem?"

"No."

"Yes," Della said at the same time Cory did. She gave her brother a smile over her shoulder—their chat about Jennika could wait. Like everything else. It wasn't important—the world still didn't revolve around her, after all—and they could get back to this later. That was the beauty of her relationship with her brother. J always made time for her. "Just something I have to deal with, J. It's not on Cory."

"Yeah, okay," her brother replied.

She turned to face Cory again, giving him the floor without saying so. "A chat, then?"

"It'll only take a minute, Della."

She doubted that.

It was okay, though.

•••

Della let Cory lead the way. The two found themselves outside in the alley beside the warehouse. With his booted foot placed in the crack of the exit door to keep it from locking them out of the warehouse, he half faced her.

"First, before anything else," Cory said, "what you did this morning isn't okay. You don't take off without letting me know where you're going first. That's not safe, and you don't need me to tell you that to know it, either."

"I know," Della said quickly.

But if he felt the need to get it out …

More power to him.

"And I'm sorry, it won't happen again," she added.

Cory's jaw flexed before he said, "Yeah, especially if you're coming to a place like this. *Really* let me know ahead of time."

Through the small crack in the door, Della could see the short hallway leading back to the mess inside the warehouse. "You knew J was here—what he's doing for … work?"

His stare remained blank and unreadable. "I know where a lot of people work—it's sort of what I fucking do, you know, when I'm not looking after entitled, frustrating women like you."

Okay.

Now he wasn't playing around.

Della's smartass came out to play even though she knew it wasn't the right time at all. "I thought you liked a challenge, Cory?"

"But I don't like fucking games, though. Especially when it means you might be in danger. Clear enough?"

Apparently, she could feel like a bigger asshole.

"I *am* sorry," she told him. "I just needed to talk to my brother today, and I didn't want you asking why … or something. Stupid. I know."

He stilled, his gaze flicking over her face even though Della refused to meet his gaze. "Were you coming to talk about me?"

She sighed.

"Yes and no. And no and yes."

Cory's expression darkened. "What?"

"I know. I confuse myself just about as much as I confuse everyone else. Surprise, I look put together but really, I'm a mess. Welcome to my world."

"Della—"

The softer tone he took on had her shaking her head. Lifting her stare, she met his so that he could *see* she was telling him the truth when she said, "Listen, I didn't mean what I said about you being a shitty guy—not really. I meant it, but it was more a reflection of what I feel about myself and less about what you've done to me or shown me. And I could give you my backstory and how every relationship I've fallen into with someone has turned to garbage, but that's not what matters. What does is that I projected my issues onto you. That's all. I needed a second to clear my head."

"Huh."

"That's what you want to say?"

Cory shrugged under his leather jacket. "Isn't that all I need to say? I didn't realize us having a bit of fun was going to cause a problem, Della."

"It didn't. *I* made it. Because we were just having fun. I got ahead of myself—scared myself."

Cory cleared his throat, his attention drifting upward to the blue sky overhead. "All right … so back to normal, then?"

"What is normal?"

"We'll figure it out. As long as it's good, what's the problem?"

Well, to start, it scared her.

Cory quickly added, "Also, I think this is what my brother, Joe, would call growth. He likes that word, the prick. He also likes pointing out my growth every chance he can."

Della laughed dryly. "My brother says it too. I have a lot of that *growth* going on lately. Just realized being here today why J doesn't tell me much about his business. I thought it was about me or—"

"They can't, Della. It's not about you. It's just what this business is sometimes. Seems like a lot of what you've done has been with family and when it came time for you to do it alone and for them to move on ... shit just got messy."

She went quiet because she'd also learned recently that listening taught her a lot more than talking did. Maybe she needed to be more grateful that she had the chance to learn—the people around her were offering that opportunity. She should put it to use more often.

"*Hey*," Cory said, his tone husky but still *sweet*.

How was that possible?

Della looked up. "Yeah?"

"Never had a chick turn me into an asshole before."

A sly grin curved her lips. "Do you mean to say I hurt your feelings?"

"I don't really *do* or talk about those."

She nodded. "Right."

"But I'm sorry, too."

"Good to know."

There was no pause between their exchange and when he leaned in closer. His lips brushed over hers, softly at first. *Searching*, she thought. There was a big part of Della that didn't like he had to search for something with her at all. Really, everything else between them had been so entirely easy when they didn't let doubts and nonsense get in the way.

She kissed him back.

Harder.

Cory seemed to like that a lot if the way he smirked against her kiss was any indication. It quickly turned hotter when his tongue swept the seam of her mouth. Then he was tasting her. Their tongues dancing while a smooth, lovely hum built in his chest.

She stepped closer.

Needed him near.

Supple, worn leather found her fingertips when she let her hands travel over his chest. His gaze stayed on hers while he took and took and took with his kiss.

It still terrified her that this man could take her heart before she realized what happened. But wasn't the beauty in how easy it could be? Della wasn't ready to think about that yet.

Cory pulled away from the kiss first. She was left trying to catch her breath, with lips still tingling that tasted of him and promised *sin*. All things she liked about this man.

He didn't move back, though. She didn't put distance between them either. They stayed close enough together that his warm, minty breath washed over her lips with his next hard exhale.

"I don't do this with women," he said. "Any of this. Being honest, and all, so you know why I fuck it up occasionally."

Della swallowed hard. "But you're doing something with me now?"

"Something. I'm not sure what."

"So as long as it's good …"

Cory watched the way her lips formed the words before murmuring, "Well, I really don't see the problem. Do you?"

Not at all.

She wasn't able to answer him. The roar of engines had both of them looking down the direction of the alleyway to the street that led to the front of the warehouse.

Two black cars—windows darkened completely from tint—raced by. She'd noticed the row of warehouses seemed quiet.

Those cars were unusual.

She just knew it.

"Cory—" Della started to say.

He didn't let her finish. "Stay where you are—don't move."

Hadn't he learned yet?

She didn't listen well.

Even when she *tried.*

It was a real problem.

THIRTEEN

TWO BLACK CARS racing down a street with dark windows wouldn't be unusual in Chicago at times. Except Cory had noticed how quiet the row of new warehouses had been that morning and the streets surrounding them. The new addition to the shipping district was still selling properties—that's how fresh the section was. Add in what he knew about J Costello's business here for an Outfit Capo, and those black cars put him on edge instantly.

The guys J had working here wouldn't cause a scene—certainly not something like acting foolishly in their vehicles. It would draw attention to who, and possibly *what*, was going down inside the warehouse. Nobody needed or wanted that.

"J!" Cory called when he headed back inside the warehouse through the side exit door.

The short hallway leading out to the main floor of the building had boxes piled high on either side. A lot like the mess between the parked cars where the crew had been readying to hide illegal prescription drugs inside the steering wheels. He imagined some of the boxes had shit inside—who knew what because it really didn't matter. Some of the boxes were probably full of nothing but packing peanuts and whatever other garbage could be thrown in. That way if anyone got inside and thought to open a box, they wouldn't find much.

Cory had done things like this before. He knew how it worked.

Unfortunately, the mess made it difficult to see where J was because he wasn't inside the office when Cory passed it by. Della was close on his heels as he came to the end of the hallway. Over the piles of boxes and cars, he found J.

Talking with Jennika across the warehouse right in front of the bay doors. Had he not heard those cars? *Because he was opening the fucking bay doors.*

"J!" Cory shouted, "Keep them closed!"

It was too late.

Even Cory knew it.

Two of the three warehouse's bay doors were already halfway opened. When bad shit went down, the same things always happened for Cory. His chest became tight. The air around him turned thinner and *colder*. Time slowed.

That was before his gut dropped. Like his heart. It was as though he could watch everything happen in excruciatingly clear detail. Not that he wanted to, but adrenaline just didn't give him a choice.

J turned to give Cory a look, finally taking his attention away from whatever conversation he'd been having with Jennika. A conversation that hadn't seemed entirely happy considering the two had been sporting expressions that warned *back off.*

"What—"

J didn't even get to finish his sentence.

Della's scream of her brother's name from behind Cory when he threw his arm up to stop her from going out of the hallway hurt his eardrums. He'd hear that for days. That he knew for sure.

Not that any of it did any good.

Jennika looked out through the opened bay door, horrified when two black cars roared to a stop. Windows rolled down on the cars; long, black barrels sticking out before light exploded, and so did the sound of gunfire. J was still looking Cory's way, though.

He didn't even see it coming.

Jennika hit the floor the second the shooting started.

Della screamed again.

"*J!* Joel!"

She tried to fight past Cory, but the moment he understood what was happening, he stopped watching. He spun around while the bullets still flew, slamming into boxes and cars and the beams, to shove her back down the hallway.

She looked a mess.

Crying already.

Her fists came at him.

She landed more than one.

"Get my brother—help my brother!"

He didn't want to tell her.

It was already too late for J.

"Cory, stop! *Stop it!*"

Probably too late for Jennika, too.

He didn't speak. Cory just did his job. He got her out, and he kept Della safe. Even when she sobbed, begging him again to help, and he had to physically lift her up to carry her through the exit door. The rest wasn't on his hands, and yet, it felt like it was.

"*My brother. My brother ... my brother ...*"

She kept saying it.

Cory wouldn't soon forget it.

•••

"I couldn't get an update from the nurses on Jennika," Cory said to Della.

She said nothing.

Didn't even look his way.

He sighed. "Not family, and all."

Although from what he understood, Della's friend had somehow managed to avoid any gunshot wounds and wasn't in the warehouse by the time the rest of the crew showed up shortly after the attack and subsequent robbery happened. They'd found her passed out in the back of the warehouse with a busted mouth and a bad gash on her forehead.

It all made Cory wonder …

The crew wasn't in—had the three of them not been there, would the end result still have been the same?

"She doesn't have family," Della said, her words coming out in monotone and her lips barely moving at all. "We are her family. Her dad died a month after we graduated high school. Her mom was never around. She doesn't have anyone. It's just us."

Well, Cory supposed that explained a lot about why Jennika and Della seemed so close.

"I'll try again in a bit," he said. "Maybe a few hundred dollars into the right hand will get us the information we want."

It was not by accident that whenever something bad happened out on the streets, and it involved the mafia, their people tended to gather. And because violence was almost always followed by a visit to an emergency room—or a surgeon on their payroll, if possible—Cory had spent more time in hospitals than he wanted to admit.

White, sterile walls. Floors that made shoes squeak. *The smell.*

All things that instantly brought a hundred memories rushing to the surface that he would much rather forget. He could still feel the backs of hard chairs biting into his shoulders, the sleeplessness that weighed down his eyes even though he wanted nothing more than to stay awake, and then horrible news that always came at the very end.

Nothing good happened in hospitals. Not like this.

"Do you want a drink of water or some—"

Della looked away from the large windows overlooking the emergency room's parking lot. He didn't like what he found staring back at him when she met his gaze. She wasn't mad—earlier, she'd even told him she understood he had just been doing his job. Now, though?

There was nothing in her eyes. Those dark brown orbs just looked *numb.*

Cory knew that feeling well, and it was hard to hide. All she gave him was a quick shake of her head before she looked back at the rest of the room and the people who had gathered.

So far.

About twenty, or so.

Della and J's parents.

The Capo—Georgie—that J had been working for. Some of the guys from the crew who showed up on time but only to find the warehouse was in flames.

J bloody on the cement floor.

Probably already dead, then.

Cory and Della were long gone.

Like the drugs inside the warehouse.

"How much?" Cory heard his uncle, Theo, ask Georgie.

"A lot, Theo."

"How much?"

"Three-quarters of a million."

It wasn't like Theo to make a trip like this—to come in when bad shit had gone down and do the rounds to put things together. Then again, his uncle was a lot like him and *hated* hospitals. He tended to do this kind of business *after* everything was said and done and people were back at home. For whatever reason, Theo was here now.

"Tommas will be coming around," Theo said. "You know when Outfit business becomes affected, he gets directly involved until it's cleared up."

As always, Cory knew.

The Capo nodded. "He might want to start with Frankie. I don't think this attack and boost on the warehouse was a plot on *me*, specifically. Heard he's been having issues with a certain gang because of … well, you know."

Georgie's words followed his stare straight to where Della stood next to Cory and the windows. She wasn't looking their way anymore—the tree outside the glass had taken her attention, but he was fine to let her do whatever she needed to get through this horrible fucking day.

Already, it was noon.

Cory knew what they were waiting for now.

The word.

Confirmation of death.

"Cory."

The sharp call of his name had Cory stepping away from Della without a word. He joined his uncle, he and Theo moving to the other side of the room where Frankie Costello currently sat on a corner chair staring at his clenched hands in his lap.

"What were you doing there?" the man asked.

Theo cleared his throat, passing Cory a questioning look. "Well?"

J's father didn't look up.

He was *mad*.

Hurting.

Stranded in a place that felt like limbo. *Knowing*—or pretty sure—that his son was dead but still holding on to some kind of hope that this could be the miracle. J could be the one miracle that God gave them.

The truth was cold, though. In the mafia, there were no miracles. Not for men like them.

"I'm not sure our presence at the warehouse made a difference to what happened today," Cory said. "Something like that—how they came in on the place and J, that was planned."

Theo made a noise. "Like they had info?"

"They would have needed it, I think."

Silence followed that revelation.

Everyone had to consider what it meant.

Theo fixed the button on his blazer through the loop and stepped away from Frankie in the chair with a quiet, "I'm sorry, old friend …"

Cory swallowed hard.

Frankie shook his head. "He's not dead—he's *not*."

"Frankie—"

"He's *not*, Theo."

His uncle nodded once but gave Cory a look that said something entirely different. "Expect your father and brother to come around. When, I can't say, but they will make their way to you. Tommas, too. He'll have questions. Before, this was just a blip on his radar. Other people could and were handling it. Now, he's going to be all over it. Behave, Cory."

"Yeah, I got it."

And he did.

What had started as a little issue had become a *huge* problem.

The Outfit would react accordingly.

Cory watched his uncle take a moment to speak with another man close to the emergency room's doors that led out to the parking lot. When he was done, Theo held one of the doors open to let a woman in that Cory recognized.

Abriella Rossi.

The boss's wife.

He couldn't hear what she said to his uncle, but when Theo pointed to the woman sitting on the row of chairs across from where Frankie sat and Cory stood, he understood well enough what Tommas's wife was there to do.

"Thank you," he saw her say.

In their world, friends tended to be other people within the life. Outsiders were harder to trust, and people who didn't have their entire world smothered by the mafia didn't understand what it was like to be these people.

He wasn't surprised that Della's mother was friends with the Outfit boss's wife.

Abriella already had her arms opened to hug Chloe Costello when she came into the woman's view. Cory felt like he was intruding on a moment that wasn't his business or concern when the two women sunk into a chair, faces wet with tears.

He could have sat down beside Frankie. Instead, he rejoined Della.

She still said nothing. Cory let her have the silence. Soon, he knew, that would change. It was the only thing the mafia did guarantee in this life. Change always came.

Cory wasn't wrong.

A doctor exited the double doors with the sign that said *HOSPITAL STAFF ONLY* with a nurse at his side who directed him to the waiting parents of a man Cory knew had been dead before he even left the warehouse.

The sounds J's mother made when the doctor apologized and confirmed the man's death? He would never stop hearing.

Chloe's screams and sobs echoed behind him when he chased Della out of the emergency room. She only needed to look at the doctor's face while he spoke with her parents to know the truth. She didn't actually wait to hear it like Cory had.

She kept walking.

Past the doors.

Over cobblestone.

Beyond the parking lot.

Cory kept walking too.

He didn't say a thing.

She walked until they couldn't be seen. Until she was sitting on the curb of a sidewalk on a road that wasn't very busy.

Cory sat down beside her. Della's hands met her face as all that strength and adrenaline finally gave way. The tension in her back let go; she hunched over her drawn-up knees when the first sob fell from her lips. He wrapped her in a hug, pulling her into his side where she could hide away from the rest of the world for as long as she needed. His chin rested on her shoulder that lifted and fell with her pain.

And finally, she cried.

Loud and aching and *broken*.

She cried—he let her.

"I'm sorry," he murmured. "I'm sorry, babe."

The sad truth?
He knew it didn't help.
Nothing would.

•••

Cory rounded the side of his bed to check on Della one more time before he headed downstairs to the main lobby of his apartment building. Then, he would need to handle yet another thing before he could finally put an end to this whole day—and now *night*, considering the late time. He barely remembered leaving the hospital, but he couldn't forget how heartbroken Della looked when he asked if she wanted to go to her place or even her parents'.

"He's there," she'd said.

Her brother, she meant.

Without asking her to explain, he already understood exactly what she meant. He bet at his place, tucked away under blankets and hidden in a mound of pillows, she was able to pretend for a little while that today hadn't happened at all. She wasn't faced with reminders of her brother on the walls in the form of pictures and forced to relive the trauma over and over again.

Reality would catch up.

It always did.

Cory would give her the night, though.

She could stay on his side of the bed if she wanted; he didn't mind. Earlier, he'd sat out in the hallway while she cried herself to sleep because he'd come to learn that Della really didn't like people seeing her emotions when she felt they were a weakness.

He didn't know how to tell her.

Grief wasn't a weakness.

That was *human*.

Nonetheless, he left her alone.

And hurt all the while.

Cory never felt worse than he did when he realized he cared for Della— of course, he already knew *that*—but couldn't help her. He wasn't accustomed to not being able to fix something when shit was all wrong.

This wouldn't be made right.

It couldn't.

Cory drifted his fingertips through the ends of Della's hair that splayed over the dark comforter. She didn't move when his fingers traveled over the curve of her naked shoulder. Her warmth gave him some sense of comfort because it was only then that he understood the part of him that was scared today.

Or rather, *why* he'd been scared.

For her.

Because he didn't want to lose her.

She was kind of a mess. A bit of a brat. And he liked it all. He just found her, and he was scared to death that he might lose her before he could even tell Della that he wanted to keep her.

"Sleep, babe," he murmured when Della shifted under the blankets. Her lax features peeked out from beneath the blankets; her eyes were still closed and those breaths of hers came out steady. "Don't let it all catch up yet."

Because once it did …

Nothing would be the same.

Though it was the last thing Cory wanted to do, he left Della behind in his apartment's master bedroom to sleep in peace while he locked the door behind him and took the elevator downstairs. When the doors opened, the first people he saw were his father and brother sitting in the leather couches that faced the receptionist desk of his building.

More surprising was the pup waiting.

Mace's ears perked and the bark left him before Cory's father or brother even noticed he'd finally come downstairs. Theo hadn't been wrong—they showed up just like he said they would. A little late in the evening, considering it was closing in on eleven at night, but he didn't care. Neither did Damian or Joe, likely.

Stepping out of the elevator, Cory kneeled down and slapped a hand to his knee. Mace broke away from Joe—who stood from the couch with their father—with his tongue hanging out and his stubby tail wagging so hard his entire rear end swayed with each flick.

It made Cory smile.

And *laugh.*

God, he needed that.

Soon, he had his pup in front of him wanting to be loved. That was the great thing about dogs. They could make anyone happy in *any* situation. It'd been far too long since he was even able to pet his damn dog, considering he wasn't home enough lately to care for him, so his family stepped up to help his sister, Mon, care for Mace.

"Hey, buddy," Cory said, running his hands all over the dog's fur. From his head to the bottoms of his feet. Mace lapped up every fucking second of it, too, his drool wetting Cory's arms but he didn't care at all. "Did you miss Dad, huh?"

That earned him more licks and excitement. By the time he stood, his father and brother had crossed the space to come and stand in front of him. Mace stayed sitting *on top* of Cory's boots, refusing to move even at the sight of his leather leash hanging from Joe's hand.

"Thought you might like to see him tonight," Joe said, shrugging.

Cory nodded, his hand drifting atop Mace's head. "Yeah, I might keep him with me for a few days. Shit is gonna be quiet, I think."

"Better be quiet," his father grumbled.

Then, Damian gave Cory a look from the side. The thing people didn't realize about the Rossi brothers' father? Damian seemed cold and unaffected from anyone on the outside of their life looking in. The boss's underboss, he couldn't afford to appear as anything other than someone who would and could kill for the slightest disrespect.

But as their father?

Damian was *everything*.

Like their ma, he was their world.

"Bit too close today," Damian said to Cory.

"Yeah, I know, Dad."

His father sighed. "I would have given you the night, but—"

"Wanted to see me alive, yeah?"

That made his father flinch.

"I chose this life, and so did you. It doesn't get easier, Cory."

Yeah, it never did.

"And," his father added, "I wanted to tell you Tommas is on it now. With what happened today, Frankie Costello's little problem just became an Outfit issue."

"Theo said the same."

"You can step back now, if you want," Damian said quietly. "I've talked to Tommas. It'll be more than just Frankie and his people going after Luis Ruiz, not to mention they've clearly got an issue with information about business being shared outside of pertinent people."

"That's a nice way of saying today was probably a setup."

Joe said nothing.

"Nonetheless," his father said, "you can step back from your job. They'll have someone else to handle what you've been doing. With Tommas putting people on this situation, it'll be over a lot quicker than anyone realizes."

Good.

That changed nothing for him.

Cory glanced down at his dog, barely considering his father's offer. "I'm not stepping back. Not while Della is still involved."

His father looked at him in a different way, then. "I heard through the grapevine you were possibly getting close to Costello's daughter. That something I need to talk to you about, or ...?"

Cory chuckled.

Joe grinned, too.

"Already done, Dad."

Damian made a thick sound under his breath. "Just ... *behave*."

"You all keep telling me that like I'm *not*."

"There was a time it didn't matter to you."

Cory nodded. "Guess I grew up, huh?"

His father gave him a ghost of a smile. "Guess so. I'm going to make some calls. You're welcome to bring Mace back to Monica whenever. She's been trying to convince me to let her steal him from you altogether."

"Never gonna happen."

"Tell her that." Then, Damian reached through the space between them, his palm clapping Cory on his left cheek. "*Be careful.* Hmm? Don't do to Lily what was done today to someone else's mother."

That hit a few nerves.

All Cory could do was nod.

It was only once their father had exited the building that Joe finally spoke.

"I've found nothing interesting on Luis yet—nothing that's going to help. I'm still looking."

Cory didn't doubt it. "What have you found?"

"A lot of business ties. The man keeps flipping his game, you know? Never stays on one thing for long. A year ago he was working with fake cash. This year he's been running whatever scheme works. You know what that means, though, right?"

"He's probably got connections."

"To almost every gang in the city. He's got a lot of friends. People act like they're not helping or doing shit for him, but they are behind the scenes."

"I wonder if that's what today was," Cory mused.

"What?"

"The drugs at the warehouse, Joe. You think the fact they were stolen was by accident just because they were there? Nah, man, not even close. That's *why* he hit the place today. Us being there was the accident, that's all."

Joe let out a hard breath. "You mean like—"

"Frankie's got a bigger problem than Luis's interest in Della. The guy's getting information from the inside. The Outfit has a dirty little rat somewhere. Someone better find who it is before they make shit a lot worse."

"How many people are attached to the warehouse?"

"Besides the people there today?"

"Yeah," Joe confirmed.

"You know those crews—could be five, could be ten. I don't have an exact number."

"I'll find it. Every fucking name. I will go through every one of them."

No doubt.

"But I missed something," Cory said, more to himself than his brother. "I knew I was missing something, Joe, and her brother's dead because of it. How am I supposed to tell her that?"

Joe cleared his throat. "Hey—"

Cory shook his head. "Don't, I'm fine. In my head, I think."

"Or your feelings."

"Well …"

"Women do that to us," Joe said when Cory couldn't find the words. "They make us messy as fuck."

"Is that what it is?"

Joe smiled faintly. "Yeah, that's what it is."

The two brothers stood there, silent. Cory felt every second tick by. Mace didn't move a muscle at his boots.

For a moment, Cory allowed himself to feel his own sadness about what happened that day, and the person who had been lost because of it. He'd been keeping it at bay; it was easier to focus and do what he needed. In that quiet span of time while he stood with his brother and his dog, he let his sadness roam free. It was rare that he could or even wanted to, but he figured … the soul lost in that warehouse was worth it.

"Could have been you," Joe said, shifting a bit on his feet so the two of them stood side by side instead of facing one another. "Dad's right—we chose this, but days like these don't get easier when it comes this close."

Cory watched Joe from the side. "It's never going to get easier. There's no way out of this life, Joe. Can't live it like we're always scared."

"Can't live it like we're bulletproof, either, Cory."

Fair enough.

"Call me when you have something that I might be able to use," Cory said.

Joe handed over Mace's leash. "Of course. Give your girl my condolences, would you? I'm sure we'll be around for the funeral whenever that happens."

"Nobody said she was mine."

"Nobody has to, bro. I just know."

FOURTEEN

"THE FIRST THING I saw when I opened my eyes this morning was your dog's *gigantic* head," Della said.

"Oh?" Cory asked.

Across the kitchen, he worked on setting a coffee pod into the machine. In nothing but sleep pants that hung low on his defined hips and ink that painted his skin, he looked entirely too tempting with messy morning hair that he ran his fingers through before pushing the button on the machine.

"Yeah," she said, looking down at the dog in question. "I thought I was dreaming for a second."

She was also currently petting said dog. On the Rottie's collar was a tag in the shape of a diamond that read his name, *Mace*, and a note that he was chipped alongside a tagged number. Likely his register number with the National Kennel Club to verify he was a purebred dog with a verified bloodline. She remembered Cory mentioned the pup in passing a couple of times, and she'd seen a picture or two.

None of those things had given Della any insight to how sweet and playful the Rottie was. The more one petted him, the happier and wigglier he became. She hadn't expected to wake up that morning with a dog looking at her considering—when she finally fell asleep the night before after crying her eyes out—there was no dog in Cory's apartment.

Nonetheless, the dog made her smile though she'd woken up ready to cry.

Wasn't that something?

"But," Cory said, glancing at her from the side with those blue eyes of his—icy or dark like storms depending on his mood—that always had her breath catching hard, "did he lick your face?"

"No."

"Or get close enough that his nose touched you?"

A grin started to form on Della's lips. "No, he didn't."

Cory's gaze dropped to the dog who was staring at his master expectantly with his black, furry bum wiggling against the floor. "Good boy—come get it."

With a sweep of his hand across the counter, Cory placed a plate of scrambled eggs covered in ketchup to the floor at the side of the island. Right beside the dog bowls with Mace's name spelled out in fire-engine red block lettering. The pup wasted no time going to his dish.

Cory shrugged at Della's light laugh. "Eggs are his weakness. Make him a plate of eggs and he'll be the best dog alive until you give it to him. I know, because I've recorded how he gets in the bed to wake me up in the morning just so my brother could laugh at me. He's barely over a year old, so he's like an unruly teenager on his best days. With an attitude to match."

Ah, Della got it.

"And that's why you love him so much—he's still a free spirit."

Cory nodded, pulling his steaming coffee away from the machine and moving down the island a bit to where he had sugar in a bowl and a spoon waiting. "He's my dude, yeah. Until I cave and give my mother her second grandchild. Joe swears he's one and done. Monica better not look at a guy until she's at least thirty. So, you know, Mace is basically like my kid until I have one of my own."

"Hmm."

His stare snapped over to her, a spoonful of sugar hovering over the steaming mug. "What?"

"You want kids?"

"A couple someday. Never saw life without it. Having a brother that—" Cory stopped talking, the amusement and happiness lighting up his handsome features dimming instantly. "Sorry, I wasn't thinking."

"Please keep saying what you were saying. It's easy, you know? And I'm just starting to realize how *easy* this is."

Cory swallowed hard. "What's easy?"

"Us. This. When we have five seconds together to just *be*. How you talk to me about anything and everything. The world disappears, and it's just you and me talking in a kitchen. So, please, keep talking for a minute. Because I don't want to rejoin reality right now."

"Okay."

She noticed he didn't disagree with her. Not about what she wanted or how she called this thing between them out.

Cory dropped the sugar into his cup, saying, "Growing up close in age with Joe made me kind of want to have a pair of rowdy boys that did the same."

Della smiled. "What if you had girls?"

"God save us all," he murmured, stirring his coffee, "because in that case ... I don't think the world is ready for two women that are half me."

She wasn't expecting that answer.

Della also kind of loved it.

"You say all the right things, Cory."

He laughed darkly. "I do what I can."

Just like that, the heaviness came back to her chest, and the kitchen grew quiet. Even Mace, who finished his eggs, drifted out of the kitchen to leave

Cory and Della alone. There was no way to distract herself from what she wasn't ready to face.

Della dragged in a shaky breath, the sound loud in the silence of the kitchen. "I'm still trying to process what happened yesterday."

"We don't have to talk about it. We can keep doing this—just talking about anything else. You don't have to go there yet, Della. Not if you don't want to."

His words made her pause. They could pretend, she knew, but it would still end. Her brother was dead. She would never go back to a time when she couldn't say those words. J would always be dead now.

"Or … could we just be quiet for a minute?" she asked. "I think I want to process."

Ten feet away, he gave her one of his grins. "Yeah, you can think. Silence it is."

He continued stirring his coffee, seemingly fine to not pay her a bit of mind even as her bare feet padded across the room to take her right where he stood. Turning around, she used her hands to pull her up to the edge of the counter where she sat.

Eventually, with the rhythmic *ting-ting* of his spoon the only noise other than their breathing, Della rested her cheek to the top of Cory's bare bicep.

She felt him look down at her, but he still didn't say a word. She understood why he was something she needed. Compared to her, he seemed like a pillar in destructive winds. *She* was the hurricane making the mess. Somehow, he felt like the steady, safe ground and she was desperate to find some traction.

Just like the day before when she couldn't bear to break down in an emergency room full of people watching her, so she walked and walked and walked until she was sure *nobody* who knew her face would see her cry. And who followed her the entire way? Who sat beside her and held her without saying a word and didn't mention it after?

Cory.

Everything in her life lately, from her business to her heart and even her pain, brought her back to this man. It was starting to feel like the universe was telling her something. It wasn't *at all* the best time, but the thing that had bloomed between them was becoming impossible to ignore all the same.

Maybe that made it hurt worse.

The rest, that was.

Because the *falling* part—falling for him?

That had been easy.

It was the *hows* of all this. *How* had Cory done this? How did her heart find a way to open up and let him in?

She had another question, too. One that only time would answer, but it had nothing to do with how she felt about Cory. Yet it had been the first thought that raced through her mind when she dared to open her eyes in bed that morning.

How would everything change?

After yesterday, her world stopped. It was turning again—of course, it kept going. The world didn't revolve around her. So, even though she'd lost the person who had been her best friend for as long as she'd been alive, life continued on.

Differently.

"Nothing is going to be the same," she whispered.

Not for them.

Or her family.

J was *gone.*

Cory stilled; his warm body turned to stone beside her before he leaned sideways a bit to press a kiss to the top of her head. His words skipped over her mussed, bed-wavy hair. "Yeah, I know. I'm sorry."

"My heart hurts."

"Time makes it a little easier to breathe, but it's too raw right now to see it. I'm sorry."

He stood straight, and she looked up to meet his gaze when she replied, "Yeah, me too."

Cory sipped on his coffee while Della retreated back inside her mind. It wasn't for long though because her mouth quickly found a reason to fill the silence.

"Checked my phone after I woke up. Missed calls from everybody. Ma was hospitalized and sedated. Dad's trying to handle everything—business and Ma and there's cops. A lot of our extended family lives outside of Illinois, but some are coming in today. Jennika sent me a bunch of voice messages; the first couple are a mess. I don't know. We're going to have a lot of attention on our family and business after this, aren't we? And … I just …"

Della trailed off and sucked in a shuddering breath that rattled. Cory set his cup to the counter and his arm snaked around her to hug tight to her side. It helped, but it was too late. The anxiety pummeled through her insides, making each and every breath shorter and shallower.

"We'll handle everything," he said, strong and sure and sounding like *nothing* that she felt at that moment. "One thing at a time—we *will.*"

She nodded.

He leaned in to nudge his nose along the hair that she'd tucked behind her ears. "Even when you feel like you're going to break, you still look like you're going to conquer the world. Just remember to breathe."

She did.

It helped.

One breath after another.

Finally, she said, "I need to go to my parents' place—my dad needs help, and there's stuff to handle."

"Okay. When?"

"Probably noon—his last message said he wouldn't be home until then. Ma, and all."

"Noon it is."

Della's stare flicked from Cory's mouth to his eyes that hadn't moved from hers. "It still *hurts.*"

"Sorry, babe."

She knew … he couldn't say anything else. What could he say?

"Can we go back to pretending like everything is okay? Like we were before so I don't spiral into a panic attack? Because it's going to hap—"

Cory's hand slipped behind Della's neck, pulling her toward him while his arm around her waist tightened. He kissed her silent as his fingers tangled into her hair and his hard, warm lines molded against her soft curves when he stepped in between her spread legs. His tongue struck out against the seam of her parting lips, taking a taste of the mint toothpaste she'd used from his bathroom earlier. Morning sunlight colored the modern kitchen in yellow tones while shivers raced over Della's skin.

Guilt raged through her while lust rammed right over it, thickening her blood and sharpening her breaths when he rolled his hips into her. His erection had her pushing forward for more while her fingers bit into his broad shoulders. She shouldn't be doing this with him right now when her family's entire world had come crashing down, but it felt *good.*

Right then, that's all she wanted.

Just to feel good.

"What did you say we were?" His tongue licked up the column of her throat before he rained hard, suckling kisses down her chest that she was sure left marks behind. "What was it, Della? That this is—"

"*Easy,*" she breathed. "This is easy."

"So let's do this. And then we'll go back to the rest of the world. Yeah?"

He always let her decide.

Even if it was selfish of her.

Selfless of him.

"Yeah," she breathed with a nod.

His hands twisted into the hem of the oversized T-shirt of his that she'd thrown on the night before when he asked, "And you like it."

"Too much."

Cory grinned and leaned in close; those hands of his dropped down to her bare thighs before flexing his fingers into her muscles to make her legs tighten around him more. The cotton panties she wore were nothing more than a thin barrier between her cunt, and the length of his erection under his sleep pants. "Me too, Della. I like *all* of this. That pussy. These curves. Your mess and your *smiles*. That sound you make when you're close. I love it all. *Lay back.*"

One of his hands raced up her stomach, fisting the T-shirt again as he shoved her back to the countertop. Her hair fell over the side of the island while his grip tightened on her shirt, making the fabric bite against her skin. She was content to lose herself in the way he shoved her panties aside, too impatient to bother with even pulling them off.

His fingers stroked her.

Awakened her.

Every tease of his fingers inside of her or toying with her clit had Della squirming harder on the counter until those noises of hers that he swore to love so much were crawling out of her throat. She came harder than ever when he shoved his pants down and used the head of his cock to stretch her open—but only just the tip—while his fingers circled her clit all the way through the orgasm.

"*Fuck yeah,* so tight," Cory groaned, his approval thick in his husky tone as he took his time sliding the rest of his cock in while Della caught her breath. His fingers splayed over her clenching stomach, pinning her in place when his deep, slow strokes started. Each snap of his hips came faster. *Then harder.* All at once, he slowed, Della couldn't help but roll her hips into him, getting more of what she wanted when he wasn't giving it to her. "*God*—this cunt's mine, babe. That's it, move that body and fuck me how you want. Show me how good that pussy looks swallowing my dick."

Her hand slipped between their bodies when he started pounding into her again. There was something sinful about feeling her wetness on his length—how *slick* it was and how hot he felt under the tips of her fingers. She used her wetness to rub circles into her clit, desperate to chase another orgasm.

Cory urged her on.

All his dark words taking her higher.

He licked the taste of her pussy from her fingers after she'd come again. Her, trembling and shaking. Him, just barely getting started.

After he'd fucked her crazy on the counter, he carried her to the bathroom. She sucked him clean in the shower, let him fuck her again, and pretended like everything else wasn't going to catch up with them.

Except it would.

Just not ... *right then.*

Della was okay with that.

•••

Della's tired stare drifted over her reflection in the pane of glass that overlooked the room just beyond her current position in the hallway. The air smelled of bleach and something else—something of *industrial* strength. Other than her eyes, one couldn't tell that just yesterday morning, her brother had been murdered and here she was standing in a hospital morgue the day after. Every hair was in place. Her booted heels and dress were set off with a black trench coat tied at the waist and a matching bag.

Appearances were everything, and Della knew that. So while she didn't put on makeup before leaving Cory's place that morning, she still had enough of a mind to get a friend to drive her over something appropriate to wear.

She didn't want to be here. Not standing in the sterile-smelling, gray hallway looking through a window at a room that sported metal cabinets, a tiled floor, and a drain right in the middle. The wall of cabinets at the far end was so clear in their square shape with small windows and white numbers on each.

The morgue wasn't a happy place to be.

Della shouldn't have been there in the first place, but in the mess of everything … someone had missed signing paperwork at the hospital. Her father was still with her mother while Frankie's men scrambled to handle business. Della was the next of kin available to come down and sign whatever was needed with the lawyer who'd been available.

Except Cory wasn't allowed beyond reception. Neither was the lawyer after they'd been signed in. She realized the paperwork said her brother's body had yet to be moved.

Della couldn't stop herself from asking, "Would I be allowed to see him?"

Had she really wanted to?

Could she handle that?

Alone?

And that's how she found herself down in the belly of the hospital, standing in front of the window while she waited to view her brother's body.

She imagined he'd been washed—*maybe.* If he hadn't been moved from the hospital yet, then the coroner for the district hadn't viewed him as he worked out of another facility. A note in the paperwork was clear that his body shouldn't be released to the family because the police still considered J's remains evidence they needed until the coroner signed off.

That bothered her a lot.

Once her mother was back at home, the first thing she'd want to do was begin work on giving her son a proper goodbye. So, now Della was going to have to go home to her parents and explain that, just to rub salt in the wound, who knew when they would have J's remains to bury?

This day wasn't getting easier. Della was hyperaware of her loneliness. Of the *sadness*. The ache wouldn't leave her chest.

A little over twenty-four hours ago, she'd been standing in that office with her brother because he did the same thing for her that he always did. He was the best big brother she could have ever wanted—her heart was missing a *huge* piece. Just like the hole that was now going to be in her life because J was no longer there to fill it.

The movement on the right side of the room had Della's attention switching there in an instant. Her thoughts silenced all at once when the large blue doors were opened for the two morgue workers who were currently pushing a rolling metal table that was long enough to be a bed. The human-shaped form under a tucked-in white sheet had her heart thundering. Even her breaths came in and out a little sharper.

They came to a stop in front of the windows.

Now or never, she thought.

A part of her had maybe still been trying to pretend like J wasn't gone. Like yesterday was a dream and at some point, she would wake up, and the nightmare would be over.

The men glanced her way on the other side of the window. This was never going to be over. They waited for her. It took her ten seconds to nod. When they pulled the sheet back to let her view Joel's ashen body from his neck up, Della was grateful for only one thing.

His face wasn't bloody. Nothing else was good or right, though.

She just wanted to be in *there*—with him. Arms tight around him, she'd beg God to let her brother's heart beat again. Even if it was only for one more minute.

So, then she could say thank you and tell him she loved him. Promise to be a better sister.

All of it.

And more.

Instead, she pulled her sunglasses back down so even the men beyond the window wouldn't see her cry. Because goddammit, heartbroken or not, Costellos wouldn't ever be seen as weak, and even in his death, J would expect and respect nothing less from Della.

She didn't know anything else, either.

•••

The elevator doors opened to the reception area of the hospital's morgue as Jennika's final voice message from the night before played on Della's phone. The shortest of the ten or so that her friend sent, it was also the easiest to understand. The others had the wind in the background, or her friend slurred too much.

She'd messaged her back, and tried to call since the morning with no answer and no reply. As she made her way back to where Cory was waiting for her, a reply finally did come in from her friend. It only said *I'm not okay—sorry.*

Della kind of figured that out on her own when she heard Jennika's mess of messages. The last one had simply been her friend mumbling, "I loved him, Della, *fuck.* Okay?" Followed by crackling static in the speaker before it cut off entirely.

"Is that Jennika?"

Della glanced up from her phone to realize a couple of things. She still hadn't exited the elevator, Cory was waiting just three feet away from her where he leaned against the wall, and the lawyer was now gone. No doubt, she or her father would be seeing the man again soon. The damn cops were all over *everything.* Like fucking fleas.

Della waved her phone as she stepped out of the elevator. Pushing her sunglasses up to the top of her head, she wasn't worried about Cory seeing her bloodshot eyes, or the dampness left behind from her most recent tears. He wouldn't say a thing.

In fact, he didn't say anything about her crying when he wiped the dampness away with the pads of his thumbs when she came close enough for him to reach out and do it.

This man …

He was something else.

Tipping her head up to meet his stare, she said, "Yeah. I don't know how she got out of the hospital last night, but she's not taking what happened well at all. I think she and J were … a thing, or something and she's spiraling a bit. Not the first time she's done something like this, really, but it's a bad time for it."

Cory chewed on his cheek like he was considering his next words. "Huh."

"I'm worried about her. She doesn't have anybody. She won't pick up a call."

"Listen, sometimes a mess is just a mess. And you have to let people live in their mess when they want to."

"That's fine as long as someone has good coping mechanisms for their mess. She doesn't."

Cory frowned. "You're worried."

"A little."

He nodded. "I'll get Joe to put a bead on her. He's already working on something related to the warehouse anyway. Somebody had info about that place, and they gave that info to Luis. We need to know who it is."

"He's claimed it, then?"

Cory chuckled dryly. "Made a few calls while you were down there. And yeah, word on the street this morning is Luis's crew claimed the hit on the warehouse, but it's already radio silence on where he or his people are. They're playing a dangerous game now, and they know it."

Rage filled her. It must have radiated in her tension or even showed in her eyes because Cory nodded when he muttered, "Yeah, I feel that."

"Did anything else come from your calls?"

"Your mother is home—asking for you. Frankie also mentioned business needs to be figured out over the next little while considering everything."

The lump in her throat came back. Even when her father was handling his wife having a mental breakdown and the death of his son, he still put mob business front row and center for his attention. It was only that moment when Della finally learned to appreciate what it meant to be these people living this life. They sacrificed in ways others couldn't imagine.

"Okay," she said.

Cory stroked her cheeks with his thumbs. "Get some color into you. You're going to need it."

"For what?"

"The lawyer let me know there were a couple of news trucks pulling up when he stepped out for a smoke before he finished his business at the desk and headed out. I checked—there's more. Someone must have let the media know someone from the Costello family was at the morgue."

Della's teeth clenched. "I didn't check the news this morning."

"You don't want to. The Outfit is all over it."

Great.

"And so is your family's name and connections," Cory muttered lower. "Listen, just give them all that *I'll-stomp-your-fucking-ass-out* look that you like so much, I'll get you to the car, and we're gone. We'll be at your parents' place in no time, and I'll call Joe on the way to deal with your crazy ass friend."

A part of her adored him for having an answer to everything. She pushed down the ache in her chest at the idea of reporters throwing questions at her at a time like this. "You like that look of mine, too."

Cory grinned. "There she is. Are you good? Did you find what you needed down there?"

She understood what he meant.

Della sniffled and dropped her sunglasses down over her eyes. "I just needed to say goodbye. Let's go."

FIFTEEN

"DELLA, I'M NOT sure anything will make me smile right now, sweetheart. I'm just … sad. I want my son."

"Well, give him a chance, okay?" Della asked her mother in the sitting room of the Costello family home. "And it *is* okay to smile, Ma. You know that's what J loved you to do the most. You were always, *always* smiling at us."

From his position, hidden in the entry hallway to the Costello home, with Mace waiting patiently at his boots, Cory cleared his throat and tried to ignore the conversation happening just a few feet away through an unfortunately thin wall. He'd always thought, and still did, that moments of grief in families should be private. He was here because of circumstance and not the fact he had actually spent any time behind the walls of this home.

He was an intruder to a private moment between Della and her mother, even if both women knew he was in the hallway. It didn't really matter.

He wouldn't want someone—who was essentially a stranger, if he was being real—to overhear his own mother's pain while she grieved over the loss of her son. At the moment, it couldn't be helped.

Frankie had greeted his daughter and Cory for just long enough to say hello before he stepped away to make a call. Probably *many* calls. That was the nature of things like murders, an eventual funeral, and the mafia, in general.

The first thing Della did when she arrived?

Went to her mom.

She introduced Cory, and while he wasn't offended that the woman didn't seem interested in visitors, the irony of it all wasn't lost on him. The first time he ever properly met the parents of a woman he had an interest in had to be this moment.

Just his fucking luck.

Right?

Yeah.

Cory put his attention back on Mace as the conversation continued in the sitting room. Della had the bright idea, after an awkward stretch of silence, that maybe Mace would make her mom smile. He was *absolutely* willing to try that.

Anything to make the situation better.

"Dell—"

"Ma, I *promise.*" Just as fast, Della called out, "Come here, Mace."

Cory's pup sat a little straighter, and his head tipped up. Those big eyes of Mace's locked on his master, and when Cory nodded, the dog didn't hesitate to dart forward into view of the sitting room's entry. Della called for Mace again, sending him flying all too happily into the room where hands were waiting to pet him until he acted drunk and foolish.

He was quick to follow behind the dog, and didn't even need to see Chloe Costello's face to know how happy the dog made her.

"*Look at him*—so pretty. Such a pretty, pretty boy."

Cory came to lean in the entryway, grinning at the sight of Mace acting like a total fool on the chaise where Chloe rested with pillows, a blanket, and her daughter. The more someone petted Mace, the more he wanted.

Greedy dog.

People seemed to love it, though.

"Hey, *mind,*" Cory said, keeping his tone sharp but not moving an inch.

Instantly, Mace relaxed on the chaise. Stretching his muscular body out across Della's legs and her mother's to be loved some more.

Chloe smiled.

A *real* one.

Seemed her daughter had been right.

"He's still practically a puppy," the woman said.

Cory chuckled. "Barely over a year old."

"I love dogs."

Della gave Cory a look. "J was allergic."

It took Cory a second.

The thought fleeting in his mind.

"That makes sense," he said out loud.

Both women looked his way.

He shrugged, feeling silly when he said, "Always said he liked Mace—never touched him, though. Some people don't …I mean, *look at him*, you know? Hadn't realized it was something else."

Chloe stared at Cory, quiet and contemplative. Another time, it might have set him on edge but right then, he was content to let this woman do whatever she wanted considering her current state and all.

"You two used to play together as boys. I haven't seen you in years, Cory. I wondered if you two were still friends."

"We ran in similar circles, Mrs. Costello."

Della gave a small smile.

Chloe sighed and went back to petting Mace. "Well … thank you for bringing him in to see me. He did make me smile, after all."

That was all that mattered.

•••

Cory stepped back from the front door of the Costello home to let a familiar man inside. Closing the door behind the Outfit boss, he offered a hand to take the black tweed coat Tommas wore when the man was ready to remove it.

"Cory," his father's cousin greeted.

"Boss," he replied.

"Working today?"

Cory smirked.

Only a little.

"Working until I'm told otherwise," Cory said.

Tommas nodded. "Isn't that what we're all doing?"

And that statement alone brought Cory back to the reality of why the Outfit's boss was currently standing in the front foyer of the Costello family home. Not that business was ever particularly far from his mind, but when grief mixed with business … sometimes it was hard to tell the difference between which was which when they overlapped more often than they didn't.

"Frankie is in his office," Cory said.

"And his daughter?"

He took the coat Tommas finally shrugged off. "With her mother in the sitting room."

"Have her join the discussion, please."

"Tom—"

Tommas's gaze cut to Cory, and his brow raised. He often found familiarity in the man's face because of the blood relation between Tommas and his father. As a young boy, the friendship between his parents and the other high-ranking members of the Outfit blurred lines for the boys of the family who later joined the business.

After all, this man currently standing in front of Cory had also once taken him trick-or-treating, let him have sleepovers with his own son, and even taught him how to slice an apple safely with a pocketknife. Tommas was also now one of the only men in his life who could give the word for Cory to kill someone or be killed himself.

It was a bit of a complex.

Or the making of one.

"This can't wait a day?" Cory asked. "Her mother just got out of the hospital. Her brother died. Frankie's not stopped with the phone since we got here earlier, and—"

"And business comes first, Cory. In the Outfit, it must. It also seems like I have a lot to catch up on with my Capo and his different business ventures, so I would rather just get it out of the way and continue with removing the current issue *my* organization faces because of his affiliations. Or his daughter's, for that matter. Are you about finished?"

He could ask Tommas the same.

Could.

He didn't.

Cory was a smartass.

Not stupid.

"If you are finished," Tommas said when Cory hung up his coat on a waiting hook, "take me in to see Chloe. My wife had to meet up with her sister this morning, and I don't want Chloe to think she isn't coming to spend the afternoon with her like she promised to do. Despite what you might think about my business for being here, the Costellos are old friends. They also need their friends right now, Cory."

Right.

"Yeah, sure, boss."

Mace was still soaking up every second of the love and attention that he could get from Della and her mother when Cory and Tommas came to stand in the entryway. It took the ladies a minute to notice they were no longer alone.

He wasn't sure if he expected anger from Chloe to see the Outfit's boss standing there, but a sad smile colored the woman's expression.

"Tommas," she said softly.

Beside him, Tommas loosened his stance a bit. "Ella's a little late. She's coming, though."

"Good."

"With that tea you like, too."

Chloe managed a laugh. "As long as somebody finds me some whiskey to chase it with."

"Ma, I'm not sure you should be drinking," Della said carefully.

"It's due," Tommas put in before anyone else could say anything else. "I'm sorry, Chloe. J was a good one—you made sure of that."

Just as fast as she'd been staring up from the chaise, Chloe's head dipped low, and her hand came up to wipe away the trail of wetness slipping down her cheek. "I tried. Frankie's upstairs, Tommas."

"Yeah, I know."

Turning on the heels of his leather loafers, Tommas gave Cory a nod when he said, "Have your woman join us upstairs, please."

The silence from the room couldn't be missed. Neither were the words Tommas chose to use in that moment. *Your woman.* A detail Cory had only really ever thought about, next to the conversation or two he had with his brother.

Had Joe talked to their dad, who then went to Tommas?

Or was this shit just written on Cory's face?

Tommas smiled a bit, lifting two fingers to point between the side of his head and Cory's, answering the unspoken question rattling in his mind. "I make time to learn everything about everyone—people often forget how far a boss's hand extends when it counts. Have her join us."

The boss headed down the hall.

Cory looked to Della.

Calm and unbothered, she stared back.

Inside, he bet she was screaming.

Oh, well.

Time for business.

"Leave Mace with your ma," Cory said. "Work calls."

•••

Cory remained by the doorway of the office. The conversation inside the space between a Capo and the Outfit's boss passed along the information dealing with the attack on the warehouse and what Frankie was currently planning to do for his own business. It really wasn't a conversation that Cory had any place stepping in considering it wasn't where he worked with the Outfit, and he was really only there with the Costello's for one reason.

She was sitting beside Tommas.

Opposite to her father.

Della glanced over her shoulder at him. Cory gave her a wink. That had her turning back around fast. On another day, he might have laughed.

Not on this one.

"The very nature of this business—"

"Tommas, my family has been in the loansharking business since before you became the boss of this organization. And when it was you and yours tearing the streets apart to rebuild the mess that those who came before you had created, *my* family stayed firmly behind your line. We had your back. Don't tell me about the nature of this business when I know it all too well."

"Then, what do you plan to do?" Tommas asked.

Frankie sighed and leaned back in his chair. "J and I were in the process of merging it all."

"And now?"

"It'll take a little longer."

Cory felt like he missed something.

Apparently, so did Della.

"Merging what?" she asked.

Frankie's gaze cut to his daughter.

Tommas didn't look away from his Capo.

"Every person handling loans from the Costellos," her father said. "The plan was to move every moving part under the same umbrella of control. *Yours.* Meaning—"

"I deal with everything. Everyone," Della said quietly.

"It was the only option that made sense when J sat down and explained everything to me about how you had been handling things."

"But it's a big operation," Tommas added. "How much a year?"

"Thirty million," Frankie said. "She only handled a small part, Tommas. You're talking moving her from one aspect of the business to heading the entire thing. *Alone*, now, however, because the original intention was for J to also—"

"J is dead, and so you will do what you have to. You will because she can, and she will learn. You cannot be everywhere at once, Frankie. You were already trying to do that, and it got messy. J was picking up the slack where he needed to while you worked out how you wanted to hand off the rest to your daughter, but now we're down to the wire. I'm no longer giving you the option. Start to merge it under her, sit back, relax, and collect our money. It's time."

"Wait," Della said, moving to the edge of her seat and staring at her father. "Why didn't you explain this to me before? Or tell me that's what you wanted to—"

"Because I wasn't ready."

Frankie's answer came out flat, but *honest.*

Della sat back into her chair with a sigh. "Well."

"And what is *your* plan?" Tommas asked.

He only looked to Della for an answer.

Cory still felt like a fly on the wall.

"*My* plan?"

"I said you, didn't I?" Tommas frowned openly. "One of your partners is dead—where's your other? You work with another girl ... a friend, yes?"

"Jennika, yeah. She's, uh ... what about it?"

Cory didn't miss how Della was careful not to expose the fact her friend was currently MIA while she was having a sit-down with the Outfit boss. Nothing was ever easy. Friendships made shit like business particularly hard sometimes.

"Bit of a brat, isn't she?" Tommas asked, still looking at Della but his question was meant for the man sitting across the desk. "Mouthy, quick with a response ... toes the line a bit. That's what it is, Cory, isn't it?"

All at once, Tommas turned around in his chair to stare at Cory from across the room. The other pairs of eyes quickly followed.

"What?" Cory asked.

"She's ... well, she's a lot like you, isn't she? Or how you *were* not long ago. Grew up a bit, I think."

Cory cleared his throat. "I mean—"

"Back to business." Just as fast, Tommas swung back around and put his attention on Della whose eyes were about as wide as saucers. "She *is* a bit of a brat, Frankie."

Della gaped. "I am *not*."

"A little," Frankie muttered. "You can't look to her for answers on the operation as a whole when like I said, she only handled her part. Getting her up to date on all the rest is going to take a bit of time."

Tommas hummed, nodding as he gave Della a shrug. "You won't have long to catch up—money can't stop moving on these streets, not unless you want someone else to pick up where you have started to slack. Do you understand me, Della Costello?"

"I—"

"*Get back to work.* Be on the streets. No one is going to run up on you when the attention on all of us is this hot. There's no good end to that. First and foremost, we keep business moving in times like these because it flexes our control. Your father has people—people who will take orders, who know how shit is done, and who will do it for you where you cannot. *Use them.* There is only one appropriate answer here. Your money is mine, girl, and I will not wait for it."

Well.

Tommas really wasn't playing around now.

Della dragged in a heavy breath. "Yes, I understand."

"Good." Nodding across the way to Frankie, Tommas added, "And Damian ... has asked after Cory. I said I would bring it up while I was here."

Della's father glanced his way. "What about him?"

"You're aware there's something ... going on in private, yes?"

"Could have asked *me* that," Cory spoke up.

Especially since Tommas didn't have to say it straight up for his point to be clear. He was asking Frankie if he knew something was going on between Cory and Della beyond his job here. As if *he* hadn't taken the information to the man in the first place quite a while ago.

"I know how to act, Tommas," he muttered.

"But do you?" the boss returned. "Frankie?"

"Cory is fine," Frankie said, every word measured. "I would let you know first, otherwise."

"He'll remain in his position, then?"

"Until told otherwise, Tommas," Frankie agreed.

Tommas nodded. "Good. Let's finish up business. For the sake of it." That was that.

Knowing he was really no longer needed with the conversation in the office—and if he was, it wasn't like he would be going far without Della—

Cory headed downstairs to check on Mace. He wasn't at all surprised to find the dog was still happy and pleased in Chloe's lap while the woman's hand stroked the pup from head to tail.

"How long is he staying?" she asked when she noticed Cory in the entryway.

"Unfortunately, not much longer. I'm working—he needs to go back to his dog-sitter until everything is a little more stable day to day. I hate making him jump around from place to place. It confuses him and then I can't really blame him when he acts out about it, you know?"

Chloe smiled. "*Cory* Rossi."

He arched a brow. "What about it?"

"Growing up, young man, you gave your parents and the rest of us plenty of things to talk about, didn't you?"

Some of it, he would never live down.

That was Cory, though.

He owned it.

"I'm happy to see you've finally grown up," Chloe said, her gaze drifting back down to his pup. "Also, thank you."

That had Cory confused.

"For what?" he asked.

Chloe lifted her shoulder under the blanket draped over them. "For looking after her like you've been doing ... and for looking *at her* the way you do."

Cory stilled.

Della's mother exhaled shakily. "Bring him back to visit again? He made this awful day a little better."

He nodded. "Soon. Absolutely, Mrs. Costello."

"Call me Chloe. You always did when you were a boy, anyway. Just because the Outfit grew you up into this man in front of me doesn't mean the rest of us forgot how you were before everything changed, Cory."

He'd remember that.

SIXTEEN

THE BEAUTIFUL, three-level home in the gated suburb seemed as quiet and welcoming as the rest of the properties on the block. Towering trees gave the large Rossi home a sense of privacy from the neighbors.

Della had never been to the home before—only passed it once before with her mother, who pointed out the names of the people who lived there now and *before*. Chloe's generation always seemed to talk about the Outfit in that way.

The Outfit *before*.

The Outfit *now*.

Della didn't really understand either.

On another day, she might have asked Cory if she could come inside with him as he dropped his dog off. Mace would stay with Monica, Cory's younger sister, until they were back at a point where he was going to be staying the night in the same house for longer than a couple of days at a time. She didn't blame him.

That day, she just had a lot on her mind.

She needed a second to herself to process it all. Cory didn't seem to mind that she opted to stay in the car while he passed the pup off to his sister. She was so lost in her thoughts, in fact, that she didn't even realize he had come out of the house again and crossed the entire circular driveway to come and stand beside the vehicle on the passenger side where she sat inside. She rolled down the window when he gestured for her to do so.

Della sighed. "You ready?"

Cory gave her a look. "Yes and no."

"What's that mean?"

His grin had her own growing.

Not that she knew why.

He just made her smile.

"You're not in your head about some of the shit Tommas was saying earlier, are you?" he asked.

Well …

"A little, maybe," she said.

"You'll handle the business, Della. You've *been* handling it."

"Not all of it. Just—"

"It'll be a lot less footwork, more *conversation*," Cory interjected. "It's to your benefit, all things considered."

"I know that."

"Then, what's the problem?"

God.

Pink heated her cheeks.

Cory didn't miss it, if his laugh was any indication.

"If a *mob boss* calls you a brat, does that say something?"

"I'm sure you've met Tommas's wife in passing."

"And?" Della asked.

Cory tipped his chin down, and said in a chuckle, "The man has an appreciation for difficult women. Just because he used a specific term for you doesn't mean anything one way or another. You're young—it's more appropriate to him, likely. And yes, you can be a brat. It's something you'll grow out of in this business quickly once shit starts to really pick up with what your father has planned for you and the Outfit. You'll learn how to communicate your assertiveness in a better way. We all do."

Yeah.

She knew.

It was just a lot to process.

It might be easier if J was there—because none of this was what Della thought would happen.

"As for the other bit ..." Cory glanced back at the house as he trailed off before his attention came right back to her. That grin of his softened into something she wasn't expecting. "My ma asked, so I can't *not* ask you. She knows you might not be in the mood, or whatever, but—"

"Hey, stop rambling."

Cory quieted all at once and swallowed nervously.

"Just say it," she told him.

"So, clearly people have been talking about us because people can't just let adults be adults and all."

"*Cory.*"

He laughed. "My ma knows you're out here—she's cooking supper and wants you to join us, but she knows you might not be up for it. She's willing to give you a pass tonight considering the circumstances. She is, *however*, over the moon because when she asked if I liked you, I said yes."

Della smiled. "How ... *simple.*"

"Right?"

He grinned, too.

"It's sweet," she whispered.

"We don't have to go in. You don't have to do this tonight. Okay?"

"Are we really doing this whole *thing* together now?"

"I guess," Cory said. "It sure seems like we are, yeah."

Della let out a weighted exhale—her sadness rattled in the sound. The heaviness didn't leave her shoulders, though, and she couldn't quite shake her nerves. "After tonight, everything has to go back to some kind of normal, right? Work. Luis. *Business*. Without my brother."

"Nothing stops and waits, no."

"Then if I don't get a choice in that, I'd really like to choose something about tonight. I would love to meet your family, Cory."

That grin came back. "Yeah?"

"They won't make things sad, right?"

"Not our style."

Della nodded. "Then, yeah, let's do it."

"My dad's on his way home. Apparently, my brother, his wife, and their baby are coming as well. My sister has a shoe fetish—she'll want to know everything about the boots on your feet—so be warned."

He pulled the car door open while she laughed. Already, they were off to a good start. Nothing he told her proved to be a lie, either.

His mother met her with a hug and smile. She let Lily Rossi play twenty questions, slyly prying in a way only a mom could, while she helped to finish supper. His father never said a word about business though she knew he had to know everything going on around them considering his place in the Outfit. She got to hold the baby; babies and puppies could make anyone smile. His little sister managed to make sure *someone* was going to buy her the same boots Della owned as a gift for her upcoming birthday.

For a little while, she wasn't sad. The Rossi house came to life.

Reality always waited to catch up.

•••

Reality came with a heavy hand.

Calls with lawyers.

Avoiding police.

Money that needed to be handled; people who needed direction. Her mother who needed her even though Chloe didn't want to say it. Her father who couldn't afford for their family to fuck up again. One day bled into two, and then three and four quickly followed.

"Joe's bead on some shit came through," Cory said quietly.

Della glanced up from the papers that were currently spread over her workspace. A desk that she hadn't used all that often in her place. Mostly because, often, she found herself working directly on the streets to get shit done. Handing out loans, or collecting when a particular debtor didn't pay.

Now, she was reorganizing so that *others* did that for her while she kept track of everything else involved in her father's books. And it was a lot.

A lot more than she realized.

"And?" Della asked.

"The drugs that were boosted are gone. For sure."

"That fast," she noted to herself.

"Like that was the purpose, hmm?"

Exactly.

"He's still working on some other info there," Cory said. "Because right now, we can't find Luis or his crew. At all. It's like they're ghosts, and that's not how it works in Chicago when the Outfit goes looking for somebody. This is looking like it was planned for a lot longer than we think."

"Yeah, it does."

Which bothered her more.

"And Jennika popped up this morning. At one of her regular haunts not far from her place. She was out of it like you said she would be when we finally found her."

Della swallowed the lump that formed in her throat at the news. She wasn't surprised. After days of no contact with her best friend, she had basically deduced that Jennika went into another one of her spirals and literally nothing would bring the girl from it except a hard and cold rock bottom.

That didn't make it easier.

It *really* sucked that it had to be now that her friend decided to say *fuck this* to life and have a breakdown, all things considered. She could really use Jennika where work was concerned, and just as a fucking friend. Where was her best friend with a bottle of wine and a blunt to let her drown all her sadness and cry on her shoulder?

Della was trying a new thing, though.

Not being selfish.

Her friend was going through shit, too. That much was clear. So, instead of feeling the brief bitterness at the news of Jennika showing up again, she tried to find the silver lining instead.

"At least, she's safe," Della said. "I'll text her later."

"Joe sent over a friend. He'll clean her up over the next couple days. See how it goes from there. Maybe she'll be ready to get back to work, or whatever."

Della pulled the papers into a pile and closed the file on top of them. "She doesn't have a choice. I'm no longer in a position to work around her. I need her to start working for me, or I need to put someone else in her place. Right?"

She glanced up from the desk.

Cory stared across the office, calm as always. "As long as you make the business keep working, then you're doing it right."

He kept telling her things like that. She tried to remember it even when at every new turn, she felt like a baby deer on new legs trying to navigate unknown terrain. *Nobody learns how to do your father's kind of work overnight, Della,* he had told her more than once, *but you're luckier to know more than most, so don't forget it.*

"He's not going to try something, is he?" she asked.

"Luis?"

"Or people for him. I don't know." Della let out a sigh. "Ma's … handling what she can. We're just waiting for the release of J's body. What if that's why he's so quiet, Cory, and it's not that he disappeared at all? What if he's just waiting for the calm to pass, so he can come in like a storm all over again?"

The window overlooking the backyard of her townhouse caught her eye. The colored leaves that were just beginning to fall from the trees mirrored her current state.

Things were changing.

She had to roll with it.

Time would bring *good* things.

It was just hard right now.

She didn't miss how Cory hadn't answered her question. He was still staring at her from across the room when she looked his way again.

"Well—what if he's just waiting for the moment when I'm weak?" she asked.

"Della."

"What?"

"Babe … you were never weak."

He said it so frankly.

Like it just *was.*

Della felt that in her fucking chest.

"That's how people like Luis work—the only way they can manipulate you is to tell you lies about yourself and make you believe them. It's how they do what they do to anybody they think they can use. They make it seem like they built you up so of course, they know the things to do or say to tear you down in the fastest way possible. Who gives a fuck where he is, Della, or what he might do? *We'll handle it.* He's toxic; he only knows how to make others be the same. Don't let him in your head when he's not paying rent to be there."

Della didn't reply.

She didn't really need to.

Cory gave it a moment before he asked, "You've had four meetings today, and took more phone calls than I am years old. Can I take you away from all this and make you forget all of this shit even exists now?"

Her next breath ached in her chest.

She would never tell him no.

Not for that.

"Yeah, take me away, Cory."

•••

In the chaos that had become Della's life in the days following her brother's murder, the one reprieve she found was *always* Cory. He wasn't the next man to sit across from her desk, ready to try to flex his masculinity all over her new position under her father's name. He wasn't someone who needed her support, or to cry on her shoulder when she'd just finished drying her own tears. He didn't take or ask for anything.

The man only gave.

It was not lost on Della how Cory had gone from being something that gave her anxiety first thing in the morning ... to being the one person who calmed her simply by looking her way.

He was just there, still doing his job. That job, though? It'd definitely changed. Or maybe *evolved.* Della wasn't sorry for that at all.

Cory was her soft place to fall. Where she didn't have to feel sad or guilty or *not good enough.* When the day finally came to an end, and he pulled her beneath him, everything went away and nothing mattered. The world silenced. Her heart stopped hurting. Breathing came easier.

He provided her the escape. She took it.

"*Oh, my God,*" she breathed, smoke coming out heavy past her lips as her next orgasm clawed closer and closer to the surface. She could feel every single one of Cory's fingers digging into the cheeks of her ass while his mouth did the best kinds of things to her pussy. On her knees with her face turned sideways into the pillow, so she could smoke what remained of his earlier blunt, there was no better way to get her pussy ate. "Jesus Christ, *Cory.*"

Somewhere, her phone rang. She just ... *didn't move.*

Couldn't might have been a better way to describe it. That orgasm finally arrived, shattering through her body with pins and needles as Cory pulled away from her pussy with one of his dark, satisfying laughs. That tongue of his lapped higher—all over-sensitive tissues and the cheek of her ass. Hot and wet and leaving the taste of her behind.

Had he heard her phone ring?

Maybe she'd imagined it.

He pulled the little roach from her fingers, tossing it to the bedstand before those expansive hands of his were back on her body. He pulled and squeezed and *teased* in all the right spots. Sometimes with his palms and fingers or with just his fingertips like when he grazed the spot behind her ears that he seemed to like so much whenever he fucked her from behind.

"*Cory,*" she breathed into the pillow.

"Hmm?"

His husky reply came the second before he fit in behind her and filled her pussy with one flex of his hips. The words that had been on the tip of Della's tongue were swallowed with her answering moan. There was something about the way he stretched her out when she was so tight from a fresh orgasm and still shaking.

It hit *every* nerve.

Didn't let her body calm.

She'd vibrate until she came.

"Shaking like a leaf already," Cory said behind her.

He liked that so much.

Fucked her harder for it, too.

He did just that. High from the smoke, still blissed from his tempting mouth and tongue, Della sunk further into the sheets. Sweat had strands of her hair sticking to her skin. His heavy breath, tasting of their sex, panted into her ear when he urged her to come again. She was all too happy to back her ass into his hand when two of his fingers found her ass and pushed deep while he pounded into her even harder.

"*Come*," he groaned.

She did.

Too high.

Too hot.

Too *everything*.

But it was still perfect.

The second she fell over that cliff into a sharp pleasure that ached around the edges, Cory shifted. He pulled her back to the edge of the bed, his feet hitting the floor with two quick smacks. His hands pushed her hips hard into the bed, and he fucked her with deep, fast strokes while what remained of her orgasm milked him to a finish.

He painted her back with warm cum. Only then did she remember her phone. Cory checked it for her because she didn't want to move. Especially not when he promised to fuck her ass next if she stayed just like that.

God.

She was going to let him do that.

Absolutely.

Then, he checked her phone.

"Body's been released," he said, glancing up from the screen. "That was your father. The lawyer let him know."

Della used her arms to make a pillow. "Time to plan a funeral."

"It'll be over soon."

But would it?

SEVENTEEN

HORENSTEIN & SONS - Funeral and Cremation.

The *only* funeral home the Outfit ever cared to do business with when dealing with death for more than one reason. The family-owned operation not only took care of the families' needs within the mob when someone met an unfortunate end, but they were also on call when, for whatever reason, someone higher up who could pay the fee needed to make a body disappear.

Many times, someone didn't want a body to just ... go away. Dead bodies usually came with messages, and the Outfit certainly liked to send those. Occasionally, however, a body needed to simply vanish and never be spoken of again.

Horenstein & Sons helped with that. Or their crematorium did.

The last time Cory visited the funeral home wasn't to plan someone's funeral. He accompanied his Uncle Theo and handled the ten-k—stacked in small bills—that Martin Horenstein demanded whenever they had a mess to clean.

Since today's business had nothing to do with getting rid of a body that would cause them trouble, and everything to do with Della planning her brother's funeral with her parents ... well, Cory thought it was probably better if he stayed outside. They could handle their family business in private, and he didn't need to pretend like only two months ago he spent an entire night sitting in the Horenstein crematorium watching a body burn.

A win-win, he thought.

As it was, his time was better spent outside where he could keep an eye on the streets. The wet smog lifting in the city was something he could do without, but it also couldn't be helped this time of year when the cold mornings met the warmer afternoons. The constant whipping of the wind had Cory leaving his leather jacket at home, so he could wear something with a bit more thickness.

Besides, he highly doubted *anyone* would be causing a problem for the Costello family while they went through the motions of preparing their son for burial. There was a certain level of disrespect for that sort of thing, and even those with the worst of intentions tended to show some courtesy for a family in mourning. Especially for a mother.

Except the streets had been *very* quiet. That usually only meant one thing.

Speaking of mothers, though ...

Cory pulled the last drag from his cigarette and tossed it to the ground as he pressed the home button on his phone to bring it to life. There, his mother's last text waited for a reply. Exhaling the gray smoke to the sign overhead that spelled out the funeral home's name in gold lettering on a black background, he replied to his ma's question about the date for J's funeral. *If they've decided yet—don't rush them or ask for me, Cory. I just want to put it on the calendar,* she'd messaged.

Another day, and he might have chuckled. His mother, forever making sure she wasn't an inconvenience to anyone else. Always supportive when she could be.

Looking like next Wednesday—eleven.

No wake, then, came her next reply.

"*No wake,*" he typed back. "*Call you later.*"

Her *I love you* response popped up soon after in a green chat bubble, and Cory shut down the screen before shoving the phone back into the pocket of his coat.

"Are you just … *always* around now?"

The random question had Cory lifting his head to find where it came from. Ten feet away, in leather knee-high boots and a jacket she cinched tight at the waist, Jennika watched Cory. Where had she even come from?

"Decided to come around, did you?" he asked.

She lifted one shoulder. Her appearance wasn't missed. Still, he showed no concern that the woman's pupils were pin-small, her hair was piled messy and high on the top of her head, and whatever remained of her makeup from the day—or night?—before was still smudged in one too many places. Calling her a mess might be too nice, but Cory opted not to say anything about it at all.

Better to let an issue fix itself, if it could.

His bead on Jennika came through when she went MIA. What else was he supposed to do? He did what he told Della he would—made sure the chick was okay, had someone get her home, and that was that. Anything after wasn't his concern, and as far as he knew, Della needed to decide what she was going to do to handle her wayward friend.

The rest wasn't up to him.

His hands were tied.

Jennika's stare cut to him, and then the waiting doors behind him. "Well, she mentioned this morning when she texted where they were going to be. Figured, why not come around and see if anybody needs something, right? Like they did for me."

Her sarcasm made sure that comment didn't quite fly over Cory's head. He knew for a fact Della had been concerned about her friend *and* tried to help as much as she could. Hence why *he* put a bead on her through his brother.

Nonetheless, if Jennika was in a mood, he wouldn't entertain it. Cory wasn't that kind of fool when it came to women, and he didn't care much for this particular one in the first place.

"I'll just ... *go in,*" Jennika said, passing Cory without as much as a look over her shoulder.

He really wasn't fucking offended.

She was a pretty thing.

But *damaged.*

A minute after she headed inside the place, someone else came out.

"God grant me the strength," came a grunt to Cory's left.

He found Della's father stepping out from the white doors leading inside the funeral home. It welcomed people into a modernly—but *comforting—* decorated reception area. To the right were the offices. Off to the left, people had to walk through another set of doors—this time, black—to enter the chapel where a majority of the wakes took place when families didn't want them at the church or at home. To the rear of the business was where people were directed for planning, to view samples, or for other needs.

For most of the morning, Frankie stayed with his wife and daughter. Cory wasn't exactly surprised to see the man outside, though. Everybody needed a break occasionally when it came to this sort of thing.

"Smoke?" Cory asked.

Della's father looked like he could use something. Since Cory didn't have any liquor—or a better kind of smoke—on him at the moment, he figured a cigarette would be just as good. Frankie must have agreed considering he took a smoke from the pack Cory offered and then his silver Zippo to light it with.

"*Grazie,*" Frankie muttered, pulling hard from the cigarette. "Casket is next—should be the last thing before we can call it a day."

"Long process," Cory noted.

"Hard on the heart, mostly."

Yeah, he bet.

Although Frankie did well to hide it, Cory knew this entire thing had to be particularly hard on the man. Not only had he lost the son he raised, but the subsequent breakdown his wife suffered certainly didn't help when piled on top of the fact the Outfit's boss was now demanding the man restructure his entire business to make things streamlined and easier for everyone involved. It was a lot to handle all at once.

Cory's main job was Della. He also didn't mind helping elsewhere. When he could, of course.

"You need something?" he asked the Capo.

Frankie shook his head at first. "Nah, I think I'm okay, kid."

Cory chuffed, but he wasn't offended. "You sure? Starbucks right down the road. All that pumpkin spice shit Della goes stupid over was on the menu. I could grab something until we have lunch."

"They would like that, wouldn't they?"

"And you know, there's nothing like black coffee to remember what's really important."

Frankie let out a laugh. "You make a good point. You don't mind?"

"Things are quiet. It's not going to hurt if I run down the block for ten minutes."

Depending on what the drive-thru looked like now.

Frankie glanced over his shoulder; the cigarette burning between his fingertips now had a lump of long, red coal at the tip and was a quarter of the way gone. He didn't waste any time, and already, the guy looked like he wanted to get back to his wife. Just beyond the glass, Cory found the woman in question sitting in one chair of many lined up against the wall with a pack of what appeared to be bookmarks in her lap.

"Never understood the point of those damn death memorials—I don't want to remember this," Frankie said under his breath. "Worst days of my fucking life."

Cory didn't think the man meant for him to reply, and so he didn't. He kept his attention on the window of the door, and the people he could see behind it from his position. Back near the hallway leading to the back, Della stood with her friend.

He couldn't see Jennika.

Or the conversation, really.

Just his girl's black dress.

Black until we bury him, she told him that morning when she picked out the outfit. *Nothing else will do.*

"Yeah," Frankie said with a wave of his hand, gaining Cory's attention again. "Go grab something for us all. I gotta get back in there."

Cory nodded, already turning to head for his waiting Mustang. "Will do."

•••

Ten minutes had been a conservative estimate. It took Cory nearly twenty minutes to get through the café's drive-thru when it was nearing noon, and Chicago was a fucking city, after all. Apparently, the Starbucks was a particular favorite of nearly everyone who worked within a three-block radius of the joint.

God.

Cory was starting to miss his regular stomping grounds. He didn't wait for shit when he walked into a place that recognized his face. Still, he put on a smile for the girl at the drive-thru window while he paid for the coffee, lattes, and bag of sweets. He didn't bother to make small talk when the chick tried, though.

Better things on my mind.

Or rather, a better woman.

Cory was just pulling out of the drive-thru and taking a sip from his coffee when a call rang through the Bluetooth speaker in his ear.

"Call from Joe," the robotic female voice said in his ear.

Cory set the coffee down and hit the button as he waited to pull out onto the street. Cars kept going, one after another, with no break in sight for him to possibly slip his Mustang in between. He didn't take chances with his car—but especially not when his newest pearl black paint job was less than a year old.

"Yeah, what's up, bro?" Cory asked.

"Frankie's got a *real* fucking problem, that's what."

It took Cory a second to reply. If only because he wanted to be sure he heard his brother right, and he understood what it might mean. Just to be sure, he asked, "The bead on the connections came through?"

"Took a second. Too fucking long."

Cory sighed. "Yeah, but do we know who was feeding Luis and his crew the info on the warehouse and Costello's business? Or what?"

Because that's what mattered.

It's what everybody in the Outfit had been waiting for.

"Yeah, I just got confirmation," Joe said. "Called you first—I'll make the call to Dad after, so he can let the boss know, and whoever else."

"Joe—spit it out. How close was the issue?"

"Really close, man," Joe said. "She's been there the whole time. Shit, I could have taken care of her days ago when my guy first found her after she popped back up. But no worries because now that we know who was feeding Luis info, it'll be handled before the sun sets."

Wait, *what?*

Cory's mind went quiet.

Joe, on the other hand, did not. "I think this Luis shit went deeper than we realized. The guy had a woman he was fucking on every corner, Cory. Every one of them had a connection to someone or *something* bigger than him. None of them were really connected to each other. I don't think Della and Jennika were different ... except for the fact that they knew each other. And as for Tommas wanting to get his hands on the drugs stolen from the warehouse—or Luis—well, that's probably not going to happen. Every lead came back the same. That shit is long gone, and so is your old friend. Neither him, nor those drugs, are in the states right now."

He still couldn't get his car out onto the road. More cars were coming.

Time ticked by.

Cory's heart *raged.*

His panic swelled.

"You mean, *Jennika* was the connection to Luis?" he asked quietly.

Joe cleared his throat, and a paper shuffled on the other end. "Yeah, it took some digging, but I found the connection. His name on a place she rented just outside of the city. I had like fifteen people to go through. Why would I look at her first?"

Right.

Because none of them did.

None of them looked at Jennika first.

Pretty things always told lies.

Never fucking failed.

"I gotta go," Cory said.

"What, why—"

Because that bitch was with Della.

At that very moment.

With her.

Cory wasn't—he was in his car a whole block away. Not with her. Not doing his job. Why did it feel like it might already be too late?

His brother didn't finish his sentence before Cory hung up the phone. He also didn't wait for an opening on the road before he just pulled the hell out. Horns blazed. Someone nearly clipped the side of his Mustang.

The engine roared louder.

Even that wasn't a comfort.

Nothing would be.

Not until this was over.

EIGHTEEN

JENNIKA'S EVER-PRESENT sense of entitlement hadn't been something that really bothered Della before. Then, her friend had to stomp her way into a funeral home and demand to speak with her about *that fucking text you sent me this morning*.

There was no respect in it.

No decorum.

Della's mother grieved across the room, and Jennika didn't give a shit. Chloe was the same woman who had let Jennika sleep in their home every single night that she couldn't get into her own. Her mom had fed her friend when she needed it; anything Chloe could do to help Jennika, she did it without question.

Jennika didn't seem to remember those things which should have been the first clue to Della that something was seriously wrong.

She ignored it.

"Why would you do this today of all days?" Della demanded, tempering her tone but still shooting a look at her mother who was now speaking to Mr. Horenstein. While the undertaker had her mother's attention handled for a second, she put hers back on *Jennika*. "You really thought right now was the best time for us to have this chat?"

Haggard would be a good description for her friend in that moment. She preferred to call it as it was—Jennika looked a damn mess.

"I'm not ignoring you," Jennika said. "I just—listen, that message you sent me this morning made me realize we needed to talk."

Della rolled her eyes, and stepped closer to the black double doors. Outside, her father chatted with Cory. Downstairs, beyond the rows of caskets they still had to pick from for J, was a room where they were currently keeping her brother's *body*. Her mother was still trying to decide which picture of her son she wanted to put on keepsake bookmarks that would tell guests at the funeral of J's life.

And here Jennika was.

Pissed off because of a *text*.

It couldn't be more stupid.

That was her friend, though. Before, it used to be something Della liked about Jennika. Something in the girl that reminded her of herself. That *selfishness*. She once thought selfishness wasn't really all that different than ambition. Except it was because one was a confidence that was earned, and

152

the other came with pettiness that looked well on no one. Especially not on a woman like her.

What had been a thing that they bonded over had now become something Della *hated* in her friend. Something she hoped didn't reflect in her own actions and behavior. She didn't want to be that woman now.

"You know the world doesn't revolve around you, right?" Della asked sharply.

Maybe a little too loudly considering her mother *and* the undertaker looked Della and Jennika's way. All she needed to see was that line of wetness in Chloe's eyes. Her stomach twisted into guilty knots because … *Jesus.*

"Everything okay?" the undertaker asked, his soft voice belying his rather *large* size. He towered high at over six and a half feet tall, at least. His shoulders were as wide as the doorways. The last thing she wanted was a problem with a man who also dealt with death on a regular basis. In more ways than one, according to her father.

And her mom didn't need this shit.

At all.

"Yeah," Della said, plastering a smile on her face. Not that it stopped her mother's gaze from traveling between the two girls. Chloe wasn't buying her bullshit, and she didn't look pleased. Why would she? She was trying to plan her son's *funeral*. *Fine.* They would just take it elsewhere. "We're going to head downstairs and look at the caskets. You wanted black, right, Ma?"

"Why not?" Jennika asked, clicking her tongue and giving Della a smile. "Let's find something black to shove in the ground, *Dell.*"

Jennika used the nickname Luis gave Della—that she hated so very much—*far* too easily. Her hand twitched to slap Jennika. She'd deserve it. Clearly, her friend was having a moment, and it was something that needed to be dealt with, but she only wanted to make it clear to Jennika that she wasn't welcome here right now.

Della controlled herself for the whole slapping bit, but just barely.

For now.

"Della," Chloe called as she and Jennika turned for the hallway, "why not outside instead?"

She didn't answer her mother.

What did it matter?

"This isn't the right time," she told Jennika.

"You texted me to say that if I couldn't even call you back, to call someone else when I need work," Jennika said, each word coming out slow and measured. Like she had read that text message Della sent that morning after yet another day of no response or even a smoke signal from her friend.

J just died; *Jennika* almost died. Luis was MIA. The Outfit was out a lot of money because of the warehouse, and people were probably going to look at her father to replace the cost of what was lost. A whole new world of business was dropped into Della's lap, and she was expected to learn it before she even understood what it meant to be in her hands.

But where had her friend been?

Getting drunk.

Probably popping something.

"I sent you that message this morning because I can't keep cleaning up after you. Especially not right now. I needed you to understand. I can't do it anymore," Della said when they entered the stairwell at the end of the hallway leading to a lower floor. "I told you what I was doing today because I hoped you would get the point—I can't worry about you right now when I have to deal with everything else. You're a big girl, I'm not going to chase you for weeks while you go on one of your benders. I have shit to do, Jenn, *God.* Did you see my ma upstairs? She didn't need this today."

She could feel the difference in temperature from upstairs to down below. While the walls were finished, she had no doubt if someone peeled back the paint and plaster, one would find nothing but the cement of a basement.

The air even had that dampness.

"I, I, I, I," Jennika said, her almost *happy*, sing-song tone making Della grow cold as they passed the double doors beyond the stairs leading into the room where caskets sat on display in five rows. "It's always about you, right?"

A familiar *clack* had Della spinning around. She knew what made the sound before her gaze even landed on the Glock in Jennika's hand. Terror swelled in her heart, but she did her very best not to show it in that second. She'd been stupid enough to let her emotions get the best of her, and she made a mistake because of it. Without even thinking.

Jennika lifted the gun a little, jerking the barrel to the right. "That one's black."

Della didn't look behind herself; she made that mistake once today and let Jennika get behind her when her back was unprotected and weak. Here they were.

"Silver handles?" she asked. "Ma wanted silver."

The girl who had been there the night Della had her first period—the same girl who had been the first person she called when she lost her virginity—made a face like something stunk, and a disgusted noise followed. "Really, *silver* for J? Gold would be better. Or even a pine box. What does it matter, he's just going to *rot.*"

Della dragged in a quick breath and ignored the way it caught and tripped going through her throat into her lungs. Was she scared? That goddamn gun was still pointed at her. So, yeah. A little. She didn't plan on showing it.

She glanced past Jennika to the hallway and the stairwell at the far end. If she shouted loud enough—screamed for all she was worth—then at least she could warn the people upstairs about the danger down below.

The quiet tittering from Jennika had her swallowing the scream when she told Della, "Is that really what you want—for your scream to be the last sound your mother ever hears you make? While she's here planning the funeral of her son, Della? *Really?*"

"You don't care."

That much was clear.

Jennika smirked. "No, but *you* do. And I'm not done talking, so give me the chance to do that before I ruin your mother's life for a second time, hmm?"

What?

She didn't get the chance to ask the question.

Jennika was already talking *again.* "He didn't love me—I didn't know it until that day in the warehouse, though. I should have because why was *I* special, right?"

"J said once that he didn't fuck with you at all. Why would you think he loved you?"

Blazing eyes turned on her.

Then, Jennika laughed.

The sound?

Crazy.

Manic, even.

"Not J," Jennika said, keeping the gun pointed at Della as she closed the double doors behind her to shut out the hallway and stairwell. Then, she put her attention back to Della as she tossed aside her small purse. Neither of them looked to see where it landed. "Your brother wouldn't get down with me like that—even though I tried."

So, J hadn't lied.

"See, he was just … always trying to look out for me, and sometimes he gave away too much. Thought we were friends, maybe. Like us, you know?"

"Not like us," Della murmured.

Jennika cocked a brow at that. "Well, *yeah.* And I meant Luis. *He* didn't love me, but I didn't know until it was too late. Good dick makes us stupid. God, he was fucking everything and anything with a hole just because it benefitted him not even because he wanted to. But I was the only one he said he loved; he only stayed the night with me. I was giving him things they weren't. I helped his hustle. I was better. That bitch, Dell."

She swallowed hard.

God.

Things were starting to make sense now.

It was terrifying.

How had she missed this?

Jennika's eyes, smudged with whatever dark makeup she'd worn the night before, darted back to Della when she said, "Have you figured it out yet?"

"You were fucking Luis when he was with me?"

It was really the only thing that hurt. Not the *actual* cheating, of course—it'd been what ended their relationship along with Luis's constant manipulation. And she never let him touch her without wearing a rubber. Still, with her *best friend?* That was a new low.

"Oh, don't get sentimental about it. We were fucking *long* before you met him. A year or so. You were just getting ... *boring*. Still being your daddy's good girl. Not yet pushing your lines. We got you there, though, right? And then we had an idea. For you. And us."

Della blinked. "Us?"

"Me and Luis. Keep up."

That gun waved wildly.

She kept her eyes on the prize.

"Luis just needed to flip his game—get money and go. Start over new. He gave me something to do, I guess."

"But he lied," Della said quietly.

She didn't need Jennika to say it.

It's *who* Luis was.

It's what he did.

Jennika's jaw tensed, and the anger came back in her steely expression as she leveled it on Della. "*You* were just a pawn—something he could hustle. I didn't see what it mattered, or why I should care. I had him, right? I came up with the idea of boosting something from one of the warehouses the Outfit owns. See, I like to listen when the guys are around. You learn a lot. Luis said if we could nab something good, he had the contacts to sell it. We'd bounce before shit even really hit the fan."

"*The warehouse.*"

Everything became so painfully clear. Only the barrel of the gun answered her back. It met the middle of Della's forehead harder than she expected. Jennika went from looking *mildly* crazy to full out fucking insane in a matter of two seconds. Della didn't even have time to catch her breath before her friend was screaming in her fucking face.

"I wasn't even supposed to be inside the damn warehouse! And he still hit it—he knew I was in there, and he *still fucking hit the place!*"

Jennika stumbled back, one shaking hand pointing the gun at Della while her other pulled at the mess of her hair. "You all could have been a bonus," she spat, the gun jerking with her words. "A mess we wouldn't have even needed to fucking worry about. But he didn't care—he didn't even answer me back when I said I was inside and to wait a minute. He just … lit it all up."

"Hurts to know someone you love doesn't give a shit about you, huh?" Della asked.

Wrong thing to say.

Jennika came at her again. Della's forehead gave the gun's barrel a soft spot to land. This time, she wasn't quite as afraid as she had been moments earlier. She really wished that she didn't recognize the pain and desperation in Jennika, but she did.

She knew that all too well.

And how much it hurt.

Thing was … Jennika didn't pull the trigger.

Della counted the seconds.

She had all the time in the world.

Do it.

Just fucking do it.

She was mad—*hurt and bitter.* It was devastating to realize someone who meant everything to you thought you were nothing. Maybe she blamed Della. Fuck. It was possible her friend was just *sick.* In her mind. Because all her life, people left her; she never had anyone except herself, and that could really do a number on someone's sense of self-worth

She didn't pull the trigger, though.

"*Just do it!*" Della shouted, vibrating from head to toe.

The gun bit harder into her forehead.

The trigger didn't click.

Neither girl looked away.

"Because you *can't,*" Della said.

Jennika's arm trembled, and her teeth clenched as a sound escaped that ached. "You don't fucking know anything. You just—"

"Because what are you going to do after this? Do you think you're making it out of here?" Della was the one laughing then, the sound bouncing from wall to wall in the room and back again. She was sure that she looked just as fucking crazy as Jennika in that moment, but she couldn't find it in herself to care, either. "After you killed me, what were you going to do then? Did you even think about that? You never did plan for the follow through very well, Jenn."

She could see the girl's finger twitch on the trigger. Della wouldn't give her the chance to pull it.

"You never planned beyond this," Della said, her hands coming up fast between them to grab the butt of the gun and Jennika's wrist at the same time. She bent both the gun and Jennika's wrist back while the other woman was distracted by her emotions. Those were always a person's weakest spot. Her finger wrapped around Jennika's on the trigger, and she fought to pull it back as she shoved the barrel up hard. It found the middle of Jennika's jaw when the two slammed into the doors. "We're all you fucking had—he's gone, we wouldn't take you back once we knew the truth. *Where were you gonna go?* You've got no one and you knew it. You're *nobody*."

They were all Jennika had. It was worth repeating. She didn't plan to make it out of here alive.

Except all the thoughts shattered in Della's mind when she finally pulled the trigger back on the gun. The bang was explosive. In sound, and action. Her ears rang as all at once, Jennika's body slumped between her and the door. Blood sprayed from the exit wound and dribbled from the spot where it had entered under her chin.

A lot of blood, really.

Della watched the pooling crimson grow as she stepped away from the door. The gun, and Jennika fell to the floor.

In the background, Della could hear shouting.

Familiar voices.

The after spray of the gunshot must have hit her in the face because she tasted blood when she licked her lips. Unmoving, unseeing eyes stared upward from the bleeding heap of what used to be her friend on the floor.

Della was still trying to digest it all.

Process everything.

By the time her father, the undertaker, *and* Cory got the double doors open, Della had found a spot on the floor a few feet away from her friend's body. She stayed just out of reach of the puddling blood while she lit a cigarette from the purse Jennika had tossed aside when they first entered the room.

"Holy fuck," Cory mumbled, stumbling over the body toward her. "*Della!*"

"I'm fine, Daddy," she said.

Too quietly, maybe. They all watched her as though she had been spun from glass and ready to shatter into a million little pieces.

Hell.

She kind of felt like that.

Smoke circled up from her fingers, drawing her attention there. She looked to the undertaker who was currently surveying the mess and the body. She was sure this wasn't how he planned to spend his workday. Then again, if she was to trust what her dad told her about the man's business, maybe this was exactly how he planned to spend his day.

"Sorry," she said to the large, silent man, "I just really needed a smoke."

Cory coughed out a laugh, and his gaze darted between her and the undertaker as he kneeled. "Babe, nobody's worried about the cigarette right now."

Right.

"Everybody's a fucking liar, Cory," she whispered. Everybody told lies; some were meant to protect her or even, help her in some way; others were nothing more than beautiful distractions so the snakes could curl in closer around her heart. Those pretty lies had been the ones that hurt the worst. They did the most damage. "Even my best friend."

He reached for her, then.

She just let him.

"Not me," he told her.

Not him.

Not him. Not him. Not him.

He'd not proven her otherwise. She *still* reminded herself of that fact. A part of her wished she didn't feel like she had to keep doing that at all. Hadn't he proved his worth to her time and time again in a far shorter period than the people who betrayed her?

Oh, well.

Cory deserved it—*he* was worth going against what had now seemed to become Della's instincts when it came to other people. She only wanted to protect herself; build walls as high as the sky. Except with him. He climbed over every single one of them just because he could.

"I left my bag upstairs," Della said to her father when he came to sit beside her.

Cory sat on the other side, silent.

"With your knife?" her father asked.

"Yeah."

"Should really consider a full-time guard at this point. It's non-negotiable. Your mother is probably upstairs; at least she listened to me this damn time to stay... *Lord.*"

Cory held up a finger. "Agreed. On the guard bit, for the record."

"Frankie, where am I sending the bill?"

Della glanced up, surprised at the question. The undertaker, who had taken a black satin blanket from a nearby casket to throw over the body on the floor, stared the three of them down. They were all still trying to figure out how this happened.

The undertaker didn't seem to have that problem.

"Well?" the man asked.

"Just put it on my account," Frankie said, pushing up from the floor, "and that'll be the end of it. Now, where the fuck is my wife?"

Della got up, and followed her dad. Cory was right on her heels. She stepped over the body, but she didn't look down at the heap of bloodstained satin. It would be gone soon, like the bloodstains on the floor and wall, and the memory of Jennika in the Costellos' lives.

She didn't mind leaving her feelings about it all behind, too. They could burn those with the body.

Della no longer cared.

NINETEEN

"WHERE ARE YOU right now?"

Two things that never waited—not for anything? Duty and family.

It was just Cory's luck that the two things intermingled more often than they didn't. That was the nature of his life when it was so engrained in the mafia. There really wasn't any way to escape it, so while it annoyed him, he dealt with it. After all, he did choose this.

"Did you hear me?" his father asked again.

"Home," Cory said. "I'm home."

Specifically, *his* own home. Because of all the places Della wanted to go to clean up and spend the night before—all over again—life kept moving forward after theirs almost ended, here was where she chose. How in the hell was he supposed to tell her no after everything?

He was *tired*.

Nearly fucking lost her today.

The one time he didn't do his job—his *only fucking job to have her back*—and look what happened. He wasn't going to forgive himself for that mistake even if it was nothing more than circumstance and someone else's crazy plans that hadn't even worked out in the end. None of it mattered. He fucked up; she almost paid for it.

Cory would have been satisfied with a room at a hotel that he'd used in the past and enjoyed. The place had bomb rooms, good service, and they knew his name. Which was all he really gave a fuck about at the end of the day. When people knew his name, he didn't even have to *try*. Everybody else jumped to do shit for him. He could use that right now. Della, too.

But no.

Here they were at his place.

"I'm coming to pick up Mace tomorrow," Cory said. "Let Mon know so she can get his stuff together."

"Cory—"

"He's going to start thinking his home is somewhere else. Maybe I'll just pay an enforcer to babysit him in the day instead. You know what I mean?"

He was rambling.

Talking about *anything*.

All things except today.

"Cory, it all ended well," his father said quietly. "Joe filled me in on all the details. Tommas also called the funeral home—he'll pick up *all* bills for Frankie."

161

"Costello isn't worried about the money."

They all had more than they knew what to do with, honestly.

"It's more the respect of the matter," Damian said gruffly. "You know how this business goes. Cory, are you pacing again?"

His walk in the front hallway of his apartment came to an abrupt stop. *No*, he wanted to say. It partly would have been a lie, but it also would have been the truth. He wasn't actually pacing—something he did when he was trying to process shit or figure something out—he was just cleaning.

Picking shit up in his place. Thinking of who he knew in the Outfit that would be the right pick to tail Della on a daily basis when he could no longer do it because he had shit to get back to. Cory couldn't watch her back forever even though the two of them didn't talk about it. He was also ignoring the fact that the shower down the hall still hadn't turned on. Despite the fact that it was the first thing Della said she wanted to do an hour ago when they got back was clean up.

"I'm not pacing," he said.

Damian chuckled; the sound came off familiar to Cory in both good and bad ways. There was something about the Rossi boys' father that Cory and his brother could never get away from. Their dad just always knew when something was up with one of them. He paid too much attention to things that others overlooked, and he liked to point them out.

"But you are overthinking," Damian eventually replied.

Cory stared into the dimness of his apartment. The water still wasn't running for the shower. He missed seeing water and food in Mace's bowl or hearing the Rottie's nails click on the floor when he came looking for his master.

He was over sneaky people.

And fuckups.

All of it.

"It ended well," his father repeated with a tone that was sure and smooth. Cory swallowed hard, knowing his father wouldn't expect a response because that's not what Damian was trying to do when he knew his boys as well as he did. "And that's where you have to land, Cory. Not on what ifs or what-could-have-beens … just what is."

Right.

"As far as we know, this is over," Damian continued. "Any drugs from the warehouse are gone—certainly off American soil because we can't find them. The same with your old friend. Good riddance to trash; if he knows what's best for him, that fuck will stay gone, too. It is time to get back to normal, Cory. Or whatever version of normal you're looking at now, son. Hmm?"

He thought about that.

Everything his father said.

"A lot's changed," he said.

"Has it?"

Cory sighed. "Yeah."

How could it not?

Della changed *everything*. His new normal would now include her because he didn't even consider anything else. Wasn't that entirely different?

Off to the side, an item he'd hung on the wall caught his attention. The scuffed, worn leather with all its buckles and pins and patches it had gathered over the years made a weight settle on Cory's shoulders. His father was right where Luis was concerned. It would be best if the guy stayed gone. If the Chicago Outfit caught wind of him anywhere, he'd be a dead man. He already was, really.

But the past was a bitch. And the two of them had never been done.

Everybody else wanted all of this to be finished—it should be. For it all to be over. He knew the truth, though.

"It's not over until it's over," he told his father. "There's still unfinished business. We should be ready for that when it happens."

"It never ends."

Well …

It was their life.

They wanted it.

"Are you good?" his father asked.

Cory headed for the direction of the bathroom. "Yeah, Dad, I'm good."

●●●

The bathroom door wasn't even closed. Della sat in the bucket chair beside the clawfoot tub, a cigarette dangling from her fingertips while she stared at the black tiles on the wall. In the doorway, Cory watched her.

He wasn't the only one who liked silence when his mind decided it was time to overthink something to death and back.

With one leg drawn up so her foot could rest on the edge, Della had set her chin atop her arm lying across her bent knee. Her other leg hung over the edge of the chair, bare toes grazing the floor. Those bloody clothes of hers had made a pile in the middle of the bathroom. She had used his white cotton robe to cover her naked body but hadn't bothered to tie it at the middle.

Flicking the ash from her cigarette to the small to-go cup of coffee that she'd picked up from the place down the street, Della's shoulders lifted and fell with a heavy exhale. Cory didn't doubt she had a lot of things on her mind considering the current weight of his own.

"That is not an ashtray," Cory noted.

Della's attention finally drifted away from the wall. "You don't smoke enough for me to use something more appropriate."

"Neither do you."

"That's fair."

That pack of emergency cigarettes was nearly half gone, now, though. Not just because of Della, but for him, too. Cigarettes became far more appealing when something stressful was involved. That was just a fact.

"It's on my face, isn't it?" Della asked. "I didn't want to look."

Cory leaned against the doorjamb, his bicep acting as the cushion to keep him mostly comfortable. "The blood?"

"Yeah."

"A bit of spatter."

Across her forehead—dotting her eyelids. She must have wiped at a spot near the corner of her mouth because a line of blood had smeared upward at the very edge like a morbid smirk. Nothing too bad. He'd seen much worse. Hell, *he* had walked out of situations looking far worse than she did. That didn't mean this was any better for her. Taking a life was still taking a life. It was harder when that life once belonged to someone who meant something to the person who pulled the trigger.

"I'm so fucking *stupid*," she whispered.

The floor took her attention away from him.

Cory hated that.

"But are you? Are all of us?"

Della glanced back up. "What?"

"You're talking about Jennika, right? You missed her—didn't see her until it was too late. Yeah, but so did the rest of us. None of us were looking at her because why would we? She hadn't given us a reason to. Was she unstable? A little. Fuck, so am *I*. That's not always a reason to distrust someone, babe. We all missed her. Not just you."

She dragged in a rattling breath.

Cory felt it all over.

His words were the truth. No doubt, she knew it too and wouldn't deny it. At the very same time, it didn't make things much better. The reality was still right there staring both of them square in the fucking face.

Mistakes had been made.

They paid for them.

Did they come out on top? *Maybe.* Look at all they sacrificed for it.

"Not just her," Della muttered, giving him a smile that didn't feel entirely true. "I missed a lot more than just her. It was everything she was doing, too. Everything she had done. I thought ... well, what's it fucking matter what I thought about her, right? Bitch is ashes, now."

"It matters because it does—your heart wants an answer. Your brain might have to accept you're never going to get one that satisfies you. That's where you decide whether or not it's worth it to keep giving it energy and attention."

Her smile was real, then.

And beautiful.

"You really do say all the right things when it counts, Cory," Della murmured.

"Do I?"

"Even when it hurts."

Right.

It was a learned gift.

Cory decided to say some more things that were both right and true. Things he'd been waiting to say because life and business and everything else just seemed to keep getting in the goddamn way at every turn. He'd thought it might be selfish to focus on his feelings and what happened between him and Della while the rest of the world burned around them. It seemed so little in the grand scheme of things how he'd managed to fall entirely in love with this woman across from him.

Except it wasn't little at all.

It happened *so easily.* A part of him thought *like it was always meant to be, man.* And shit, maybe it was. Because he couldn't imagine beginning or ending his days anymore without this girl on his fucking mind.

Wasn't that crazy?

That was the shit his brother and father tried to make him understand when Cory couldn't comprehend how a man could love and fuck and keep the same woman for the rest of their lives. But he did now—he understood everything now.

He was the wind ripping them around and around until they couldn't breathe. She was the rain keeping them soaked to the bone and feeling alive. Everything between them became the storm. It kept building and building until the pressure finally let go and here they were.

"Bloody or not," Cory said, pushing away from the doorjamb to enter the bathroom, "you're still perfect to me. That's what matters."

Della's head popped up, and he felt her gaze following him as he worked in the bathroom. He turned on the bathtub and plugged the drain. Grabbing a cotton hand towel from the pile on the counter, he wet the cloth before coming to kneel in front of her.

He took his time.

One swipe, then he washed the cloth out.

More blood disappeared.

Della sat patient and quiet.

"We'll burn your clothes," he said.

"I liked that dress."

"I'll buy you three more."

She grinned. "Yeah?"

"And Birkins to match."

"Wow, pulling all the stops, huh?"

Cory's gaze snapped up and met Della's dark stare. She stilled all over when he dragged the warm washcloth over her cheek one last time to get rid of what blood remained. "Pulling nothing, babe. It's what it is."

"Cory—"

"I love you. I don't know *how* to say it, so I'm just going to say it. I can't make it amazing because it just *is*, you know? Yeah, I could wait until it's a better time, but I'm fucking tired of waiting to tell you this. I'm sorry it came close today. It won't happen again. And I love you, Adella Costello … far more than I should."

Her chin quivered, and he didn't move when her fingertips glided over the line of his jaw while the two of them stared at one another.

"That's a terrifying thing," she said.

"I don't think so."

"No?"

"Nope."

Della laughed. "Do you know why I fell in love with you? Why I *do* love you?"

Cory smiled *full-blown*. Couldn't have hidden it if he tried. Someday, he'd tell her how much joy it brought his very black soul to hear her say those words.

"Tell me. *Tell me everything.* I don't think you know how much I enjoy hearing you talk."

Or maybe she did.

"I hated what I thought you were, but I fell in love with the man you couldn't help but be with me."

"Because you make me a better one. A better man."

"Or are we just a disaster waiting to happen, Cory?"

"The better question," he returned, "is are you willing to find out?"

Della leaned in for a kiss. He let her take it as he tossed away the bloodstained washcloth. Her kiss was a good enough answer for him.

He found everything he was looking for in the skim of her lips against his and then the taste of her on his tongue. She tasted of tobacco and *her*. Heat and temptation and fucking perfection. That's always how she was to him. He couldn't stop himself from moving closer when her fingernails danced over his biceps and down his shoulders. Crouching slightly over her in the chair until her back was flush with the curved back, only then did their kiss slow.

She smiled. Her lips curving against his own grinning mouth. All teeth and stained lips and *happiness*. He wanted her to do that more often. Smile, that was. Too many things had given her every single reason to cry lately but not him. He wouldn't be something else that hurt her. She would only ever smile with him.

"Do you think … this is all over now?" she asked.

Her words tickled his skin.

The urge to taste hers was strong.

"Almost," he told her. "But I don't want you to worry about that shit anyway. What's left isn't something you need to handle. I don't want one more thought in your head about people who only did you wrong. All you need to do now is be happy. Nothing else is important. Let me take care of the rest. Whatever you want, I'll do it if it means you're smiling. That's kind of the deal between you and me now, huh?"

Her glittering gaze teased him. "What, that you'll do anything for me?"

"Yeah, Della. Exactly that."

I know," she said in a breath. "That's the terrifying part I mentioned earlier. Because the only thing I really want is for you to stay. Right now. Later. I get fucking clingy, and if we're *really* doing this fucking thing together then—"

That was enough for Cory. Now she was just overthinking. He kissed her again just to shut her the fuck up. He figured it probably wouldn't be the last time, but there wasn't any need for nonsense tonight. They were fine. Everything else would work itself out. The last thing they needed to pick apart was what they had together.

It worked.

"Don't fix shit that isn't broke," Cory said, kissing her quickly between each word. "You want me to stay?"

Della nodded. "Yeah."

"Then, I'm staying."

Cory's gaze dropped between them, and he thoroughly enjoyed the view. The robe had fallen open around her curves, and she wore nothing under it. "And unless you tell me you want something else other than me, I'll be *very* good to you while I'm here."

The way her breath caught in her chest had him leaning in for another taste of her lips. She gave it to him, willing and sweet and already greedy enough to let him do whatever he wanted to her. That's how fast things could switch between the two of them. A word or a look. The *promise* of something sinful sent both of them chasing it together.

That better never change.

"You're all I want," she told him.

"You sure?"

"Absolutely."

Then, he'd give her exactly that.

"I want you to come before the tub fills," Cory explained when he grabbed Della's wrists and pinned them over her head to the wall with one hand. His other? Dipping between her already wide thighs. She had no shame with him, and he fucking loved it. He got her hot enough that she didn't care if he knew how bad she wanted it. That got him off every single damn time. "On my fingers, and then give me a taste, yeah?"

Her tongue peeked out to wet the seam of her lips when his fingertips ghosted over the soft heat of her sex. If she wasn't entirely bare, then she was neatly trimmed like right then. Her hips jerked forward when he found her clit and flicked his fingers against it.

"Is that what you want?" he asked.

His fingers moved lower to find where she was wet and silky. The longer he waited, teasing with soft strokes and the occasional flick the more she trembled and the harder she tried to stay still. Under his control, he thought she was always at her best.

Almost in control.

But not quite.

It left her *wild.*

"Hmm?" he asked. "Yeah, *this?*"

She nodded once. "Yeah, Cory."

His fingers sunk into her cunt; her responding moan had his dick aching in seconds beneath his jeans. *Fuck.* Her legs widened more, and her tongue flicked out to strike against his lips when he leaned in close enough. Every twist of his fingers along her inner walls had him so fucking happy he was going to spend the next hour *plus* getting his dick massaged by those. When he treated her right, her body gave him everything he wanted and more in return.

"Be louder next time—if the fuckers next door move out, I'll be able to buy the whole damn floor."

Della grinned. "*Make me.*"

He would.

He *did.*

In the bathtub after it filled, while her body was hot and flush from the water and covered in bubbles. He put her on top and made her ride him until he exploded because there was nothing quite like the sight of her ass bouncing in the water against his cock to make him lose all sense of life, really. And then he held her back against his chest with an arm locked around her so that he could grab her throat while he teased her clit until she was screaming his name loud enough for his neighbors down the hall to hear.

Every time she came, he wanted her to do it again. Right then. *Later.* In the fucking morning. As long as she was on his dick, or sitting on his face while she did it, then he was a happy fucking boy.

He couldn't get enough of her.

Didn't want to.

There was something viscerally attractive to him about the way Della looked when he fucked her. Something about how she looked with his hands on her, and his marks left behind. How she moaned and *whined* and asked him for more.

All of it was a drug.

He didn't mind saying he was addicted, but he didn't need any kind of help for it. She was his greatest temptation and his biggest prize. Each time he was seduced in between her thighs, he always found something wonderful.

Why on earth would he stop?

TWENTY

THE BEAUTIFULLY tragic thing about time?

It did, in fact, keep moving forward.

Those who moved with it—even when all they really wanted to do was curl into a ball and hide away from the world—were the strong ones. They all had moments when the grief caught up, and it hurt to breathe through the pain, but it was all one day at a time. From one to the next. Again and again. That was strength. A kind of strength that a lot of people didn't understand or mistook it as something else.

Passing a look down the street at the line of homes before she pushed open the front door to her parents' place, Della let out a sigh into the cold air. It felt appropriate to bury J on a mid-Autumn day like this one. With gray clouds overhead letting just a little bit of sun through. While the leaves were still changing colors on the trees, but the wind hadn't picked up enough to rip them from the branches.

Nothing was dead yet from the cold.

Sweater weather, she used to tell her brother. Pumpkin spice season. She could still hear the way he used to laugh, see *his* signature grin form when he replied, "*Girl shit, man.*"

He wasn't wrong. He still used to like her lattes, though.

Just before she stepped into her parents' quiet home, that last look at the street had different memories bubbling to the surface of Della's mind. Of her brother, of course. All the times they played in the front yard or when he chased her down the front steps after she stole his iPhone before her parents bought her own. Trick-or-treating when they were little.

God.

Shit was so much easier then.

Less complicated.

For a minute, Della would give *anything* ... She would give it all to go back to that time with her brother for one more minute. But that wasn't how life worked, and sometimes, one had to say goodbye to the people they loved sooner than they expected.

That's what today was about.

Burying her brother.

Tightening her grip on the gift bag in her hand, Della shoved the thoughts aside that had made her eyes water. It wasn't that she didn't want to feel *anything* today, but rather ... she didn't want to cry. The nights leading up to J's funeral had certainly seen more than enough of her tears, so why add more when she could do something more for her brother?

Something *better?*

She wanted to celebrate his life.

Not grieve his death.

Not today.

"Ma?" Della called down the hallway beyond the foyer. "You up?"

She sent up a quick prayer that today was a better morning for her mother than the last couple. It was a toss-up. Some days, Chloe made an effort to not get lost in the new, ever-present sadness in her heart. Other days, she tried to drown in it all. Della didn't wonder why or feel any bitterness about her mother's grief ... she never wanted to lose her own child. She couldn't imagine what this was doing to her mother. She did wish she could help more often, though, but sometimes that just couldn't be helped.

It was the nature of her current life. The new responsibilities on Della's plate where her father's business was concerned kept her running from one side of the city to the other just so that every single fuck working under the Costello family knew who was in charge now. And the bitch wore heels when she arrived. Nonetheless, she made time for her mom.

Chloe needed it even if she wouldn't ask her daughter for it.

"In the kitchen," her ma called back.

That was a good sign.

She even smiled.

Della followed the new, faint smell of chocolate and nutmeg to the kitchen. Her mother stood straight up from the stove with a sheet of chocolate cookies in her hand. At her questioning stare, Chloe shrugged and laughed.

"I just ... remember when I used to make you guys cookies for the morning on weekends?" her mother asked.

Della took a few steps into the kitchen and shrugged off her coat. Placing her jacket and purse to a stool along with the small gift bag, she waved a hand at those cookies. "I do—they're the best. Hand one over."

Her mother arched a brow. "Excuse me? Not with that attitude."

"*Please.*"

That had her ma smiling.

It's all she wanted to see.

"Let them cool first," Chloe said. "And aren't you supposed to be at the church with a certain someone to make sure all the flowers come in?"

"He's handled that."

Chloe grabbed a spatula and began to slowly remove the cookies from the sheet to a waiting cooling rack. "So, are we not talking about the fact that you've spent as many nights at your place as you have at his place this week, then?"

"You could just ask if I'm fucking Cory, Ma."

Her mother gasped and widened her eyes in mock shock. "I would *never.*"

"I like him."

"Oh?"

"He's gonna be around a lot."

Chloe's gaze flicked to her. "Well, okay."

That was that.

It wasn't lost on her that her mom managed to give her special attention at a time when—honestly—Della should be the last thing on Chloe's mind. But that was her mother—that was all moms in a nutshell. Even when their soul was being eaten by agony, they still managed to show up, put on a smile, and make their kid feel amazing.

"I love you, Ma," Della told Chloe.

"Forever and ever?"

That was something she used to say to Della and J when they were kids as she put them to bed. Della couldn't forget it or how it ended.

"And ever and ever," she said quietly.

Silence answered her back.

Because usually, in the background of the house somewhere, if J heard it, he would reply, "*And ever!*" As loud as he could just because he could. He was never going to say that again now. They still stopped and waited for him to do it, though.

Chloe made a soft sound. "It's not the same, is it?"

"No."

"We're still going to do it, though, right?"

Della nodded, feeling the tears come back but she blinked them away. "Yeah, Ma. We'll still say it."

"Are we crying in here?"

The new voice had Della laughing as she used the sleeves of her black silk dress to wipe away any wetness that might have escaped from her eyes. Turning, she faced her approaching father who already had his arms opened to take a hug from her. The second Frankie's arms wrapped around Della, she was five again, home smelled like her father's cologne, and her dad could scare away every bad dream that dared to haunt her nights.

"It's a beautiful day to say goodbye, isn't it?" Frankie asked, hugging her tighter. "His favorite time of the year, Della."

"Yeah, Dad."

They didn't want to say goodbye.

It was still a beautiful day to do it.

•••

"You'll miss him the most when you least expect it," came a soft voice from Della's left.

Though she'd prepared mentally as much as possible for the moment when her brother's casket would be lowered into the ground, she'd not actually been ready when it finally happened. She dared to glance away from the hole dug in dirt, but was grateful for the large rim of her hat and the birdcage veil that kept her face hidden from the crowd. Or rather, what was left of it.

A few feet away, her parents accepted hugs from friends. The priest chatted with those that remained near her brother's headstone that had only been finished the night before and placed just that morning. White lilies covered the ground and the casket that now rested at the bottom of the hole.

"Why is that?" Della asked.

Cory's mother came to stand a little closer to her side, but Lily Rossi didn't offer any other sense of comfort. No hug or even a pat to the back. Della was grateful because frankly, she'd hugged and said *thank you* to more people than she cared to admit that day.

"When I lost one of my older brothers as a young woman," Lily said with a quiet sigh, "I was just starting out in my adult life, really. It hurt when I buried him. Still kills me to see his name carved into marble when I visit. But it hurt worse when time passed, and I realized how much they were missing. Dino would have *loved* Joe—that kid reminded me so much of him. All the worry Cory put us through while he grew up, Dino would have laughed and said that was just the DeLuca side of him coming out. He wouldn't be wrong. But that's when it hurt the most."

"And nothing makes it better or easier, I imagine."

Lily glanced over at Della, and for the first time that day, she allowed someone to look her straight in the face and see the tears she kept hiding. "No—but better I tell you now and you expect the pain to come than to stumble into it over and over again the way I did. My son thinks you're a very special young woman, Della."

"So he keeps telling me."

"I hate seeing the past repeat itself."

"Or is it just the life we chose?" Della asked back.

Lily considered that, her attention turning back on the grave. "Does it make a difference if the end result is still the same? It all comes full circle. One way or another. I'll see you at the Trentini mansion later for dinner, hmm? We'll talk more. Someone's coming this way, and if you hadn't noticed, he didn't want to leave your side at all earlier."

From the right, Della watched Cory approach.

White lily in hand.

"Did you find your brother?" Lily asked her son.

He reached for his mother and gave her a kiss on the cheek before taking the spot at Della's right. "I did, Ma. Dad's waiting with the car."

"Perfect. Della, I'm sorry."

She gave Cory's mother a smile. Thank you wasn't appropriate. She bet Lily knew that better than anyone. "I know."

Cory's arm found Della's waist, and her head laid against his bicep. It wasn't lost on her how he wore a three-piece suit and leather loafers instead of his usual leather, jeans and boots. She wanted to admire him looking like sin poured into a suit with his hair slicked back, and a single cross stud in his earlobe. Even his nose ring had been changed to be the same silver as the stud in his ear.

He held out the lily for her to take.

"I saved one extra," he said. "From the splash over the casket."

She took it with trembling fingers.

"Take it home," Cory told her, bending down to press a kiss against the top of her head. She closed her eyes, and a tear escaped. Before she'd even blinked, his hand slipped up under her veil to wipe the tear away with the pad of his thumb. He never even smudged her makeup. She grabbed his wrist and kissed the tip of the digit, her silent *thanks*. "Put the lily in water, and I'll make sure you never see it wilt."

Della smiled a bit. "*How?*"

"Magic."

"Do you mean to say you'll always replace it so I never have to?"

Cory shrugged and stared out over the grave and beyond the small hill to where rows and rows of cars were parked in the church's lot. "Maybe, or maybe it's just like I said."

"Right, *magic*."

This man *was* kind of magical.

In his own way.

The vehicles had started to thin out of the parking lot, but there were still quite a few. They had to keep all eyes peeled lately. Chances were, they weren't the only people watching. Cory wanted to be ready if that was the case. Della didn't blame him.

"Any news on Luis?" she asked.

He was still MIA.

Della didn't trust that at all.

Cory's attention came back to her in an instant. "Not yet, but that's okay."

"Oh?"

"None of this is ever random, babe. Remember that."

She would.

Or try.

•••

The two weeks following J's funeral passed faster than Della expected during the moments she thought would be the hardest after burying her brother. She contributed it to the fact her family and their friends rallied in their own way. Late dinners. Coffee runs. Random check-ins just because. Phone calls that lasted longer than they normally would.

She saw it all for what it was.

The way someone asked *are you okay?*

She wasn't.

Neither were her parents.

It was getting better.

"I'll take Mace for a walk around the block," Cory said in her ear as she stepped out of her car in the driveway of her townhouse. "And then I'll be in."

He was back working with his uncle now but he was never too far from Della's mind considering her new best friend just happened to be an enforcer Cory handpicked. She didn't breathe sideways without that man knowing about it. Harry was his name—the guy was old enough to be her dad, but he certainly wouldn't put up with her shit like her father would.

He was there to keep her safe.

Not to be her friend.

Della didn't forget it.

"How far away are you?" she asked, following the pathway that led up to the front door of her place.

"Less than two minutes. Last-minute Starbucks run for a certain *someone*, you know. Saw the fucking sign as I was driving by and Mace jumped into my lap at a red light, for fuck's sake."

Her, that was.

She needed her caffeine before bed, plus she managed to get Cory's pup hooked on pumpkin bread. Now, he expected a piece at least a couple of times a week.

Della laughed. "Oh?"

"I'm not far behind. Don't worry, babe. All's good."

Right.

Depending on where they both ended up at the end of a weekday, they stayed at his place or hers. More often his than hers. She didn't mind. Tonight, he called to say they'd be going to her place regardless. And his reason for why wasn't negotiable. Still, she hadn't been expecting to come here alone. Her enforcer was posted at the end of the street. She reminded herself of that, but her nerves didn't settle.

"Is Harry still on the street?" he asked as she unlocked the front door to her place.

"Yeah, having a smoke in his car."

"Don't look back at him. Sixty seconds now, Della. It might be our last chance."

Yeah, she knew.

"Love you," she said.

His response echoed in her heart. A mirror of her own words.

She hung up the phone and opened the door. Closing it behind her, she didn't even get the chance to flick on the light before her uninvited guest made himself known. She washed the hallway in light when she flicked the switch on the wall, showcasing where Luis sat on a chair he'd pulled into the hall from the kitchen.

Black hair and equally dark eyes. Looking like death waiting for her. *Smiling.* Death always smiled. He even wore Cory's jacket.

"I hate unfinished business," Luis murmured.

He dared to grin.

Della was counting down the time.

"Aren't you happy to see me?" he asked, widening his arms. "Not really here for *you* ... but two birds, one stone, you know? Figured, when you say *fuck you* to someone like Cory Rossi, you do it with your whole damn chest, Dell. He'll understand why I'm here to do this."

"He already did," she replied, unbothered.

Coldly, even.

Luis didn't miss it when his gaze narrowed. "What does that mean?"

"Think about it."

He looked like he might get up from the chair. He even uncrossed his jean-clad leg to drop it to the floor, and then fixed the sleeve on the leather jacket. All signs of his nerves, she knew. It was easy to find when she understood what to look for now.

"I'm not here to chat," Luis said, "but I'm sure you already know that."

Yeah.

"Was she worth it?" Della asked.

That had Luis glancing her way as he pulled a switchblade from his pocket. She *really* thought he might want to go for the easy kill—a bullet straight to her brain. She wasn't all that surprised to see he wanted something more personal for her.

A knife was always personal.

"Jennika, you mean?"

"Yeah. Good pussy, or ...?"

Luis waved a hand. "*Loca*, but purpose serving. I'm going to fuck up your face first. Cut it to shreds. It was really the only thing I liked about you in the first place."

Della was done playing games.

Especially at that threat.

"No, you won't. Did you think my new guard was a coincidence? Or that I haven't sold this place yet even though I would rather be at Cory's place every night? How about the fact that my schedule hasn't changed in weeks?"

Luis walked right into the trap they set. Just like they wanted him to. He was a creature of habit in some ways. It was the downfall of better men than the one standing in front of her, so she didn't know why he thought he could be an exception to the rule.

In this life, there were no exceptions. Only consequences.

Luis's face morphed with rage at every question she threw at him. They landed like knives until he was standing from the chair and coming toward her. Della didn't move—refused to show him fear because she no longer felt any for him.

This man didn't scare her. He'd only broken her heart and even that didn't hurt now.

His hands raised, but her next words stopped him from coming close enough to actually put them on her in some violent way. "The jacket, Luis … should have checked the pocket. He knew you were coming back for it—you couldn't miss the chance. Schoolyard shit, Cory said, but you wouldn't forget it. He stopped wearing it for a reason. He put it in *my* closet for a reason. Have you figured out what that reason is yet? We showed you the way to get here and you walked right in."

The figure stepping out of the rear hallway with a skull bandana pulled high over his mouth and nose with a black pup on his heels had Della's heart racing more than the sight of Luis coming closer did.

Those sixty-seconds were up.

Della smiled when he came within feet of her in the hallway, his eyes blazing with rage and disbelief. "Because when someone watches you, you always watch back, Luis."

Cory already had the gun aimed when Luis realized they were no longer alone in the townhouse. It was already too late. "None of this shit happened by accident, man."

He spun on his heels.

The barrel of Cory's gun met his forehead.

"Remember when you used to tell me that?" Cory asked. "Jacket still fits—die in it."

"You fucking—"

Della pulled the taser from the pocket in her coat and jammed it straight in between Luis's shoulders. She pulled back the trigger, and the volts of electricity sent Luis flying to the floor in a heap. She gave the twitching body one last look before she stepped over it.

Cory lowered his gun and kissed her on the way by. "Harry will take it out the back. Nobody will see. Joe's coming to help us get rid of it."

She wished she cared.

"I'll be back before two, hopefully," he told her.

"Good." She didn't sleep well without him anymore. Della let him kiss her again, softer that time while his fingers grazed her chin. "But the better question is *where's my latte?*"

His laughter drowned out Luis's noises from the floor.

"On the table at the back door. Are you babysitting Mace?"

She gave the pup a look. He sat, his head cocked to the side, watching the twitching man on the floor.

"You don't even have to ask, Cory."

Not for anything.

She would give him everything. He'd already given exactly that to her, after all. It was her turn now.

TWENTY-ONE

BY THE TIME Luis woke up, and Cory allowed the asshole to realize he *was* awake and still alive—although in a mighty world of fucking pain—the guy was in an entirely different place. Luis's last memory was probably the way Della smiled at him, unfeeling, before he turned on Cory in that hallway. He took a sense of satisfaction in that.

Everything else was probably a bit fuzzy for the prick, though. Confusing.

Painful.

Cory smirked to himself, appreciating how little effort it actually took for them to pull this off. All because really, some shit never changed. Same with people. He'd known Luis at a very strange time in both their lives. Wasn't everyone's teenage years filled with memories that made them and shaped them? Some of it, he didn't want to remember. A lot of it, he would never be able to forget.

Back then, it had been Cory's stubborn streak that really followed him down the worst of rabbit holes. Mostly because his stubborn nature was also heavily entangled with his arrogance and curiosity, though he'd never wanted to admit it. *His* issues brought him to a place in his life where there wasn't a problem he couldn't solve.

For Luis, it had been a bit different. The guy couldn't let shit go.

Ever.

Something like that didn't get better with time. That's why he knew Luis would be back. He hadn't thought the guy would return to take a pound from Cory as soon as he had, but he prepared for the chance all the same. Because the end result would never change.

They had unfinished business. Luis just didn't get a say in the way it ended.

"*Yeesh*," Cory whistled as Luis blinked up at the darkness all around him. Other than the strobe light at the other end of the warehouse—he found keeping one in places he liked to work sometimes served him well for many reasons—everything else was bathed in black around the man on the cold cement floor. "Look at you, yeah?"

Pain was a motherfucker.

Luis groaned when the stiff bones and blooming bruises on his body wouldn't allow him to do anything more than roll to his side. Which put the asshole right in view for Cory in the darkness and how he stood directly in the path of the strobe light. The man's gaze lifted at the same time Cory grinned. Pulling down the skull bandana down from his face, he lifted the burning blunt to his lips and took a hard pull.

The smoke blinked in and out of the darkness.

Black and white.

"*Fuck you,*" Luis grunted out through bloodstained, chapped lips. His arms wrapped around his middle as he coughed out a painful rattle. "*Oh my—*"

Yeah, that pain was wicked.

"Joe broke all your ribs," Cory explained.

From the back of the warehouse where Joe sat alone in the darkness, the man called out, "Wasn't a problem—took barely any effort at all."

Luis looked like he was going to say something or *try.* Cory really didn't care to let the man even make the attempt when it wouldn't matter. What was it? More cursing? Threats? *Insults?* None of that shit changed anything now.

Look at him. The guy was already dead. *Basically.*

It was kind of sad.

Cory wasn't the type to play with his prey. *Joe* did, though. Hence the ribs and everything else.

"I had a trip in the jacket," Cory explained. "I knew the second you took it off the hook. You're just that petty. She wouldn't be enough, you wanted to really fuck with me because you thought I honestly cared about that piece of trash you're wearing. A long time ago, maybe. From my position, it doesn't look too good to be wearing it right now, though, huh? I really hoped you might let some time pass before you tried any shit with us—let J's people have their moment to say goodbye. Should have known better."

Luis opened his mouth, and one of his hands twitched when it fell to the floor like the man was going to reach out to Cory. *Fuck that noise.*

This was over.

It had been over the moment Cory got the notification from the wire that the jacket had been moved that day.

Keeping what remained of his blunt balanced between two fingers, Cory pulled the bandana up over his face again. Smoke still danced between the strobing of the light before it disappeared into the darkness.

Luis opened his mouth to shout. Or maybe scream. Cory just lifted the gun he'd kept tucked at his side where the man couldn't see in the shadows and pulled back the trigger. Bone made such a morbid sound when it cracked against cement.

He kind of liked it.

•••

"Where is your pup? Theo says he never leaves your side lately. Your sister was watching him for a while, wasn't she?"

That question had Cory smirking. "She was watching him. And he's probably sleeping on my side of the bed—Della lets him do that shit when she thinks I don't know."

Sitting across from Cory, the man who greeted him was already dressed in a three-piece suit despite the time of day.

"If you're here to talk with me this early in the morning," Tommas said, leaning into supple leather of a couch that faced a row of bookshelves, "then I assume you have good news for me?"

Cory grinned, tipping up his lukewarm to-go cup of coffee in his boss's direction. "That I do—you can call off any Outfit hounds on Luis's trail. He met the incinerator at four this morning. Joe stayed behind to discard the ashes."

Tommas let out a laugh. "Is that all?"

"Well—"

"I thought something happened. *Not* this, but I won't complain. I appreciate you, specifically, letting me know on the Luis front. How did that come about?"

He did a quick run-through of events. The replay wasn't that interesting. Frankly, it had all happened so quickly that he hadn't even bothered to make a proper call through to his boss to ask for permission, but he didn't really have to. The Outfit had put a bounty out on Luis quite a while ago. The guy was free game.

Cory was just here to give Tommas the news face to face because after the money the man lost in the warehouse, and everything else that changed their business due to Luis, it just seemed appropriate. Plus, as his Uncle Theo would say, if he had a direct line to the boss himself without having to go through other people, why not use it?

That's how the game of the Outfit was played.

"Good, good," Tommas murmured in reply to Cory, reaching for a drawer in the ornate coffee table sitting on the floor between their respective seats. He rifled through the drawer, asking, "Anything else?"

"It might be important for you to know there will be a bit of noise from the south side next week. Della made a deal with Miss Wang that will benefit both your business from loans *and* the parlors across the city."

That had Tommas glancing up. "I think you mean *Mr.* Wang."

"Nah, he has a daughter. And with her in charge of the operation, the Outfit will see a four percent increase monthly for their protection, of course."

Tommas sat a little straighter, though his hands didn't leave the drawer. "And what will Mr. Wang's daughter gain from this new arrangement?"

"Freedom. Apparently, it's worth the cost."

A soft noise echoed from Tommas's throat.

"How much was Wang in debt to Costello?" the boss asked.

"More than he should have been. There were terms made. Some agreements put through that covered interest for a time. Della had a better solution. It'll benefit everyone across the board, so when the noise picks up in the south over one little death, less concern from the mob would be appreciated."

Business never stopped.

Even when Cory had multiple balls in the air. Now with Della managing her father's operation as a whole, and Cory back on the streets with Theo to keep everything smooth for the higher ups in the Outfit, his attention had to be everywhere again.

Tommas sighed heavily. "I'll keep that in mind. Really, *four* percent higher? They're already paying us—"

"A lot," Cory said. "Yeah, I know, she did well with that one."

"Good to see her settling in, I suppose."

Wasn't that what counted?

Then, Tommas shifted direction entirely. "Which saint do you prefer—when you find yourself praying, which saint do you ask for help when it seems too trivial for *Him*?"

"Why?"

"Matter of curiosity."

Catholics.

Cory never understood the appeal, but his parents had him in the church before he could even remember, and he'd never known anything different. It was why he kept a string of rosary on his rearview mirror and on his bedpost.

Let God see all his sins, then.

Might as well.

He didn't have to think about his answer. His favorite saint had found him early in life and never left.

"Saint Anthony," Cory eventually said.

Tommas chuckled as though that didn't surprise him a bit and riffled through the drawer more. "The saint you pray to when things, or *you*, are lost. You're a walking cliché, Cory."

"Not even close."

The man nodded once. "And we all appreciate it, trust me."

Tommas finally found what he wanted. He laid all the items out on the table for Cory to see and all at once, he understood what the boss wanted to do.

A picture, the size of a playing card, of Saint Anthony faced upward with his name in gold script at the bottom. The blade closest to the edge of the coffee table glinted when it caught the light. All things one needed to make a man.

To give him his *in* to the family.

Properly.

Except …

"I'm just missing a lighter," Tommas noted.

Cory didn't think about it before pulling his favorite Zippo from the back pocket of his jeans. He handed the item over.

"I like making my men privately," Tommas said. "You could say it's become a tradition for me. I like being the only person who can say whether another man is worthy to sit beside one of mine. You understand?"

"I do."

"But you should also know, *many* men have stood and vouched for you recently." Tommas picked up the knife and pointed the very sharp tip in the direction of Cory's hands. "Is this what you want?"

Was that a real question?

"It is."

"Palm up, Cory."

•••

Cory's favorite time of the day had changed. It used to be when the sun went down—darkness made everything look a little better. A lot of things could hide in the shadows. It was also where he found most of his fun. Even in his dreams, he was restless.

Lately, though, the time of day he liked the most was first thing in the morning when the sun was still brand new, and the rest of the world wasn't waiting for him to do something. Usually, Mace would still be sleeping on his big pillow on the floor at the foot of the bed, the house was silent, and his blankets were always warmed with Della wrapped up in them.

At dawn, he learned to appreciate the stillness that came with it and what it meant for him to be able to have it at all. It just so happened to be his luck that he shared those early morning moments with Della because she hadn't lied.

Chick *was* clingy.

She wanted his attention.

Always.

The woman could blow his phone up in five minutes if she thought he was going to catch an attitude with her over anything. She changed the whole arrangement and style of his bedroom without asking, but it looked good, so he didn't say shit. Her clothes were in his closet. But fuck, she made a mean steak.

They were *basically* living together even though they hadn't explicitly said so. It seemed like a lot of their entire relationship had just been the two of them making moves that propelled them ahead together into something new. Without ever asking at all.

Cory *did* like it.

It just wasn't lost on him that it was happening.

Lost in those thoughts—while getting his dick sucked—was how Cory found himself spending his favorite time of the day. Della peeked through the curtain of her hair when she came to the head of his cock, those plump, wet lips of hers tight around his shaft. She let him go with a pop, but her fist tight around his base kept him awake like a live wire against the mattress. She rested between his relaxed legs, her head in his palm while he stroked her hair, and she got him off. There was nothing quite like the sight of her blowing him first thing in the morning.

Truly, he was blessed.

Della smiled overtop his cock. "Am I swallowing?"

"Every last drop."

He'd paint her pussy with his cum later and use it to get her off when he played with her clit. Right then, though … yeah, he just wanted to watch her swallow him down.

All of him.

Della's dark eyes flashed with pleasure before her head dipped down. He didn't sweep the hair out of her face in time to see her take his dick in her mouth again. Still felt it. All hot and tight and *wet*. She did dangerous things with that tongue of hers. On his tip. Down his shaft. Against his fucking balls when she pulled them in for a suck, too. Finally getting the hair away from her face, he was enraptured with the focus and pleasure he found in his woman while she worked to get him off.

"God, do you know what you do to me?" Cory asked, his head dropped back to the headboard.

Della hummed around his shaft. The vibrations had his balls tightening in the best way. Her fist worked his length. Just like her mouth. The teeth. *Her tongue.* The groan that came out of him was thick with pleasure and he was close to losing control.

No better way to let go.

That was for sure.

He looked down.

Della stared back.

Cory came *hard.*

It seemed never-ending.

She took every bit, too.

He was still trying to catch his breath when she finally let his cock go. Crawling up him, she showed her tongue with a laugh and smiled wide. Her brows lifted, matching his when he reached for her. His cock didn't even have the chance to soften before she climbed on top of him, taking him in all over again.

Shit.

Her inner walls?

They could work him for *hours*. As long as he could keep from blowing his load like a teenager getting his first fuck. That was always the challenge with Della.

She sat down on his length.

Cory already had her ass spread wide with two fistfuls. It stretched her out just a bit more, and she *really* felt him driving into her then.

"Wang is a go," he told her, referring to his conversation with the boss the morning before.

She nodded, her breaths all high and stuttering as he worked her back and forth on his dick. "*Good.*"

Jesus.

Why was she so perfect?

Nothing would be better than this—*than her.* The realization slammed into Cory with a weight he hadn't expected. He was never coming back from this.

From her.

She'd always be his end.

He would always keep coming back to her.

"Love you," she whispered, her chest tight to his and their lips brushing when she spoke.

Every breath she panted out, he sucked in. She'd come quickly—it would take him a bit longer this time but that was just fine. Christ, her pussy would be dripping when he was done.

"I'm marrying you," he told her.

Sure.

Absolute.

He just knew it.

The way she looked at him when he said it?

She knew it, too.

As for the rest?

It could all wait.

BIO

Bethany-Kris is a Canadian author, lover of much, and mother to four young sons, three cats, and four dogs. A small town in Eastern Canada where she was born and raised is where she has always called home. With her boys under her feet, a snuggling cat, barking dogs, and a spouse calling over his shoulder, she is nearly always writing something ... when she can find the time.

Find Bethany-Kris and where to follow her at www.bethanykris.com:

OTHER BOOKS

The Guzzi Legacy

Corrado
Alessio
Chris
Beni
Bene
Marcus

Renzo + Lucia

Privilege
Harbor
Contempt
Forever

Andino + Haven

Duty
Vow

John + Siena

Loyalty
Disgrace
John + Siena: The Complete Duet
John + Siena: Extended

Cross + Catherine

Always
Revere
Unruly
The Companion
Naz & Roz

Guzzi Duet

Unraveled, Book One
Entangled, Book Two
Cara & Gian: The Complete Duet

DeLuca Duet

Waste of Worth: Part One
Worth of Waste: Part Two

Standalone Titles

Pretty Lies
Dirty Pool
Effortless
Inflict
Cozen
Captivated
Dishonored

Donati Bloodlines

Thin Lies
Thin Lines
Thin Lives
Behind the Bloodlines
The Complete Trilogy

Filthy Marcellos

Antony
Lucian
Giovanni
Dante
Legacy
A Very Marcello Christmas
The Complete Collection

Seasons of Betrayal

Where the Sun Hides
Where the Snow Falls
Where the Wind Whispers
Seasons: The Complete Seasons of Betrayal Series

Gun Moll Trilogy

Gun Moll
Gangster Moll
Madame Moll

The Chicago War

Deathless & Divided
Reckless & Ruined
Scarless & Sacred
Breathless & Bloodstained
The Complete Series
Maldives & Mistletoe

The Russian Guns

The Arrangement
The Life
The Score
Demyan & Ana
Shattered
The Jersey Vignettes

FANTASY ROMANCE

The Hunted: A 9INE REALMS Novel

Find more on Bethany-Kris's website at www.bethanykris.com.